Short Stories by Bootheel Will

by

William Campbell

To Mrs, Alice

I hope you enjoy the book

William Campbell
Bootheel Will

RED LEAD PRESS
PITTSBURGH, PENNSYLVANIA 15222

The contents of this work including, but not limited to, the accuracy of events, people, and places depicted; opinions expressed; permission to use previously published materials included; and any advice given or actions advocated are solely the responsibility of the author, who assumes all liability for said work and indemnifies the publisher against any claims stemming from publication of the work.

ISBN: 978-1-4349-6114-3
Printed in the United States of America

First Printing

For more information or to order additional books, please contact:
Red Lead Press
701 Smithfield Street
Pittsburgh, Pennsylvania 15222
U.S.A.
1-800-834-1803
www.redleadbooks.com

These stories are about history, struggle and survival. Though most of the characters are not real ,the opinions and traditions they convey are. These are stories of common man trying to live a common life and keep their history alive. They are intended to inspire and entertain and perhaps coax one to take the journey to his or her own family history. when i first started writing these stories I knew very little of my own families history . Now i am content in knowing the part my ancestors played . I hope you enjoy them as you read them .There are many more to follow these.

" BOOTHEEL WILL"

And One Walked Back

THIS STORY IS PURELY FICTIONAL ,HOWEVER THE REFERENCES TO THE HISTORICAL EVENTS ARE NOT ,THE REFERENCES TO THE BELIEFS AND LANGUAGE RETOLD IN THIS STORY ARE BASED ON DIFFERENT LITERATURES AND HISTORICAL RECORD. PERHAPS SOME OF YOUR OWN ANCESTERS MADE THIS JOURNEY.

WRITTEN BY WILLIAM CAMPBELL ,
"BOOTHEEL WILL"

A young wife stands in her kitchen discussing ,the fate of her husband's father .Both very concerned about his wellbeing and both worried and feeling that he's been spending too much time alone. Their conversation intense and both almost in a yell ,it was apparent that neither would give any ground soon. Look dear ,he's old and true to the old ways of his people. He did not ask to come here ,that was all our idea. He said that he was happy just where he was, and we did not listen. I know he makes you mad , but he doesn't mean to.

Often Walter Stoutman had trouble getting his wife Anne to try to understand, that his father wasn't interested in any modern ways.

Your father could at least thank us for getting him out of that, god forsaken shack that had been, condemned for three years. Does he realize how much money you spent building that new addition that he lives in?

Dear i'm not saying he owes us anything ,it's just ——— well he has all that stuff in his part of the house to keep him occupied and all he wants to do is sit on that cliff ,by a fire and talk to the sky.

He's seventy years old dear, he's not like your average old man ,he is not just set in his ways, because he wants to be stubborn. The way he is ,is how he was raised ,it is how every Indian in our tribe was raised to be, for many generations in the past. Don't take this the wrong way ,but you couldn't even begin to understand how our people were.

Having said that , Walter knew that he was about to get an ear full now. Anne's face seemed to change to three different shades of red, and she began to tense up .The look on her face changed from frustration to angry. Your people! What do you mean your people?!! You haven't even claimed to be Indian in ten years,,,,it's almost like your embarrassed to even be one.

Now you wait just a minute Anne, i'm proud to be Native American, i just don't choose to hold on to the old ways like my dad. This is a totally different time and era, If i say i'm an Indian when people offer me a new opportunity, all i get is what they would offer an Indian, not what i have earned. This house, our cars and everything we have, is not because i'm an Indian . It's because i earned it on my merits. Listen dear ,i don't want to argue over this, because you know as well as i do, my dad is going to do as he wants to no matter what we say.

I'M sorry ,i don't want to argue either. ANNE replies . You know that he's starting to tell Charlie about all these old stories ?

Yes Anne i know, he used to tell them to me too ,when i was his age. Don't worry they are harmless, most of them are just exaggerated legends anyway.

Anne and Walter made up and went back to their usual routine. Working and earning the money they needed to pay for their more than modest home. They were both successful and earned a good living . Several days had passed and on this particular occasion Anne and Walter happened to be coming home from work ,each approaching the spot in the hills where Walters father likes to sit and gaze across the cliffs and bluffs in the foothills of lower Colorado, not far from the Oklahoma panhandle. This time was a little different though, Charlie was on the cliffs with his grandfather and as far the parents new ,this was a first .They didn't live far from this site ,so they continued home each entering their drive at the same time. When Anne got out of her car it was more than obvious , she was more than perturbed by what she just saw.

Although Walter was calm and leaned more to wonder why his son was spending time like this with his grandfather, instead of playing video games the way he always does. He seemed to like the idea and even had a slight smile from it.

Did you see ,what I just saw Walter? He's got our ten year old son on that cliff ! What if something happens ? He knows how dangerous those cliffs are ! I think you need to go down there and get him before something happens.

Dear you are over reacting ,dad isn't going to let any thing happen to Charlie ,he's been climbing and walking cliffs his whole life. Hell, he can get around on them better than we can. Do not worry, it will be alright.

What if something happens to your dad,? What then?

It will be alright dear .Now lets go inside and i'll help you cook supper when you rest some.

They went inside and rested some ,then decided to cook their evening meal ,Anne was still worried ,and growing more tense. It was now near dark and Charlie and his grandfather hadn't shown yet. Anne pointed at Walter and with a stern stare in her eyes said ;Walter you need to go and find them ,now ! I don't like this one bit ,he knows better than to keep him out after dark.

I told you dear they'll be here any————-

Just as Walter was about to finish his sentence Charlie and John Walter Stoutman walked in the front door, giving it a slam as they entered.

See ANNE ! I told you it would be o.k.

John Walter and Charlie walked into the kitchen and instantly ,John could tell there was tension between the two of them , even though he didn't say anything ,he knew it was because of him. It was quiet , up until they all sat down for supper, then Charlie started telling his parents about the story his grandfather had been telling him this afternoon . He was too young to realize the conversation he was trying to start, was only fueling the tension already present.

EAT YOUR SUPPER !! Anne snapped out in anger.

What did i do mom ? Charlie ask.

Even though Anne's next statement didn't match her character and it was rare that she would even raise her voice to Charlie, but this time she did.

I SAID SHUT UP AND EAT!! Anne was furious and this confused everyone at the table.

Walter as surprised as he was started to say something , when John interrupted. Wait son, let the boy finish his food ,then we will all talk, i know what's going on and we can discuss it later.

The rest of the meal time was quiet ,everyone just stared down at their plates while they ate ,as each one finished their meal they took their plates to the kitchen and cleaned them up.

Charlie , why don't you go into the den while your mom, dad and i talk? It'll be ok ,we just have some things to discuss. I will come and see you later.

Walter was building a head of steam, it was clear that he wasn't happy about his wife's anger , and did not understand where it came from.

Anne ,what was that all about ,at dinner?

Anne started to speak ,when John cut her short in sentence. Wait Anne ,i know what's bothering you .You think i'm teaching your son , bad things. I assure you that i would never tell that boy anything, that would hurt him in any way. The ways of the Cherokee are simple ,and they go back farther than when this country was discovered much ,much farther. I tell Charlie these things so they won't be forgotten , just as i have told Walter. I know your family has only been in this country a couple of generations, so you do not understand .

Dad i don't think that has anything to do with anything ! Walter quickly butts in .

It doesn't son, when you are talking about things in general, but we are talking about a different culture ,and when someone doesn't understand a different culture they push it away or try to change it .It isn't any different today ,than it was two hundred years ago. If we don't like who you are, we'll put you on a reservation and we won't have to deal with you .That is how it's been, and how people have thought for many, many years. The truth is, you two have done well for yourselves, and you don't want anything to change that. I understand that. The boy is interested in what i have to tell him, and it won't cause him any harm.

MR.STOUTMAN? Anne says sternly ,I don't want Charlie's head filled notions of spirits ,or people dieing .He doesn't have to know how a bird thinks or why a coyote runs in packs ,these things are irrelevant in today's society. What he needs to know is how to read well, and write well, he needs to know how to work different gadgets and how to be successful. He needs to be smart, so he can go to collage and get a degree.

Anne as long you think that way ,maybe you are the one who needs an education, and i'm not talking about anything you can learn from a book.

Having said that John Walter quietly, but hastily leaves the room and goes out to the patio to sit alone. Anne and Walter are left standing in the kitchen ,each one arguing back and forth about their opinions and what should be done about the situation with John Walter.

Several days pass and all seemed to be back to normal, and they continued on the way they always have .One afternoon, late evening the sun had nearly set , leaving the most beautiful array of colors on the horizon . It looked as if the sun seemed to have found a spot to rest in between a clearing in a cliffy landscape. Oranges ,reds, yellows , blues mixed together to paint the sky ,leaving the sun to dimly light up and create a skyline that wouldn't last but a few more minutes , giving it all away to darkness. Walter walks up to where his father was sitting on the ground of the cliff ,he always sat on.

Beautiful evening isn't it dad ? I can see why you sit up here so much.

Sit and join me by the fire son ,lets talk awhile .

Walter did as he was ask ,although it was quiet for a few moments, when John noticed a somewhat puzzling look on Walter's face. He knew something was troubling him and wanted to ease his mind if he could.

Let's have it Walter ? What's got you so troubled ,that you came up here? Just tell me what's on your mind and don't hold back any thing.

Well ,alright then dad . Anne and i have been talking ,we want you to spend all the time with Charlie you want too. It's just ———————- well it's ,we don't care for you telling him all those old legends , We don't want to confuse him, it's difficult enough on him already. Dad i know that the old ways are important to you and that's fine ,but people don't live that way any more.

That's my point exactly son, our people don't live ,that way any more! The traditions we had and the beliefs we lived by are what kept our people together and strong. When the last one of our people that knows these ways, die .It will be like we never existed to begin with. The borders of our reservations will be erased and our land ,that i might add keeps getting smaller every day ,will be sold to the highest bidder . I fought in two wars to protect the American way of life and being an American ,that gave me the right to hold on to the ways of our people .It gave me a right to be who i am and it gave me a right to be proud of what i am . I am an American Native in both senses of the word. If you and Anne don't want me to pass on, what i know, to Charlie, i will try to respect that. I want you to remember one thing ,when you let him watch those westerns on TV. and in the movies, no matter how entertaining they are, they were made to make money,,, not to tell the truth .If someone doesn't tell him the truth then he will always think that Indians are savages and all Indians lived in tee pees and killed people viciously . If that is what you want him to believe, then i have no choice but respect your wish.

Dad i hadn't thought about it that way, but Anne will never understand it that way. She's my wife and i have to go along with her wishes, whether i like them or not.

Because she's your wife, it's very important that both of you teach your son both of your cultures, then he will have enough knowledge to choose his own path. I hope i have helped to ease your troubles, but i want to be alone now .

Walter walks back to his home leaving his father to himself. He enters the living room where Anne is watching TV., she notices he is there and points out the humor of the program she is watching . Walter isn't really interested and is deep in thought from the conversation he and his dad just had . He decides go to bed and after he kisses Anne goodnight he stops by Charlie's room to tell him goodnight . Still deep in thought he turns in for the night.

The next morning Walter was awaken by Charlie with a hard shake ,his voice was frantic and he was near in tears.

DAD! DAD! Grandfather is leaving ,he's packing his belongings and he says he's going back home . I thought this was his home?

Walter sprang up from his sleep and at the same time. Anne also heard what was going on and quickly followed Walter downstairs to the new addition where, John was staying. Both looked confused as they entered John's bedroom.

What are you doing Mr. Stoutman ? Why are you leaving ? Your son had this new addition built on the house for you and you don't want to live in it. I don't understand you ,at all, you should be grateful to have this nice place to live.

Dad what's going on? We can work this out .Let's talk for a minute. Walter was worried and puzzled at his dads actions. His fear was his dad would go back to his old shack, that had been condemned for several years. He remembered how hard it was to talk him out of it the first time.

Anne breaks in again . Mr. Stoutman look at what you are doing to your grandson !!

This is my reason for doing what i'm doing ,if i tell him something or i show him something you say i'm doing something to him. You have not even, one time, sense i have been here, told me i was doing something for him. I only agreed to live here so that you didn't have to drive so far to visit and make you feel better. I was fine where i was at. Let me tell you this also,, young lady ,you've been calling me Mr. Stoutman for eleven years now, if we were friends on the street that would be respectful ,but i'm your father in law . And you've not once acknowledged that. As for you Walter ,you built this add on for your benefit ,not mine.!

You felt that it would keep you from having to put me in an old peoples home. Plus it couldn't hurt the value of the house either. You felt i could cause you less trouble here . I didn't live in that shack because i had too ,i lived there because i wanted too!! I have plenty of money to do anything i want. If you'll remember correctly, i have always had a good job.

So now give me a hug u-gv-wi-yu-hi {CHIEF} and i'll be on my way. John says to Charlie as he throws his bag over his shoulder and starts to leave the room.

Wait grand pa , Charlie calls out. When will i see you again ?

Soon son, soon, i won't be that far away.

John Walter walks down the long narrow stretch of road that leads to his son's home, leaving his son and daughter in law with their heads hug low, neither one feeling good about themselves, because they each knew in their hearts, all that he had said was mostly true.

John didn't look back, he just kept walking .

As sad as they all were Charlie would stand to lose the most ,his time with his grandfather was special to him. He loved to hear the stories and old legends and looked forward to them each day. Even though he was to young to know what he was feeling, he knew he felt different when he was on the cliffs with John, and he liked sitting by the fire and just talking and asking questions. The most important part to him was ,he was getting answers to his questions.

Several weeks passed by, leaving a void in the lives of Walter and his family. Things just weren't the same without John Walter. School was near the end of it's year and would be letting out for the summer soon. Walter knew this would leave Charlie alone while they worked. Charlie was responsible ,and could take care of himself a few hours a day ,he just didn't seem the same since his grandfather left.

Anne missed John, but not like the others. Her routine didn't change much one way or the other. One evening while watching the news she saw something that caught her by surprise.

WALTER ! ,WALTER COME IN HERE QUICK ,YOUR DAD IS ON THE NEWS WITH A COUPLE OF OTHER OLD MEN.

Walter rushes into where his wife was and just as he entered the room the news cast was over. What was it all about dear ? What did they say?

I didn't catch all of it . They said something about they were veterans of some war, and they were all Native Americans and, something about taking some sort of trip, that was all i heard .

My dad was in Korea and VIET NAM ,he was part of some special tribal group or something . I don't really know, because he didn't talk about it . Those other men must have been in the same group.

Walter doesn't think too much about it for the rest of the evening and continues to go about his evening as he normally would. Walter wakes the next morning and dresses for work. He is almost at the front door to leave when the phone rings .This call would leave him shocked . Anne walks by on her way out for work and notices the look on Walters face.

What's wrong dear? Anne asks .

That was my dad's doctor, he said dad needs to come in for an operation, it seems dad has a couple of tumors that needs to be removed .I don't think i need to give you the, or else part. Apparently dad has known about this for a long time. The doctor said he hasn't been in for an appointment in several months and was wondering, well you know ,if he was still alive.

Did you know anything about a doctor?

NO! HE DIDN'T TALK TO ME ,THAT MUCH! Anne replied harshly.

I'm going to go to the reservation and see if i can find him, call my work and tell them i'm going to take some time off, and i'll call them later to explain. Give me a kiss ,and i'll see you when i get back, i don't know how long it will take me to find him. He could be anywhere with in hundred mile radius at the reservation .

Walter speeds out of his driveway as if he were in a race of some sort . He arrives at the reservation that is a couple hours away. Only after asking several people and spending several hours looking does he locate the where abouts of John Walter and goes to the cliffs where he's been camping sense he left Walters home. Walter walks down a little trail to the bluffs until he comes up on his father sitting by a fire. Walter stops a few feet behind him and looks at how at ease his dad is. He notices that his dad is dressed in traditional Cherokee clothing .Which is something he'd only seen him do one other time, when his mother passed away several years before. As he stands there quietly watching and listening to John Walter chanting and praying in the Cherokee language, he isn't even sure his dad knows that he's there. John Walter finishes his prayer and without turning around speaks to Walter.

Hello ka-nu-nu {Bullfrog}, come and sit with me by the fire .

Dad you haven't called me that sense i was a teenager .The reason i'm here —-

I know why you are here .The spirits told me you were coming, they said you would be sad and try to make me come back with you. They told me not to go back with you.

Did the spirits tell you that you were going to die, if you don't go back with me.

They did not have to ,when my mother ,my father ,and my brothers and sisters died ,i knew this would also ,be my destiny , "ka-nu-nu" the spirits have told me 'to keep someone alive against their destiny is selfish, to wish someone to die is evil ,to let someone die with honor and dignity, is love.' When i earn my place in the upper spirit world ,i will see my mother and father ,brothers and sisters again. I will get to walk and hunt with my grandfather, and i will get to hear the songs of my wife "wa-le-lu" { HUMMING BIRD } again.

Dad ,you said 'earn my place? What is that supposed to mean ? I can see that you miss mom and the rest of our family, and i understand that , but what makes me leery, is when an old Indian says earn. What are you up to dad? I know you got some, half crazy, half baked sceam planed.

Because you do not live by the old ways ,you may not understand what i am going to do, and it's not a sceam. It is my destiny. It is my rite of passage to the upper world. This is what i have been waiting on , the spirits to tell me what to do. Our people must remember the suffering ,they must know ,about the sorrow our ancestors endured ,they must know, how it was and remember, so the way it will be, can only be better.

Dad i hate when you talk in riddles ! Because i do not have the slightest idea, of what you are talking about.

Knowledge comes to those who listen and do not talk. A vision comes to those that look but can not see, and patience comes to those that wait and do not hurry, Walter.

Dammit dad ,!There you go again! WHAT IN THE HELL, ARE YOU TALKING ABOUT!!?

ALRIGHT WALTER ! SHUT UP- WAIT AND WATCH ,THEN YOU WILL SEE WHAT I'M GOING TO DO!! BUT DO NOT RAISE YOUR VOICE TO ME IN DISRESPECT AGAIN!!!

I'm sorry dad ,you just have me confused ,is all. It will never happen again.

John Walter may have medical problems, but he by all means was not a weak man, in any since of the word. His will was strong and he knew what he wanted to do. He was somewhere in between stubborn and determined ,he had been given a vision and nothing and no one would stop him from achieving his destiny,, or rite of passage. His beliefs in the old traditional Cherokee ways were never stronger than they are now. His beliefs are what kept him alive, they kept him proud and gave him courage when he had to have it the most. They also may very well be the reason he has the strength to live out his destiny and to die with dignity.

"ka-nu-nu " Grab some wood and build the fire up high .I am going to tell you some things i have never told you before. When you were little, you were too young to hear them and when you were older, you were too busy to listen. The fire will be bright enough for you to see a vision of what i am explaining to you.

When i was young ,before i went to war, i was told part of my destiny by the spirits. They told me ,that i must be brave, that i must be a fearless warrior and i must prove to them that i was worthy of my destiny.

When the war in Korea started, i joined the Army along with some of the other natives .They needed someone to run the front lines and relay messages to those who couldn't use the radios, because they made too much noise. We also had to fight single handed against several North Koreans many times. We spent most of our time in the forests and jungle alone. We were watching the Koreans and they didn't even know we were there. There were seven of us, all natives ,all warriors from different Indian nations. Each of us had very strong traditional beliefs.

Anne said she saw you and some other men on the news ?

She did, they wanted to honor the seven of us with medals ,we took them, so they would not feel bad, but the spirits didn't need them, we proved ourselves and the spirits saw our bravery. All seven of us came home after the war and found jobs working up high, building skyscrapers. The spirits of the 'a-wo-ha-li '{Eagles} kept us safe and made us unafraid. Then a few years later our country joined the war in VIET NAM ,once again we volunteered .We met and all seven went in at one time even though we operated separately in the war, the spirits kept us safe as if we were one unit. We were able to go some places the other troupes could not. We could move like the possum and the raccoon do at night, in and out of trees without a sound. We could scurry quickly across the ground like a field mouse, then attack like the panther .The Army used us, because they could not train anyone to do these things, the spirits show us in our visions. When we were all together ,we were like the coyote and we would confuse them and attack them all at once.

Thanks for telling me that dad ,i understand more now than i did, but i still want to know why you won't let the doctors operate. They can remove the tumors and you have a better chance of living.

The only chance at living you have, is to live while you are alive and i have done that. Do not confuse existing with living ,they are not the same. Existing breaks a man's spirit and it weakens his soul .To live you
must out run the bear, because he is fast. To live you must out think the fox ,because he is smart. You must soar higher than an Eagle, because he is fearless. The spirits have given me my path and if they want the tumors gone, then they will take them away. If i let the doctors operate on me,, it will change my destiny. I don't want to just exist ,i want to go to the next part of my life.

Walter still disapproves of his dads decision, but he knows he has no choice ,but except them. OK dad i know you are going to do, what you want to do . So will you tell me what it is ?

Sure Walter , i am going to walk back the way we came.

Dad you are doing that riddle thing again.

The 'Nunna Daul Tsuny' i am going to walk back the way our people came on the TRAIL OF TEARS, this will complete my destiny . Walter when you and Anne didn't want me to tell Charlie the old legends ,the spirits told me there were many like you . The ones like me are old now and many of them are completing their destiny . So that leaves very few of us to carry on the traditions. Sense there are more like you, than me, our memory will not survive much longer. The spirits tell me, my walk back will get the attention of our younger people and this will help keep the traditions alive. There is a big gathering of the Cherokee Nations in East Tennessee in the fall, and i'm going to be there for it.

Are you sure, you are going to do this dad?

Yes i am, it is my rite of passage. Its my destiny. It's living and not existing.

Very well then ,i won't try to stop you, but if you can't complete the journey alone,, let me help you .

The spirits will help me, but you are welcome to come with me.

You know i can't because of my work. It will take you several months to do this and i can't get that much time off work. Where are you going to start at dad ?

I am going to start where the trail ended, Tahlequah Oklahoma, even though the old fort is not there anymore, i know where it was and i'll start there. My journey will take me through many towns and states , Missouri ,Illinois, Kentucky and Tennessee. It will end in what we now call Charleston Tennessee. This will be the greatest experience i will ever have had.

If you want me to dad, i will take you to the starting point and see you off.

I was hoping you would want to 'ka-nu-nu' and if Anne will let you bring 'u-gv-wi-yu-hi' ,it may be the last chance i have to see him.

I will dad .When are you going to leave?

Three days from now. Me and the other elders are going to have a vidule and the other six of my old unit will be there also, to represent their tribes as well .This isn't just about our own people, it's about all Native Americans.

O.K dad, i have to leave now ,but i will be back to take you to the starting point.

Walter told his dad by and left to go back home, even though his ride wasn't real long, a couple of hours or so. It gave Walter some time to think ,and he now had a better understanding of why his father was the way he was. After talking to his dad this time Walter couldn't help but remember his own childhood, he knew he didn't have a bad childhood ,but his life seemed to have a void and he didn't realize what it was until now. Walter could only remember a few of the stories he had been told and they were sketchy at best.

He realized why he did not know what his father was talking about most of the time, because he wasn't interested when he was younger. Walter's mind wandered the rest of his trip back home. No mater how hard he tried he couldn't piece his memories of the old legends back together .This seemed to sadden him , tears began to collect in his eyes ,he was not crying ,but something seemed to be talking to him and he didn't know what . Almost as fast as he became confused, it became clear to him why his father was doing what he was doing.

Walter was nearing the outer borders of the reservation when he saw some young kids playing and gathering .They were a mixture of teenagers and near teenagers, some were playing basketball with an old bicycle rim for a goal and a partially flat ball .The rest were just sitting on benches and make shift seats talking and acting like teenagers do . Walter stopped ,turned around and pulled up to where they were . When he got out of his truck they hardly paid any attention to him until he cleared his throat .

Excuse me? Walter said kind of loud.

They seemed to ignore him at first until he got louder .
EXCUSE ME !I WANT TO ASK YOU SOME QUESTIONS!!.

This got their attention, then a couple of the older teenagers walked over to him ,by the way they looked at him he knew they didn't trust him and their posture assured him of it.

What are you up to dude ? The largest of them ask .You a cop or something, or are you crazy??

No i am neither one .I just want to ask a couple of simple questions and i'll pay five bucks for each correct answer. Anyone interested ?

Yeh !!They all seemed to answer back at once. Go ahead ask your questions, but you better pay up or you'll get jacked up .The bigger one said with a serious look in his eyes.

Can anyone tell me where the 'Nunna Daul Tsuny' is??
No one answered

Alright then, how about "Stand Waite" or John Ross? How about Major Ridge ? Does anyone know who they are?
Still no one answered.

O.K. i'm sorry i'll just ask one more, then i'll leave you young people be.
Does anyone know where the 'TRAIL OF TEARS ' is ??

They all seemed to shrudge their shoulders ,Walter knew that his dad wasn't exaggerating now . Then one of the younger children walked up to Walter .

Mister, i know the answers .Do you want me to tell you ?
No little fellow ,here is ten dollars anyway . Walter starts to get in his truck and leave when he hollered for the big ones to come back. Listen i'm sorry i bothered you kids, here is a hundred dollars .Can i trust you to go and buy you kids a new ball goal and basketball?

For sure mister ,and you can ask us questions anytime you want.

Walter returned home ,however the next few days weren't the same, he was distant and always in deep thought, Anne noticed his change and seemed concerned, when finally she confronts him about it .

I've never seen you like this .What is bothering you, is it your dad or work ? Maybe i can help you .

I told you about my dads plan and the kids on the reservation and the questions i ask them .

Yeh that's sad, but what makes you think you can do anything about it ?

I don't know if i can or not, but i know i grew up on that reservation and i know how hard it was sometimes . When dad came back from Viet Nam we had to move into the city so he could find work, he took good care of me and mom .We pretty well got what we wanted because of his hard work .I got my work ethic from him, so i have to say i have what i have because of him. What i am getting at is ,even though i don't understand his beliefs. I am still part of him and Charlie is part of him, so i have to respect that . No matter how hard it is to believe . I am Cherokee and so is my son and we will learn the way of the Cherokee, weather we live it or not . No matter who likes or doesn't like it. I have to pick him up tomorrow morning and take him to TAHLEQUA , i'll be leaving real early .

WAIT JUST A MINUTE WALTER!! ? YOU'RE GOING WITH HIM AREN'T YOU ? THEN THERE WILL BE TWO CRAZY INDIANS OUT THERE!!

This infuriated Walter, he hasn't gotten this upset sense he and ANNE met ,but this time her not understanding pushed a button that she had never pushed before. He tried to hold in his anger, but it was impossible .

NO I AM NOT GOING WITH MY DAD !! HE IS NOT CRAZY AND NIETHER AM I, DON'T EVER!! AND I MEAN !! EVER !! refer to me or my dad as CRAZY INDIANS!! AGIAN !!!

This caught Anne by surprise, for the first time in their entire relationship Walter had lost control of his emotions and she was afraid of it .She began to cry and tremble ,her hands began to shake to the point where Walter grabbed them to hold them still. As he did he pulled her close to him and gave her a hug and kiss on the forehead .Walter held on to her tight ,he had an enormous amount of remorse ,because his anger caught him by surprise too.

That afternoon Anne and Walter settled what differences they had and Walter told Anne some of the stories his dad had told him .Most of them were just how the Cherokee lived and where they originally came from ,he told her how they were primarily farmers and hunters ,that they lived in log homes and solid built dome huts .The information he gave her was basic and didn't have many details. Anne told him what it was like being a third generation American and how difficult it was for her grandfather to get citizenship when he came to the U.S. from Russia. Because of his political ties he was exiled .She told him how she was primarily raised in a Russian community in New York City. Anne was educated by her parents and grandparents and tested for college on her on .

Walter most of what I know about Russia ,i heard on the news .The information my family gave me was highly filtered. This country is no different than there, people are persecuted because of who they are and where they came from ,their religion, race, nationality always seem to separate them. I don't know why, but i didn't want Charlie exposed to that ,it will be hard enough on him as it is .

They finished their conversation and went about their normal routine until bed time. Then they both turned in for the night .They awoke early the next morning as planned and Walter woke Charlie so that he could go with him and see his grandfather off .On the trip Charlie had a lot of questions that were hard for Walter to answer. As hard as it was for Walter to restrain himself, Charlie left him vulnerable .Walter finally answered as many as he could, but the final straw was when he ask if his grandfather was going to die .Other than tell him that everybody does sooner or later, he tried to act like he didn't hear him.

Dad! Charlie said getting louder . I know about the tumors, what are they anyway?

Almost instantly Walter slammed on the brakes and pulled the truck over to the side of the road. WHO, IN THE HELL TOLD YOU ABOUT THAT ? Walter quickly responded . If that damn doctor said anything I'll —

Wait dad,, it was on the answering machine one day when i got home from school. A lady was trying to get a hold of grandpa and i just overheard is all . Are they bad for you ?

Yes son, they can be if they aren't treated . When i see your grandfather again he's going to get a piece of my mind for making me have to answer these questions. Better yet son when we get there, you ask him, these questions.

I'm sorry i made you mad dad ,i was just curious is all .

You didn't make me mad son , it's just your grandfather has a way of leaving things up for grabs sometimes .

It was quiet the rest of the trip to the reservation . When they entered the reservation Charlie had a curious look on his face .This was his first trip there and it was apparent that it wasn't what he expected. He looked at his dad with kind of a sigh as if he didn't know what to say.

I know what you are thinking son, where are all the horses or teepees ? How come there aren't any kids playing ball ? How come most of the houses are in bad shape. Things like that . Well son our government considers the reservations soveren nations which means they have a separate leader or chief and operate under their own laws . Then they don't have to give the same assistance the rest of the country gets. It gets really complicated after that and even me being a legal major in college ,i don't understand it very well.

Walter arrived where his father was waiting for him .John Walter's fellow army buddies were there as well as the other elders and various people from the reservation. A small news paper operated by someone on the reservation was there taking down names in order to have something to fill it's pages .John Walter was dressed in traditional Cherokee clothing a bright colored head scarf tied so that both hanging parts hung to one side of his head. His shirt was bright colored mostly white with beads and buttons sewn in various shapes. His pants were made of a soft brown leather with fringes hanging from the entire length of the legs. Although there weren't any headdresses of feathers ,the men representing the other tribes were dressed in their own traditional wear.

Walter and Charlie got out of the truck and Charlie ran over to his grandfather .Grandfather we came to take you to Tahlequah ,are you ready?

Yes Chief i am, but first you must meet some friends of mine. These six men here are all elders of other tribes like the Lakota ,Sioux ,Apache ,Chickasaw, Creek and Choctaw. Their blood is mixed many times with other tribes ,so you could say all Native Americans are represented here today.

I will call them by their tribal name .The first one is 'Runs Quickly' he is a Lakota elder, the second one is LINCOLN NIGHTHAWK he is a Chief of the SOUIX . The man to his right is an APACHIE warrior ,in the Viet Nam war he was the bravest man i have ever saw. It was his job to go behind the lines of the enemy and capture officers for interrogation . He also rescued many of our fellow soldiers and brought them back to safety, when no one else could. We call him 'DE-WA-' ''[FLYING SQUIRREL] He had an ability to jump from tree to tree in the jungle with out ever being noticed .One particular time he captured three officers and rescued twenty wounded soldiers in one trip.

The man to his right is" CHICASAW "CHARLES HOUSE he is a direct descendent of the first of our people to survive 'THE TRAIL WHERE THEY CRIED" and a medicine man of his tribe. Robert White standing next to him is of the Creek, his people are also Survivors of the walk here. The last of my unit, we just call him "U-HO-I——-SV-GA-TA "BAD APPLE" he could get us in more trouble without even trying . When we were resting sometimes, if we saw the enemy ,we would have orders not to confront them . DO NOT DRAW ANY ATTENTION TO YOURSELVES !! they would say. But for him that was like saying .Go ahead,!! Get captured !!!! and he did many times, but he always escaped bringing others with him. He is Choctaw. He is the only Indian that I have ever seen, that couldn't sneak up on anyone. HA!HA!!

Charlie these men that you see before you ,weren't really part of any unit ,we were expendable ,so were many other men of all types, we were no different than anyone else, except we all went in alive and we all came out alive. Many people do not believe as we do, but it was the spirits of our ancestors that kept us brave and safe.

Of course Charlie being the age he was, sometimes would ask questions that he shouldn't.

WOW!! HOW MANY PEOPLE DID YOU KILL.? Charlie ask excitedly

John then looked at Walter not knowing how to answer that question. They were quiet for a moment each looking at each other in awe. Then FLYING SQUIRREL spoke up.

Young warrior, it was not our job to kill anyone ,our job was to save lives and deliver messages, quickly and quietly. If we had to kill anyone it was because we had to, not because we wanted to .Your grandfather

probably saved the lives of several thousand men, as we all did. Always remember ,being a warrior is not about how many people you can kill. It is about how brave you are and how many people you can save. To be a warrior is to be afraid, but have courage, to fight ,but if possible ,not harm . When you are a warrior, your people know that they are safe when you are with them. A warrior must always protect those that can not protect themselves. He cares for the old and the sick, he teaches the children compassion and pride . But most importantly a warrior must always remain alive to help his people.

Flying Squirrel saying what he said took the pressure off everyone else .Walter told his dad that they needed to get going because they had a long drive ahead of them. John agreed and shook hands with all of his old friends each one giving him a little trinket to carry with him on his journey. John put the trinkets in a small bag and put them in the truck along with a large shoulder mounted back pack. The back pack had tied to it all the accessories he would need for the walk ahead a bedroll, canteen ,length of rope, small fishing pole, were just some of the items .They drove away leaving all of them cheering and waving as they passed through the reservation.

Three generations were in the truck, each with a different idea of what to believe in ,this probably no different than any other family. Each generation leaving out a part of the history of the generation before and causing a void for those who follow. Sometimes when this happens an entire family history and the culture of an entire people are erased. John's fear was that this might very well happen to his own family and tribe. The quest he was about to under go ,he hoped would open the minds of generations to come. His goal was to bring some life back into his people and country that was so dear to him.

John's last war would be fought against an invisible enemy. This enemy had the weapon to erase the memory ,the pride and strength that had been passed down from his ancestors .He knew that the only way to preserve this history ,was to make a statement . Not by talking, but by opening a door to a room full of old and ancient ideas. John felt that if he opened the minds of not only his own culture ,but all cultures. Pride ,faith, hope and determination could be restored. He felt that all people need not just survive ,but be alive in their hearts.

Not long after they left the reservation Charlie fell asleep like most kids do on long trips. Walter and John mostly reminisced about when each were young how the reservation had changed and how people in general had changed. They passed through towns and John showed Walter some of the high rises he helped to build. Sometimes they didn't say a word for several minutes and when they did it was just small talk. Walter was deep in thought and appeared distant at times ,it was like he was trying to make up his mind about something, but couldn't. When they arrived in Tahlequah they decided to rent a room for the night, so John Walter could get a fresh start the next morning.

The next morning John awoke and started to wake the other two but Walter was not in his bed, he looked out the window and Walter's truck was gone. Sadness had started to fall on him when he turned on the light and saw Charlie was still asleep on the floor .Then he turned to see a brand new back pack in the corner with a note pinned on it .

Dear dad, I awoke early and went and bought these supplies for Charlie, he has everything in there he should need .I put him a brand new hunting knife in the side pouch and it's o.k. for him to wear it. I had it engraved to mark the date of probably the most important thing he will ever do in his life. Me letting him go with you is the most important thing ,i have ever done. Only you can teach him what he needs to know .Take care of him and tell him i said to take care of you .I will catch you, somewhere on the trip . YOUR SON " KA -NU- NU ".

John Walter and Charlie were happy at the decision Walter had made .They got packed and ready to begin their journey ,after they ate breakfast, they were just outside Tahlequah, John begins to tell Charlie the story of The Trail of Tears ,and where they were headed first on the trail.

Charlie seemed to be having trouble with his pack, he didn't know to wear it high on his shoulders. The weight was hanging too low, causing him loss of balance and minor pain .John made the adjustments needed and they began to increase their pace.

Chief when you want to stop and rest tell me and we will rest. I do not want you to get too tired, we have a long way to go.

It's o.k. grandfather a warrior doesn't complain, he does what he has to, to help his people.

This is good y-gv-wa-yu hi ,you are brave and you were listening back at the reservation .

Where do we have to go first grandfather ?

Our trek will take us to Springfield Missouri first, but there are many stops before we get to Charleston Tennessee . There, is where our people began the walk, this way. There were a couple of trails our people were forced to take. One of the trails began south west of Charleston Tennessee near the Alabama border and dipped down into Mississippi then made its way north into western Tennessee then finally North into Kentucky and southern Illinois. Then they took the Mississippi River way south to the mouth of the Arkansas and finally north and west again. The other went almost straight across from Charleston to Tahlequah only crossing the Mississippi River once. But the one we are taking is the second longest one.

How long will it take us to get there grandfather?

If we can walk twenty mile a day, maybe only two months, but the spirits don't want us to go that fast. Our mission is to give a message to all our people .We must remind them to remember, not only the pain the five tribes suffered but the pride and traditions we had. The spirits tell me this is the end of my destiny .Now they are telling me this is the beginning of yours. Chief this may sound like a drastic way to get them to see. But many ,many years ago warriors were not much older than you, when they started their visions. The ghost of our ancestors can be seen by those that believe, and they are invisible to those that do not.

John and Charlie walked at a good pace on their first day, stopping only to eat and view sights along the way. By late afternoon Walter had made it home and he knew Anne would not be happy about his decision and expected trouble from her ,for it. Walter walked into his house and his wife met him in the hallway on his way looking for her .

Walter where is Charlie? She asked not thinking anything at first. Wait a minute ! Walter you didn't let him do what i think? Did you ?Tell me he is outside somewhere!

Before you say anything, hear me out first? I left him with his grandfather, he needs to be with him right now . My dad can teach him things, i don't know how to teach him . If i hadn't let him go he may not have seen him again .

WHAT IF SOMETHING HAPPENS?!! DID YOU THINK ABOUT THAT!!? HE'S A TEN YEAR OLD BOY !NOT A STUBBERN OLD MAN !!

Calm down ,i know how old he is, that's why i did it . Look i knew you might not agree. The reason i didn't call and tell you is i didn't think about , even letting him go until early this morning. I didn't even tell my father by ,i couldn't bare it .They both will be safe .

WALTER !! IF SOMETHING HAPPENS TO HIM ,I WILL NEVER FORGIVE YOU !!

I know Anne .That's why i hired a couple of ex body guards and police officers to follow them .The good part is dad and chief won't even know they are there .They are only supposed to follow .They are experts in this type of thing. They will not let anything happen to them. You and i are going to take sometime off in a couple of weeks and follow them . I have plenty of vacation time coming and so do you and this is a perfect way to use it. You don't have to worry. They are going to follow them every step of the way.

Grandfather ——-?

Wait y-gv- wa- yu- hi if you are going to be a teacher of our culture you must learn the tongue of our people. In Cherokee i am called ta-li u- gi -da-li '{ Two Feather} . You will have plenty of time to learn on the walk back. You will get to learn many things. I will tell you about the three worlds of our people UPPER , LOWER and the one we live in. I will tell you about THE LITTLE PEOPLE and some stories and legends of chiefs. . But first a-gi-yo-si-ha {'i am hungry'}, lets do some fishing in that stream up there.

But we don't have any bait .

We do not need any, i will tell the spirits to throw them out of the water for us.

For real!! I got a see that !!

NO chief ,,John said as he was laughing .We will find some bait by the bank or we will use spears and gigs. Chief there is always a way to accomplish the things you want to do, if you think first . Sometimes you have to look under rocks and fallen trees or in piles of leaves. You can find bait right where you are going to fish.

John and Charlie had good luck with their fishing , Charlie was having a blast on his first night away from home .John couldn't be any happier either the way he was laughing and joking with Charlie at how he was trying to eat fish from the stick he used to cook their meal over a fire. Charlie was grimacing at the thought of the smoke covered fish, he was eating .This humored John immensely causing him to laugh aloud at him.

Why are you laughing at me ?

Because you were supposed to take the scales off before you started eating it. Didn't your dad show you anything?

Yes grandfather, he showed me where he kept the number to the pizza delivery guy.

Once again they broke into laughter. After they finished their meal John began telling him some stories ,Charlie listened closely taking in every word. Like any kid his age, he kept plenty of wood on the fire lighting up the whole creek bank they would camp on for the night. They were getting ready to go to bed when a highway patrol officer pulled up and turned on his lights. After shining the spot light in their eyes he walked over to where they sitting .

Good evening gentlemen. The officer said in a loud voice. You fellows homeless ?

No officer we are on a journey, a pilgrimage of sort. Why, are we doing something wrong ?

No not really, except your fire's a little high and the grass is a little dry this time of year, we haven't had our spring rains yet.

John slowed the fire to a low glow and asked the officer to sit with them and he would tell him the details of the trip. The officer did and seemed interested in it, until he asked John for some identification.

All i have is my social security card and some credit cards. Will they do? Listen Mr. Stoutman it's very unusual for an old man and a small child to be out on the highway like this, at this time of night .These cards don't really prove who you are and there's all kinds of people in this world now, i'm going to have to call this in .If something happens i don't want to be responsible .You two wait right here while i go to my car .

Charlie was getting a little scared and it showed .His grandfather noticed and told him to not worry they weren't breaking any laws.

The officer went to his car and was gone several minutes before he returned.

I'm sorry sir, for holding you up ,everything checks out .You two be careful and have a safe trip.

The next morning the two of them woke up and began their journey once again .Cleaning their camp site as if they weren't even there .Their trip took them over a hilly terrain and slowed Charlie down leaving John waiting on him at times. Are you o.k. Charlie? John asked

Yes i am fine, these hills are a little steep is all .

There is a little town up ahead, we'll stop there and make it a little easier on us . I'm getting hungry anyway.

Ta-li u-gi-da-li ? Are we going to hunt for our food ,like they did.?

Yes, y-gv-wa-yu-hi all animals leave a track to follow, and if you are patient, food is not hard to find. There are many things we can find to eat . Small animals are sometimes the easiest to catch in snares or traps. We can eat berries and all types of nuts from the trees. Tree bark ,some types of roots, grubs worms ,and insects will do in a desperate situation. You must be careful i am on a trail now, it has left large tracks to follow, it won't take us but a few minutes to find our breakfast.

What is it grandfather a rabbit or squirrel or something.?

No Charlie ,it's that cafe up there these tracks lead right to it. HA!HA!HA!

I thought you said we were going to hunt for our food 'ta-li u-gi-da-li '?

Charlie true warriors , will only kill when it is necessary to .When you kill an animal needlessly, you kill part of your own spirit .When an animal gives you his life ,so you can survive ,then his spirit becomes part of you . It then goes to the upper world. I will show you our ways to hunt, but there is not any need to kill. People have been killing animals without a need for too many years now, they hunt them now for their horns and heads to hang on a wall , their spirits are dieing a little at a time and they may not get into the upper world.

John Walter and Charlie traveled at a good pace for two weeks finally reaching Springfield Mo. Although not a giant city but larger than any they had been through thus far. Charlie was amazed at all the rushing around going on .They walked near to the center of town to do a little sight seeing before going on ,however John wanted to get out of the city before night fall. They weren't dressed according to the norm and people began staring and pointing at them, sometimes even making comments like' hey where's the rain dance '?Anything for people to be cruel was happening and it unnerved John. As they were starting to leave the outskirts of the city they were approached by some hoodlums ,who started harassing them.

"Hey chief where's your squaw "? Things of this nature. You got money old man? One of them asked. Just give us your money and we'll let you go .

Want to go ahead and help them out , one of the body guards asked the other .

No not yet, the old man looks pretty tough ,let's wait a second and see what happens, we are not supposed to blow our cover ,unless we just have to.

John Walter pulled Charlie behind him and his posture changed, he began to change to a defensive stance .

Young men you will save your selves a lot of pain, if you just walk away now, and leave us be .

To these thugs was this sounded more like a challenge than a warning. I guess we will just have to take your money old man, one said as he took a swing at John . John ducked and grabbed the boy by his arm as it passed in front of him spinning the boy and twisting his arm behind him . John pushed the boys arm up as high as he could with out breaking it .Leaving the boy in severe pain, nearly in tears the boy tells his friends who were about to help him. Stop he'll break it if you don't back off . Please mister we will leave, if you let me go . John's anger was at it's highest sense he was in the war and he had a blank look on his face, almost as if he weren't looking at anything.

It's too late now boy, i warned you not to bother us ,now your not so tough are you?

We had better stop him ,i've seen that look before, he is going to hurt that boy real bad, if we don't . One of the men following them said . Look follow my lead and get out your badge . As they drove up closer, they jumped out of the car .STOP! POLICE ! LET THE BOY GO SIR? WE WILL TAKE OVER FROM HERE !

John did as he was asked coming back to his senses .Sorry officers i don't know what got into me, i was just protecting the boy is all .

It's o.k. sir, we'll take it from here ,you and the boy are free to go .

The two body guards watched as John and Charlie walked and turned a corner out of sight .Then they turned to the thugs still standing there . Since they were getting paid, they assumed they needed to earn it. WELL BOYS, YOU MADE TWO MISTAKES TONIGHT .One, you took on an old man who knows how to defend himself. And the worst one you believed we were cops. We get paid to fight ,so welcome to your first free ass whooping tonight!

The two body guards beat the thugs up a bit , not hurting them, but teaching them a lesson. After that they decided they needed to find a new car .

I'm going to find a car rental and get us a new car, the old timer knows this one now. The driver of the car said. Hey how did you know the old man was going to hurt the boy? The other one asked.

The move he used on the thug ,was only taught to an elite special forces squad .We called them Night Stalkers. Because they mostly moved at night .There were only seven of them, all Indians and all as ruthless and deadly as a rattler. If we hadn't stopped him, that boy would be dead right now! His next move was to rip that boy's arm out of his shoulder socket and break his neck at the same time.

The man that hired us said we had to protect the old man and boy, but it looks like we may have to protect every one else from him. HA!Ha!HA!!

The two men changed cars and continued to follow the two travelers at a safe distance and for the next few days all was quiet. John and Charlie seemed to be speeding up some as Charlie was getting stronger and able carry his pack easier.

Charlie we are going to leave the highway now and go into the wilderness, so we can stay on the trail .We will stop up here and get some supplies, our loads will get heavier and it will be more dangerous. You must be very careful at all times.

John Walter was in the store while Charlie stayed outside sitting on a bench watching their packs and enjoying the rest, after near a half days walk. A van pulls up near where he was sitting and a lady dressed in a business suit walked over to where he was sitting.

Hello young man you sure do look cute in your costume. Are you going to a party or something?

NO MAM , my grandfather and i are walking the NUNNA DAUL TSUNY back to where it started .

What is that? She asked

You know mam, The Trail of Tears it's an old Indian trail . He is teaching me my heritage .

Wait a second young man ? Where is your grandfather at now?

He's coming out of the store right now. Grandpa these people want to talk to you .

She stuck her hand out and introduced herself and Walter did the same.

I'm from the local news paper ,i would like to hear more about your trip if you have time .I would also like to put it in tomorrows paper .I think this would be a great public interest story.

John thought for a second,,, Yes mam, my grandson and i are trying to get a point across ,you might be just what we need to get people to take interest in their heritage.

The reporter asked John several questions about his trek and he explained part of the story of the Trail of Tears .He held her interest and she wrote down everything he was saying .The photographer took some pictures .They all shook hands and John and Charlie continued on their way .After entering the Mark Twain national forest their scenery changed and a calmness seemed to overtake them. The two of them now ready to rest for the night once again, found a good spot to camp .The stream was clear and you could see fish swimming by with ease. The ground was laidened with small pebbles and stones which seemed to make it feel cooler than it actually was as dusk began to set in.

Y-GV-WA-YU-HI ,it is your turn to build us a fire, but tonight i will show you how to build it the way the old tribal council built theirs . Arrange the logs in an x .This will let the smoke rise in a circle and carry our words to the spirits. After that we will bathe ,then eat.

Charlie did as he was asked, gathering enough wood to last the night After bathing and eating Charlie and John started talking, Charlie starts to put a cedar log on the fire to build it up.

WAIT! Charlie that wood is sacred to our people, they only use it in certain ceremonies.

I'm sorry grandfather ,i didn't know.

It's o.k. Y-gv- wa -yu- hi that particular kind is cedar, it is the most sacred of all the wood, to the Cherokee, it is the only one that has the colors red and white in it's veins. There are other woods important to our people like spruce ,pine, holly and laurel ,but we use the wood from the cedar tree to honor our dead. During the seven days of creation these trees were the only ones to achieve the highest level of sacredness, because they were able to stay awake while all the others fell asleep .These trees are used in our medicine and ceremonies.

What do you mean ta-li u-gi-da-li ,fell asleep?

You know how in the winter time all the trees loose their leaves, these trees do not. So we say they stay awake .The numbers galiqougi and nvgi " 7 and 4" are also very special to The Cherokee .

Although not very late ,the sun had just started setting behind the trees and John was getting ready to tell Charlie a lot more details about the significance of the two numbers.

Hey you by the fire !! Can i come up ?

Who are you ?John replied not being able to see who was yelling to him and Charlie.

I'm the scout leader for the local cub scout troupe and my troupe and i saw your fire .They are trying to earn their fire safety badges and some others .I wondered if we might look at yours only for educational purposes ,we won't cause you any trouble .

You and your troupe are welcome at my camp, so come on up .

The scout troupe walked into John's camp, they introduced themselves and looked around trying to determine if John and Charlie were making any mistakes in their camp site. Each one of the scouts looked and gave their ideas and opinions on what they thought should or should not be .When they were done the leader told John what their opinion was of his camp site.

My troupe here, thinks you done the best job on a camp site they have ever seen .And so do i .

One of the boys was trying to get the attention of the scout master discreetly and tugged on his pant leg and gestured for him to bend down so he could whispers something in his ear. John noticed and saw the boy was a little nervous. John had a small grin on his face and was amused at how the boy was reacting.

Don't worry young man, i haven't taken any scalps in years. John and the scout master laughs setting the young one at ease .

Ask him your self the scout leader replied after the boy was done whispering in his ear.

UM, AH ,UM ??

Spit it out young man i won't hurt you .

Are you a real Indian Mister.?

Well i am as real an Indian as you can be now days. I am Cherokee, full blooded in fact. John had an idea, Listen if you and your troop want to ,i was just about to tell my grandson some old traditions and stories, you are more than welcome to sit and listen .This is actually why, he and i are here .

Cool ! and Awesome! were just some of the reactions John heard from the small group of young boys in his presence .They all looked at the leader for approval and he nodded his head in agreement. The happiness was apparent of John, by the look he had as he started to tell his story to an audience of interested listeners.

The Cherokee have been here in this country many years before the people in the big boats thought they discovered it. Sense we were already here in this country, it was already discovered. When they came we shared our land with them . We showed them many of our ways to live and get by ,and how to live on a new type of land. We helped them plant their crops and showed them new ways to plant. We joined the offices of their leaders so we could become involved in what we thought might be a better way to live. And for awhile it was but the more people that came the more things changed. Some of them were greedier and so was some of ours .

When they told our people to leave our land, we didn't want to. They tried to trade us land but some of our people resisted, and they sent their soldiers to remove us by force. Even when our people gave them land , they wanted more, especially when gold was found in Georgia .There were five tribes removed by force ,to a fort in Charleston Tenn. This is where the lives of one hundred thousand Indians changed drastically. Charlie and i are walking back the way they came. We are not trying to change history or make any kind of protest . Charlie and i just want our young people to not forget the eight thousand that died on the trail. The elements were very hard on our people ,disease, starvation and bitter cold were just some of the things that claimed their lives.

Some of the people were able to go by boat on the' Long Man '{rivers} but for the most part, most of them took a couple of routes chosen by the government. The route we are taking is the second longest one.

The Cherokee are very spiritual people, we don't believe in the supernatural, but the ghost of our ancestors can be seen by those who believe in our old ways. We believe in the Little People that live under rocks ,in thickets and caves among other places. They have long hair and can only be seen, if they want you to see them .They don't like being bothered so most have never seen them. We shouldn't even be talking about them after dark .Sometimes when a child is lost, they help them find their way.

We hold the numbers seven and four important in our beliefs .The number seven represents the seven clans of the Cherokee . The number four ,refers to the four winds east ,west, north and south along with these there are three other directions ,up for upper world, down for lower world and center for where we live. There are many other references to these two numbers but you don't have time to hear them all. The owl and the cougar are special to us also, they were the only animals to stay awake during the seven years of creation .That is why they are out almost only at night. These are only a small part of the things important to our people .When you go back home find a book on 'The Nunna Daul Tsuny'. You will read about the Five Civilized Tribes and the states they were from. All of these are known as the Cherokee nation. Remember young fellows you might even be, part Indian because many ,many are ,and don't even know it.

By my Indian name i am called ta-li u gi da li and i call my grandson y -gv-wa-yu-hi. I really do thank you for sitting and listening, i hope you enjoyed it.

John and Charlie chatted for the rest of the evening keeping the fire burning to a low glow .Charlie had a lot of new questions and John did his best to answer them.

I wonder how mom and dad are doing grandfather ?

I would assume they are fine, probably worried, but fine. Your father said he would meet us on the trail somewhere .I expect he has to wait for time off from work I used to take your father camping when he was young like you. He loved to build fires and climb rocks and trees . Let's get some sleep chief, tomorrow i will show you how to make a bow and arrow.

Ok grandfather, i'm kind of tired anyway.

John and Charlie slept for the night, leaving Charlie dreaming of the stories he had heard earlier that evening. They awoke early like they have been doing sense they started their trip. After eating breakfast, they cleaned their camp site and decided to move on .While they were walking

John kept hearing twigs snap on the path they were taking . The sounds were a long distance behind them, but John knew someone was following them. He wasn't worried ,but more curious and started plotting how to find out who or what it was behind him.

They had traveled several days through the woods and needed to restock up on some supplies. John was getting a little slower, but only he could notice it .

Chief, there should be a town up ahead lets veer off the trail and get some supplies, we only have a couple of days until we get to the Trail Of Tears State Park next to the river where our people crossed from the east to the west. We will rest there a few days and build our strength back up before we cross the river.

By this time they were nearly half way into their trip and John wasn't positive he had accomplished anything . John and Charlie now nearing where they were going to rest kept noticing little signs on the small highway they were walking on .

IF YOU SEE THEM CALL 555-TRAIL OF or another one they saw THEY ARE ON THEIR WAY it seemed to John like he was seeing one of these signs every half mile and they were interesting to him, but he had no idea they were about him.

John and Charlie were about a half mile from the entrance of the park, sense it was a state park and late spring they weren't paying any attention to all the vehicles with different liciece plates on them entering the park.

Listen up everyone, they are almost here, a reporter from the local television station said aloud. Let's give them time to come back here where we are, at the camping area.

TA-LI U-GI-DA-LI there are cars from everywhere parked here, wonder who they all are ?

They are tourist grandson, this is a state park there are always a lot of people at state parks.

For the first time on the trail John was wrong and he had no idea at the reception he was about to receive. All of these people were here to see the two people that had just completed part of an almost
imposable journey .Even though they were only about half way, a trip like this in modern times would be very difficult to achieve. In some cases even harder than those that made it the first time.

TA-LI- U- GI- DA- LI ! That sign says grave of princess Otahki, was she Cherokee ?

Yes she died here on the trail ,i will tell you more about her later, let's go rest now.

It was mid afternoon as John and Charlie walked around a curve, there were hundreds of people waiting for them, they were taken by surprise and overwhelmed at the response they were getting. John had no idea he would cause this much attention to him and his grandson. By the look on his face he knew that what he wanted to happen, was coming true.

Mr. Stoutman ,may i have a few minutes of your time? A man walks up to him and asks. I am from the local T.V. station WE HAVE BEEN FOLLOWING YOUR PROGRESS SINSE WE READ AN ARTICAL IN A NEWS PAPER A COUPLE OF WEEKS AGO ??The reporter said as the crowd cheered louder and louder. As you can see, you have caused quite a stir ,these people are here from all over the United States. Before i ask you some questions there is some one here that wants to see the both of you.

From behind the news van walks out Walter and Anne, she is already crying and grabs Charlie and hugs him nearly out of breath . She went through the normal mother thing ,I MISSED YOU. ARE YOU OK ? HAVE YOU BEEN EATING RIGHT? things of that nature.

Yes, mom he replied ,we've been eating bugs and worms and tree bark ,you know the healthy stuff.

Right then Anne looked at John with a look that could melt a rock . She started to point her finger at him when Charlie starts laughing.

I'm just kidding mom . ha ha ha! We been eating real good, fish and potatoes and what ever else we wanted. We took real good care of ourselves, you wouldn't believe how much i learned on this trip so far. I will tell you all about it later.

Walter walked up to his dad shook his hand and John pulled him in and gave him a hug .They didn't say much at first then, John ask Walter how everything was at home.

I hope you didn't get into too much hot water with Anne ? I did at first dad, but we kept up with you two on the news ,there was something on it, almost every day.

Them two men you have following me didn't hurt any either did it son ?

How did you know about that dad ?

With all of them westerns you watch , don't you know by now a white man can't sneak up on an Indian? By the way Walter ,you might want to let them off the hook, i would imagine they are wore out by now.

I will take care of that, but dad there are so many elders here from other tribes and reservations .I think you should go and thank them ,there is a stage set up for you .Some of these people have been here for a week or more.

As Walter and John were talking a convoy of police cars came speeding past them with their lights flashing and sirens blaring, they didn't know what was happening .Behind the police cars were several black sedans and SUV's . One of them stopped in front of John and Walter and a man wearing a gun and small microphone headset got out of the vehicle.

Mr. Stoutman you and your grandson and family please follow me.

There is someone that wants to meet you.

They turned to do as they were asked when they noticed the police and other men were clearing a large circle of people away from the area. They heard a loud chopping noise coming from just beyond a group of trees .Once they recognized that it was a helicopter being followed by two others. They became tense wondering who it was flying into the park. As the helicopter lands and the props slow down several more men dressed liked the one that was leading them to the stage got out and formed a small circle ,as the first helicopter left ,the other two landed in the same spot as the first. The anticipation was very high, when Charlie yelled out.

HEY IT'S THE PRESIDENT!! Grand father the president is here. .

The secret service men surrounded the stage where John and his family were waiting .The president enters the stage and shook hands with John and his family ,and then they began to realize just how powerful a statement they made.

John i think what you and your grandson are dong is very commendable myself have a small amount of Native American blood in my veins. As i think many Americans do. Over the last several days congress ,the office of Indian affairs and i have been working on some steps to improve and secure relations among the American Natives. I know it sounds like i'm making a speech ,but the condition of our country's moral, needs a kick in the pants and i think you and your grandson are doing just that. As you can see the support you have is overwhelming, i have been informed that not only here, but other places along the trail are watching this historical event on satellite. You have inspired me immensely, you have made me think about how i am supposed to be doing the job i was elected to do. I have realized that with all the technology we have created, the price we paid may very well be tearing down the walls of our imagination I' VE HEARD IT SAID THAT A GREAT LEADER ISN'T REMEMBERED FOR HOW MANY MEN HE HAS LEAD, BUT FOR HOW WELL HE LEAD THEM, one last thing. First i want to thank you . I may be the president of the United States, but it will take someone like you to be the chief . I think i can speech for many of the people in this country, sense that's what i was elected to do. We are proud of you and your grandson.

After the president exits the stage and shakes hands with several people in the crowd he gets in his helicopter and flies away. The whole crowd gets quiet for a few seconds then John Walter starts to speak in the microphone .As he does he sees his military friends walking out of the crowd toward the stage. John pauses for a second .

I REALY WANT TO THANK ALL OF YOU FOR TAKING TIME OUT OF YOUR LIVES AND COMING HERE TO MEET MY GRANDSON AND I !! YOU DON'T KNOW HOW HAPPY THIS MAKES ME !! The spirits told me it was not too late. And now i truly believe them. These six men that have came up here to the stage ,i had the honor to serve in two wars with them. All seven of us are from different tribes. All seven of us have been given a destiny by the spirits.

I want each of you to look around you, take notice of everyone, that is our age. In thirty years most of us will be dead. Many of you will be our age and your children will be your age. Hats three generations of memories, by the time the forth generation is born the three generations ahead of it will have left out part of the history, of the one before. A very large portion of an entire family history will be lost. It doesn't matter what nationality or race you are from. John looks at Anne ,it doesn't matter if some or all of your history is bad or all of it is good .The generations after it, can not learn from it, or keep it going, if they don't know anything about it.

This very park that we are standing in marks a very important change in the lives of not only the American Indian. It marks a change in history ,of this entire country, many bad things happened during this time, as well as many good things. You can only now, learn from the past, you can not change it .The future can be saved by those that know about the past. This is why my grandson and i, wanted to get your attention.

John stepped back in line with the rest of his family, as he did, he began to notice the elders and older people of the crowd all approach the stage. They were clapping their hands in approval of what they had just heard .John's friends walked onto the stage, and one of them steps up to the microphone .

MAY I HAVE YOUR ATTENTION PLEASE !? He pauses waiting for the crowd to stop clapping. John said that he was honored to serve with us six, to me that is the other way around. There were times in the wars that most of us doubted our faith and beliefs. John was our leading officer, because he never once doubted his ,he kept us strong by not letting us forget who we were. A couple of times he had to knock us back into belief. We are still alive because of it . Inspiration is the most powerful weapon you can have at any time. I see many elders and chiefs in this crowd ,and I see many young children here as well. If these two have not inspired you to sit by your fires tonight and share the knowledge that you have collected through the years with the young people, that are going to carry on these traditions into the future ,he paused for a brief moment and stared at the crowd .THEN YOU HAVE CAME HERE FOR NO REASON!!

After he finished what he was saying the crowd all started clapping again .The cheers were even louder than before .John and his friends and family gather up and introduced them selves to Anne .The crowd all came by and said some type of encouragement and show of gratitude .The excitement was that of a state fair or a movie star coming to town. For an hour or more John talked to as many people as he could but as the afternoon grew later and later the more people started to separate and go to their own camps and fires .John and his family began to set up their own camp site .As nightfall came you could hear chants and songs echoing all over the park. Many of the people were now wearing their own traditional clothing and head dresses .Some were dancing around their fires others were showing their young their trinkets and keepsakes .Each one showing the purpose or explaining it's use. John just like the just was telling his own stories. Walter, Anne and Charlie along with the two bodyguards were surrounding their fire listening as John was telling his story. John stopped for a minute to talk to the bodyguards.

Before i go on , i thought i should tell you my son has hired you but if you don't want to, you don't have to stay .I appreciate what you did for us in Springfield , but i can make this trip alone if need be. Anne and Walter will probably be taking Chief back with them. I however ,must complete this trip.

Dad ?Anne said John gave her a look of surprise. Dad, we are going to finish this trip with you. First you want us to join you ,then you want to run us off. Anne says jokingly, Make up your mind. HA HA HA !

John's face lit up even brighter ,everything he had dreamed of just came true. Nothing could top the excitement he was feeling now. Then one of the body guards spoke up.

Mr. Stoutman my folks were part Apache and i don't know hardly anything about our past, they never really talked about it. If you don't mind, i think i will go with you and your family, at no charge of coarse.
Then the other spoke up.

I've got some kin people over in Tennessee, i haven't seen in ten years ,If it's ok i will stay on the trail until then.

Sure fellows ! Over one hundred thousand made this trip the first time and as far as i'm concerned, that many can make it this time. Charlie you wanted to know earlier who Princess Otahki was ,well the Cherokee don't have princesses or princes in their ranking system, but there are legends that she was either the daughter of Reverend Bushyhead ,who married an Indian maiden or the daughter of a chief. It is said when they were trying to cross the river just over there, the river was very icy and the boat they were on, being overloaded turned over drowning many people, about three hundred or more. Otahki was one of them. There are many names associated with the trail. Chief John Ross and Major Ridge were both leaders of The Cherokee and involved in the government. Stand Waite also tried to stop this removal by force. It wasn't only the Cherokee that were removed. White people that were adopted by the tribes were taken prisoner and made to make the walk as well. History books tell of different numbers of people dieing on the trail. There's no telling of how many died during the evictions from their land and at the forts before the trail. The Cherokee people were not nomads, they liked stability and education they wanted to read and write and believed in god. They were hunters and farmers and caused little problem to anyone.

There were five tribes involved in this journey all from the other side of that river right there. The Cherokee ,Choctaw, Creek ,Chickasaw and Seminoles all moved to a land they call RED PEOPLE Oklahoma" as long as the grass is green and the river flows this will be your land, they said. The tribes were called The Five Civilized Tribes but there were more than just us removed The Illinois Configuration The Quapaw and Osage were also part of the Indian removal act .These tribes were the original residents of Tennessee, of Georgia ,Florida, Mississippi, Alabama, Missouri and Arkansas. After we settled in Oklahoma on our new land, the whites started coming as they did when we lived in the east. Our land got smaller and smaller because of many broken treaties. That is why we now live on reservations and are called a sovern nation. John stopped for a second ,I am going to get some rest now, i will tell you more tomorrow.

All of the stories being told that night were intriguing, each one unique in it's own way, poor childhoods ,struggle ,hardships, predgudist ,ridicule, were just some of the obstacles that had been placed in their path .Each one overcoming it and moving on to a better life. As each one finished they once again, separated to their own fires .The next day younger ones seemed to be strolling around stopping by different campsites, watching the elders make different crafts .Some were making beaded items, others making clothing from animal hides or store bought leathers, dream catchers with different colored feathers tied into the woven circle of nets ornamented the campsites .Blankets ,rugs and baskets sitting on tables and hanging from makeshift racks all with patterns and designs relating to lost Indian culture were on display, some being sold and others were just there to look at. A group of elders sat around one particular fire chipping stones and straighting short sticks with homemade tools from the area.

What are they doing ta-li- u-ga-da-li ?

They are making arrows and bows ,lances or spears, axes or tomahawks. These are the tools our people used to survive . At first they were for hunting and farming, but we had to adapt them for fighting and war. Our bows had to grow longer and our arrows had to be longer to keep our enemies farther away. Our lances became stronger with longer points at the tip for close fighting .The tomahawks we used for cutting wood had to become sharper so that when we threw them they would Pearce and lodge into our enemy. Our knives were crude but they could enable you to skin an animal quickly ,then we had to make them longer and sharper to defend ourselves. For century's these tools were just tools, until we were forced to make weapons out of them, once that happened many of the tribes were called savages, because they did not have guns to kill other people with. In the worst case situation these tools we have used for centuries, can still be used in many ways for survival today.

Once again night fall fell upon the camp ground with little change from the night before, as the people all calmed their fires and finished their songs . A hush fell on the entire site. John knew this was his last night on the west side of the “long man” and even though he wasn’t going to cross it in the historical spot ,he was still on edge and nervous anticipating he and his families quest to complete the trip. When they awoke the next morning a large portion of the supporters had already left the site .John and his family cleaned their site and were wondering where Walter had went. A brief period of time passed when a taxi pulled up to their campsite. Walter and the two body guards got out and joined Anne ,Charlie and John.

Dad i took the vehicles to town and put them in storage, they will be fine until we get back. We also had to get some more packs for Bill and Allen here .

If you are still paying them dad, they can carry mine. You know how heavy these things get after a couple of days? Charlie jokingly replied. ha! ha ha!!

This struck Bill by surprise the little guy had made a joke at his expense. But he knew they were closer and better friends because of it.
Charlie having said that left the door open for verbal retaliation .

I can lighten the load some, for us if you want me too Charlie?
How’s that Bill ?

By throwing your little butt off the bridge when we get to it.

This got a laugh out of everyone ,but Charlie, he just sort of tensed up and looked at his dad with a blank look.

You started it son ,don’t look at me. Walter said sort of grinning .

It seemed, this morning, would leave everyone mischievous and picking at each other as they began walking out of the park toward town. They walked about a half mile or so when Charlie turned around and looked behind him .

Ta-li- u-ga-da-li you better look behind us. Charlie said in surprize.

The remaining people in the campground had all lined up forming a parade behind them .Hundreds, of them most walking ,leaving one to drive the vehicles. Aside from the vehicles the original walk must have looked similar in size . An event like this could only cause John and his party to swell up in pride dawning a look of major achievement on their faces. Them and the parade of natives neared town after a half mornings walk. They began to notice the flood walls as they approached the edge of town and the river boats all seemed to be sitting idle in the middle of the river. Just over the horizon, the bridge they were going to cross became visible, and more and more citizens of CAPE GEAUARDO MISSOURI began gathering on the sidewalks in front of their homes.

As they entered the first block of business buildings, they were met with a convoy of vehicles, police cars, all with their lights and sirens flashing and blaring as bright and loud as possible. Fire trucks ,military vehicles ,tanks , motor cycles ,limousines, vehicles of all types, joined in the rare event taking place. Banners with all types of encouraging slogans hang from the building and homes. Joy only hastened their walk and as they continued through town. The crowd was enraged with excitement .The closer they got to the bridge the more they noticed how many armed service men it took to hold the crowds of cheering people back .Now entering the half mile or so before the bridge, a man walks into the parade shakes Johns hand .

I 'm the mayor of this town, if it's ok with you, before you cross the bridge into Illinois, i would like to say a few words and walk across with you.

John agreed and they kept the pace, until they reached another stage ,set up for their benefit. John and his family stood as the mayor began his speech ,listening to his every word.

This marks another historical moment for our ever growing town. For the second time in history, a what should never be forgotten event, is according within our borders. Let our historians add this day to the chapters of our books. Write down in your own family history books and memoirs this date and occasion ,for your grandchildren and those who will follow to read about. Jessie James, Bonnie and Clyde, Generals, Grant and Lee among many other notorious people have been said, to walk down these sidewalks and streets in this town. But not one has made an impact for our nations future such as this. Never have i since i was born, seen a statement of this magnitude take place. And until i die, probably never will again. So i ask that when you cross our new bridge and place a historical significance on it ,that it be the one to wipe the tears and help heal the pain felt by so many. GOD BLESS YOU MR. STOUTMAN. THANK YOU, TO EVERY ONE.

The mayor stepped down from the podium and took a place beside John .People in the crowd began wiping tears from their eyes. A young Native American soldier looks at his commanding officer, as if he were asking permission to join the walk .The officer nods in approval and the young soldier hands one of his fellow soldiers his gun and helmet. As he does this, it is noticed by several other native soldiers, all with that same look for approval and they too were given a nod of ok . Through out the crowd, soldiers of what seemed like all nations of American Indians ran to take a place along side John and the rest of those ,who were about cross the bridge connecting the east and west border of Indian nations.

Down in the Mississippi River, river boats were all lined up with their half mile long trains of barges sitting idle on both sides of the bridge ,some going up river and some going down river, to deliver what ever raw material or grain they may be transporting to what ever river port city or town. Neither boat would pierce the enormous shadow cast from the bridge to the river. The crews of these boats, were all standing on the decks at near attention, each one flying the flag of our country or state in which they came from. Emotions seemed to be increasing and anticipation growing with every second passing .

The first young soldier had already taken his place not in line, but as an escort or century along the outside lines of the parade of walkers ,he notices an elder with a canister of paint or powder in his hand and looks over to him .He sticks his hand out and asks if he can use it and the elder hands it to him. The young soldier opens it and sticks two fingers in it then takes both fingers and wipes them across his cheeks on each side of his face. Leaving two lines marked as if he were preparing for a battle like those seen in the movies. After passing the canister behind him, to the next soldier enticing him to do the same, then the next one ,so on and so on .The first soldier then removes his shirt and under shirt, leaving him only wearing his camoflaudge pants and black polished boots. Once again causing a chain reaction of those behind him. The six of John's fellow military friends follow suit in what the young soldiers are doing , and then form a line spanning from rail to rail across the bridge in front of John and his family as they begin to walk across to the Illinois side .The entire parade starts to move and as it does it gives the appearance that a group of warriors are prepared to engage in battle, just as the group starts to move .A loud yell comes from a group of on lookers, no one really sure where it came from.

SHOULLLL DERRRR ARRRRMMMMMSSS !! PLAAA TOOONNN FALLL INNNNaaa! The voice seemed to get louder being heard above the whole crowd, tension was now beginning to form among the crowd of now nervous people .What could possibly be happening this was a peaceful movement ? People in the crowd were asking each other why the remaining soldiers were arming themselves and lining up in defensive stance. Surely nothing was going to happen to spoil this glorious event. The soldiers all did as ordered, their faces were blank with expression and they held their guns by the forward and stock grips placed at an angle across their chest each one staring forward awaiting the next order. The commanding officer takes in a deep breath and holds it a second. The front of the parade unaware of what's going on continues to walk .

PLAAATOOONNNAA !!! MARRRCHHAA !!!! DOUBBBBLLEEE TIIIIMMMMEEAA!! his voice was louder and raspy almost a screaming growl as he fell in behind his troupes now running toward the front of the parade forming lines on each side of the now painted soldiers ,as they raced passed the outside lines of the escort toward the center and state line of the bridge. The soldiers still blank with expression kept their position along the curb and rail of the bridge awaiting the parade to catch up with them. The walkers now only a few yards away from the half way point notice the soldiers facing away from them and standing at attention hearing another batch of orders coming from the commanding officer. PREEESENNTTTA !!! ARRMMMSA!! READY !!! AAAIMMM !! FIRE!!

The soldiers began firing their guns over the tops of the boats in the water echoing from the water each time an order was given .Every few second as the walkers continued to cross the bridge an order was given to fire. A gun salute by the military normally signifies honoring the death of a fallen soldier. Not this time, it was paying tribute to courage and perhaps honor an old painful memory putting it to rest ,and combating a new one. The native soldiers began breaking away from the parade and joining their units they were with. All of them excited at what they had just participated in, began putting the rest of their uniforms on and wiping the paint from their faces. As the last of the walkers crossed the bridge before turning back they give a yell of some kind and turn around ,came back across the bridge leaving John and his dwindling group to continue on. Each of John's friends turned back toward the town, gave John a nod of encouragement ,finally leavening John and his family and two body guards to complete the still, long journey ahead.

John and his small group picked up the original, trail passing through many ,many small towns along the way. It seemed that each one they walked through, there were little banners and signs in the yards or on buildings acknowledging their effort. At times they would stop and give an interview with some small town paper or TV. station, an quickly go on .

A couple of weeks pass and the terrain was getting more difficult to walk, as the hills were becoming increasingly steeper. John's Family began to notice a drastic change in his pace and appearance ,he was slowing down and losing weight . His face was pale and showed signs of pain, not that he let on like it. He was determined to finish what he started. Night fall was nearing on this particular evening and they had already made camp in a field for the night.

Dad i think we need to talk! Anne said as she handed Charlie a plate of food. You are not looking very well. Shouldn't we stop for a few days so you can rest? There is a motel and hospital just a few miles up the road, tomorrow we can....

Don't even think about it ,John cut her off quickly. I am just tired is all .Nothing to get your feathers ruffled over .I am going to turn in early tonight ,get some sleep and everything will be better in the morning. Look we have only got about a hundred miles or so and we don't have a lot of time before the big pow wow . So goodnight everyone and i'll see you bright and early in the morning.

John turned in as he said goodnight and went to sleep quickly leaving Anne ,Walter and the two body guards still sitting by the fire. Charlie finished his meal and decided to go to bed early too. Anne kept watch and when Charlie fell asleep she began to talk to Walter .

Walter i work in a clinic and i've seen this many times .Your father is sick, those tumors are growing and will only get worse from this point on .If you don't convince him to get medical treatment ,he may not finish the trip.

Walter dropped his head briefly and looked as if he knew the out come already. Anne ? I can't make him do anything, by the old ways, he knows what is going to happen .To him, he is not being headstrong or stubborn. He's fulfilling his destiny , he's doing what the gods are telling him to do. Dad says a person only gets to make one good statement or one good last stand in life and most people let it pass by.

What about Charlie ? How is he going to handle this ? He thinks the sun rises and sets on his grandfather. Anne ask nervously.

He's been knowing dad was going to die long before, we joined the trail . He heard the answering machine and ask me about it ,then he ask his grandfather about it .You know how dad is ,he wouldn't lie about anything. I hate to tell you this ,but he has already told Charlie what he wants done in case something happens. Now we will be the bad guys if we try to change it .We ,no matter how much we don't like it ,have to except dad's choice.

The next morning John woke just before day break ,one by one they all woke starting with Charlie. Each one joining John by the fire. Good morning dad. Good morning grandfather .Good morning Mr.Stoutman. Each one giving their greeting as they joined him by the fire drinking coffee.

How are you feeling today dad? Anne asked .

I'm ready to get started as soon as everyone else is, i'm old and as slow as you all are, i'll be in my second childhood by the time we get there.

Anne knew that this was his way of hiding the pain ,still apparent on John's face. They broke camp and began walking like normal. Now only three or four days walk from completing what seemed like an endless journey John's determination seemed even more set than when he started. With his determination as strong as it was, he himself realized he was having trouble keeping up with the others . He seemed to be wearing his pack lower and lower indicating his strength was diminishing. The hills were the steepest they had been the whole trip, and getting steeper each mile they walked. People continued to join them for brief walks at times ,causing John to hide his pain even more. Bill and Allen had watched all of this, they were going to ,it seemed as if they both had the same idea at once. John had stumbled a couple of times with out anyone noticing but the two of them.

Hey Walter ? let's stop awhile and rest .My back is hurting and we don't have that far to go .Bill called out!

Walter agreed, because they all were tired and needed rest .

They made camp early and talked mostly about what they were going to do once they got there. They began reminiscing about their entire trip the goods and the bads. Bill noticed every one was hiding the fear they had and were trying to avoid any conversation that may pop up about John's condition.

Walter, it wouldn't have been any of my business ,if i hadn't made this whole trip with your dad and Charlie, but i have watched quietly and observed some of the most amazing and unbelievable things one man should ever see. I can almost assure you, your father won't complete the trip. In the beginning of the trip, i have heard the stories that he's told Charlie. The traditions he lives by are only powerful to those who truly believe in them. I saw something very similar to this with my own grandfather, when i was a kid. He was full blooded Pawnee . By your dad's beliefs, there is something that has to be done right now ,and only Charlie can do it .

DO WHAT? ,WHY CHARLIE ? Anne and Walter quickly replied.

Because he is only a boy ,he is still a true believer ,he has not decided any path or set any ways of his own yet. To him everything his grandfather has told him is true , you said it yourself . He would not lie about anything and Charlie knows this, that is why he believes everything that's been told to him. Look ,Walter and Anne .I can't explain it to you, because i'm not a believer .You'll have to trust me on this , and for the first time you'll have to trust Charlie to do something very important, by himself. You hired me to protect them ,did you not ?

Well {pause} Yes .

Good then ,look at your father ,he's been asleep for over an hour now. Would you go over to the creek where Charlie is fishing and bring him here ?

YES ,i'll be back in a few seconds.

Walter returns with Charlie, and the atmosphere is like that of an emergency room in a hospital. John was dieing and every one knew it .Charlie looks at Bill and drops his head . Bill takes his fore finger and places it under Charlie's chin .Then he gently lifts it up and looks Charlie in the eyes with a calming stare.

Little fellow ?

YES SIR? he replies .

Do you remember what your grandfather told you back in the forest? Bill said in an almost whisper as Charlie nodded back. IT'S TIME ,LITTLE GUY. Bill says with a concerning smile.

Charlie kisses his mom and dad on the forehead and walks over to where John lays asleep ,picks up his hand with a firm grip and quietly says ,'a tsi-ge-yu-i u' {i love you} drops his head and walks into the woods alone.

Where is he going ? Anne asks Walter in a frantic voice. Stop him !

We can't! Walter replies. He will be ok.

Charlie walks deep enough into the woods ,where he could not be seen or heard by of those sitting at the camp. He comes to a clearing with several fallen trees laying on the ground. He looks around until he finds two fare size pieces of limbs from one of the fallen trees. As Charlie places them in an x and starts them on fire, a complete quiet falls on the forest and the owls and other night animals that were prowling on the forest floor ,seemed to calm at once .The leaves on the trees, that had been ruffling in the slight night breeze had came to an instant stillness.

Charlie removes his shirt and takes his shoes off , as the fire gets higher and hotter the smoke begins to rise through an opening in the canopy of the tall trees .Spiraling and swirling higher and higher, it begins to cloud up in the cool night mountain air. Charlie bends down and wipes his hand on the forest floor picking up clods of partially moist soil .Then he puts some soil in both hands, rubs them together and smears them on his face and body. Charlie then stands up in the smoke and waves it over his head ,first east then west then north and finally south. Charlie then looks at a log laidened with veins of red and white laying on the ground. CEDER!! Charlie says to himself ,as he walks over, picks it up and puts it on the fire. As Charlie stands in the smoke, now swirling faster and higher ,he looks up into the sky ,and in a low calm voice begins talking .

a-da-nv-do na ga-dv-gi-dv a-ya go-hi-sv-hi ga-dv-gi-dv a-ya a-da-do-li-s-do-ti a-li-sgo-lvdo-di na-sgi-a-sga-ya i-na-ti-wo ti-hv-e ga-lv-d-tlv , e-lo-hi ut-se-li ly-u-wa-ko-di

"GREAT SPIRITS THAT HEAR ME ,HEAR ME PRAY, ALLOW HIM INTO THE UPPER WORLD , IT'S HIS TIME"

Charlie sat back down on the log and bowed his head and started to cry. His tears began to puddle on the ground below him. Then he hears a voice, but he can't see where it's coming from.

Why do you cry little boy ?

Where are you? I can hear you ,but i can't see you .

Do not be afraid, very few people have seen us .

Us who ? Charlie once again ask.

We are the Little People your grandfather told you about. Sense you are not lost, we prefer that you do not see us. It is better this way, but we want you to know that we are here, just the same. It is a great thing ,your grandfather going to the upper world, you know? He has earned it .

You know my grandfather ?

Yes we saw him when he was a child, just like you . He became a great leader ,this trip has proven that once again . If you follow your destiny , you too will go to the upper world.

What is my destiny ? Charlie asked.

I can not tell you that ,only the spirits know the answer to that. It must be something very great or you would not be here now. Sometimes greatness, comes not from knowing your destiny ,but following your heart .This is what your grandfather did ,when he was little just like you, his grandfather told him he would make a great journey . But he did not know this would be it. Look into the fire ,you will get some of the answers you want. Look into the smoke ,visions will appear for you to see. I must go now, i have many children to keep from being lost.

Charlie was still a little in shock and disbelief at what he had just experienced, but it wasn't over yet, he began to do as he was told by the voice .He looked deep into the fire and smoke, becoming disorientated and dizzy . With out losing his composure or patience he waited for anything to appear to him, when several seconds pass an image appears in the smoke and leaves him deeply bewildered.

Grandfather ? !! I can see you !!

Yes y gv wa yu hi . I have completed my destiny , your mother and father don't know it yet ,so let them rest tonight. I want you to meet some people John said, as several more images appeared . This is your grandmother and my father and his father and his father .These are the ones who live and remembered the traditions so that we could have them and give as a gift to our grandsons and granddaughters and, theirs as well . I will tell you, just as my grandfather told me .You will be a great warrior, your, destiny is full and your own journey will be a long one. As long as you believe, the spirits will never let you fail in whatever you try to accomplish. I must go now .But always remember, a warrior is always brave ,he is always ready to teach ,and most importantly he is always there to protect those , who can not protect themselves, no matter what happens . I will see you when you are ready to join us.

Charlie was still sad, but happy at the same time, he puts the fire out and returns to the camp site with his mom and dad. As he enters the camp site he walks over to where his grandfather lay motionlessly and covers him up. With out saying a word ,he hugged his parents, smiles and goes to bed .As bad as they wanted to, Anne and Walter want to console him, and wondered where he went and what he had been doing for so long however, they did not and let him be alone. The next morning they were awaken by screams and cries from Anne and each one quickly got out of their tents and bed rolls to see what was going on.

I tried to wake him but .....

It's ok mom , he is in the upper world now .Charlie says as he hugs and consoles his mom .

Walter just drops his head and neals down to cover his dads face. He was very sad but didn't let on, he stayed strong and intended to complete his trip he started with his dad. Walter started to build some type of homemade stretcher, when seven native American men walked into their camp.

Hello,, we came to finish the trip with you all.

As you can see dad is ——

It's o.k.. We know , we are going to carry him the rest of the way.

But it is over twenty miles or so till we get there .Walter said to the young men dressed the same as John.

Sir that is not even a step, compared to the journey your father has made in over seventy years . We must get going though , there are more people, already there, than we have ever had in the past. A very special ceremony has been prepared for him and all most all Native American tribes are represented already. So please leave your packs here and some one will come back for them later today.

They all set out on the last leg of the trip, each of the young Indians took turns caring John to the pow wow .Later that evening all the different tribes paid their respects in their own traditional ways ,each one giving praise to him .They buried John on tribal land and monumented his grave. Walter and Anne along with Charlie were given a ride back to their own vehicle, and along the way Charlie wanted to stop.

CAN WE PLEASE STOP AT THIS MUESIEM FOR A MINUTE DAD ? ,There is something i want to do.

Sure son what is it .

You and mom come in with me and you'll see . They did as he ask and when they got inside Charlie walked up to the lady behind an information counter and handed her the knife that Walter bought him before he started .

She read the insignia and smiled at Charlie and thanked him .Then they turned and left. As they did Walter looked at Charlie with an asking look .

ITS O.K. DAD, IF WE KEEP IT, ONLY WE CAN READ IT, AND REMEMBER , IF THEY HAVE IT ,MAYBE NO ONE WILL EVER FORGET. THEY MUST KNOW THAT OVER ONE HUNDRED THOUSAND WERE FORCED TO WALK WEST———

"AND ONE WALKED BACK."

THE END

'BOOTHEELWILL'

Overall and Outlaws

A young man drove his car into an old narrow dirt driveway. He looks at his son and tells him to wait in the car while he goes and talks to the old man sitting on his front porch. The younger man was in his early thirties and wasn't very well kept. His cloths were torn and dirty and he kept wiping his nose with his forefinger. He walked with a slow stagger just barely picking up his feet as he took step after step. As he approached the porch where the old man was sitting quietly whittling an old stick. His voice just slightly hearable, he seemed to cock his jaw and grind his teeth as he talked .Perhaps he had some kind of tick or nervous disorder , but it was clear that the old man didn't want him there.

What are you doing here boy ? Did you think i was lying when i said, i would shoot you if you came around here again?

Though the porch wasn't falling apart, it had seen much better days .Years had passed sense it had been painted and the edges of the tin on the roof was rolled up some as if it had taken a beating over the years from the wind. The old man sat back in a high back rocking chair, not rocking, but not sitting still. The porch cracked and squeaked as he shuffled about in his chair. You could tell in every way that he was very old, by his white hair and wrinkled and blottie skin. One side of his overalls was unbuttoned leaving one strap holding them up. Though it seemed really out of place, he wore a tie and brilliant white shirt beneath his overalls and his head was covered with a wide brimmed hat that seemed to sag in the front and rear from years of wear. His shoes were shined but why, the dirt yard and rocky terrain must have kept him working on them all of the time.

Hello Deuce ,i, know you don't want me here . But please listen to me a second?

BOY !! He said in a loud voice as he pointed at him .Then he leaned forward and the younger man had to move as he spit off the porch .

I need help Deuce .

You mean you need a favor ,and i'd be aside myself if you didn't .

You want me to do something for you, but you don't want to be obligated to do anything in return. That's what you want. The old man's voice was harsh and sharp almost raspy and unforgiving . He just stared the man down as he talked .

Please Deuce i'm in trouble and i need help , you are all i have left.

You say that like you've already used everyone else up ? Course i expect you have .Where's your dad ?

He won't even talk to me, he says he don't even have a son.

I guess he'd be right ,you ain't ever acted like one . Don't waist them tears on me boy , pick your head up !! Now who's that in the sedan?

He's my son , i named him after you Deuce ,he's six years old .

What the hell does that got to do with anything ? There are five others with my name. What kind of trouble you in? Steeling , robbery, drunk driving, you owe someone money you can't pay back?

It's a long story and i don't have a lot of time .

Just as well, i don't care anyway. I bet it's got something to do with that dope though.

Deuce i need to leave Six here for a couple of hours .Is it ok?

Yep , long as you're leaving . Real funny to me though, i ain't ever even seen'em.

I'm sorry Deuce, i been real busy is all.

SHUT YOUR MOUTH BOY! ! The old man yelled as he pointed at him. Long as its closed, you can't lie. Now just go get the kid. Just so you know, running from the law and dope dealers, ain't got nothing to do with being busy.

Thanks Deuce you won't regret it. He's a good kid. He said as he slowly turned to back toward the dented up sedan and get his son. Come on son you are going to stay here with my great granddad for awhile .I'll be back in a couple of hours to get you.

He wasn't much more than knee high to his dad when he got out of the car. He was wearing overalls just like the old man .The old man noticed that he looked just like his dad standing beside him.

Looks just like you Nickel .The old man said in his raspy voice.

Yeh he looks like all of us did .

The little boy climbed up on the porch and sat in a chair next to the table beside the old man's rocker. The one he called Nickel looked as if he didn't know what to say to the boy.

I—-I AH—-I'LL, AH

Just get going Nickel ,long as you are stuttering ,you ain't lying .

Put the boys tote in the back of my truck and i'll get it later.

The old man knew he wasn't coming back in a couple of hours . Apparently he had heard the couple hours thing before. The old man propped his feet up on an old five gallon bucket and sat quietly as he watched the rusty sedan race down the dirt road. The little boy kept looking at the old man as if he wanted to say something ,but didn't know what to say. He sat there several more minutes just looking out across the pasture. Just like any kid his age he could not resist a conversation .

You know my dad sir ?

Yep , all his life .

It was quiet for few more minutes and the boy was getting to know everything around him .

That your old truck ?

Yep , sense it was brand new .

But still the old man sat quietly staring off in the distance paying little attention to the boy as he continued to whittle away at the stick.

Them your cows ?

Yep ,, sense they was born.

The young boy was trying to strike a conversation up, but didn't quite know how to go about it .The old man wasn't helping much with his short answers and he was starting to make the young boy feel uneasy .The boy began fidgeting some and pulling at the seat of his britches. It was obvious he didn't like wearing the overalls .

You like wearing these things ?

Yep , been wearing'em all my life.

The old man kept watching him out of the corner of his eye , he knew he was uncomfortable, but he just laughed under his breath as the boy pulled and tugged at his overalls.

Unlatch the top strap button on one side kiddo .Then let the strap fall to one side out of the way . Let the strap on the other side all the way out to it's longest length . Then unbutton the buttons on the side . That'll get them britches out of your hind end, i can't stand that either. There now, how's that Kiddo?

The old man said as he helped the boy let the strap out to it's longest length.

That's a whole lot better sir. Thanks . What's a kiddo ?

It's kinda like a kid, only smaller.

You know what my name is ?

Nope , we ain't been introduced yet.

My name is Marion Frank Loughary The Six!

That many, huh? What happened to the rest of 'em ?

I don't know ,i guess they weren't no good ,so they kept me .

Yep , your probably right.

Is a hundred very old ?

Yep , for an elephant it is.

Do you know how old i am ?

Nope .

I'm six , i will be till i get seven.

Ya ,don't say?

How old are you ?

I'm ninety five, i rekin.

Is that older than a hundred?

Nope , not by a long shot . Why?

My dad says were are going to see this real old guy and he says he's like a hundred years old.

Why do you need to see the old guy . Deuce ask letting on like he didn't know who the boy was talking about.

He said i needed to dress up like this, so the guy would like me .

He says i need to make him like me real fast. I don't know why but i think he plays football.

Football?

Yeh my dad says i need to make this guy like me real fast, cause he thinks he's gonna kick off anytime.

The old man knew what the kid was talking about and he still couldn't let on .He knew that a kids had a way about being honest about things with out even trying.

He said that did he?

He says the guy has so much money he don't know what to do with it all. He says if i'm nice to the guy and make him like me , he'll give me some.

Need a lot of money do ya?

I don't, but my dad says he'll hang on to it till i get old enough to spend it. Besides i got plenty of money ,i got two dollars. You know anybody like that?

Nope ,, can't say as i do.

You got anything to drink?

What do you want beer ,wine ,whiskey ,cold cola, water? .ha ha

I guess water ,my dad says i ain't old enough for the other stuff.

You've had that conversation already ,have ya? That's probably the only smart thing your ——Well , never mind that ,sit here i'll go in and get you something.

They sat there quietly again for several more minutes and the boy just kicked his feet over the side of the chair and tapped his hands on the chair arm . It was late in the afternoon and the sun was getting near the horizon and starting to make long shadows of the trees and hillsides. What's your name ?

Most folks call me Deuce or sometimes they call me Frank.

Frank can i ask you a question ?

Yep , if you can think of one. ha ha !! Deuce answered kind of hiding the laugh.

My dad ain't coming back is he? He always says a couple of hours , but i know it's a whole lot longer than that.

He probably ain't got no watch ,Six. Your dad ain't never been real good at keeping time. I wouldn't worry about it none.

It don't matter ,and i am not worried, he always comes back in a couple of days.

Hey boy, you had viddles yet ?

Viddles ? What's viddles?

Kinda like food,, only better. Let's go see if we can't scrounge up something to eat.

They entered the house and the boy was amazed at what he saw. Guns, ropes ,badges, a saddle hanging from one of the rafters . There was bicycles , toy cars and trucks, and little red wagons hang from the rafters as well. This place was like an antique barn, old furniture and radios , dolls, toy trains just anything you can imagine, he had. He kept the old hardwood floors oiled down with mineral oil to keep the dust down. Frank walked slow and kinda bent over, but all in all he got around good for a ninety year old man.

Wow ! sir you got everything in here , i ain't never seen this much stuff in one place.

Yep, i been keeping this stuff a lot a years . Some of it i found in the fields after we get them bad storms ,some of it i found in ditch dumps, some of it i found in peoples garbage cans driving down the road. Most of it i bought for one or the other of my children or grandchildren. I let them play with the toy till they got too old ,then i fixed it and handed it down to the next one.

You ain't got no kids anymore ,how come you keep them ?

Kiddo ,toys is where we get play magic from .

Play magic ? What's that?

Well a long time ago kids used to have to do a lot of work and they was sad all the time .The work ferry made their hands and feet sore and it made their backs hurt .One afternoon this fun ferry showed up with this stick and wheel she said push this wheel with this stick each time you tap the stick to the wheel you will have fun. The she said some magic words ,i don't know what she was saying, but she raised both hands in the air and started spinning around and hollering .Let every toy have a smile, behind every smile let there be a child ,to play with that toy .There must be fun in every toy ,even if the toy is broke ,it must still make a child smile, but the magic must work on all people ,if an adult plays with that toy then they must smile too .The toy gods must put enough fun magic in every toy to last for a thousand years. So that's why i keep all these toys ,they still got plenty of fun magic left in'em.

Alright kiddo what kind of sandwich you want , i got possum , squirrel , lizard , snake , bologna and ham .

Yuk ! i ain't eating that stuff ,except maybe the bologna or ham .

Why the possum is fresh , i just ran over it this morning. ha ha ha!

Alright then ham and bologna it is .What do you want on it? Mustard or mayonnaise ?

Mustard , i don't like mayonnaise .

Yeh me neither,, mayonnaise is for women and sissies . You got a girlfriend ,Six?

NO WAY !!!

Me neither .

They sat down at the table in the middle of the room and started eating their sandwiches .The boy noticed that none of the chairs matched but each one was different in it's own design .

How come all these chairs are different Frank ?

Well each time a new generation was born i bought a chair from that era .The one i'm sitting in was my pa's and the one that you are sitting in is the last generation.

The boy is looking around the room at all the pictures hanging everywhere.

Hey you got a picture of my dad hanging up there , then there's you and my grand pa ,but i don't know who them other two are.

One is my dad , and that third one is my son, we called him Tripps .

What is your whole name Frank ?

MARION FRANK LOUGHARY JUNIOR , ALSO KNOWN AS "DUECE"!

HEY THATS JUST LIKE MINE, EXCEPT FOR THAT JUNIOR

PART!!

Yep,, i'm the second one , my dad 'Ace' was the first one, your dad was the fifth one , my son Tripps he was the third one , your grand pa is the fourth and he is also my grandson.

Is there a number seven ?

Nope ,, you ain't had'em yet .

You mean like have a baby or something?

Yep .

YUK!! I ain't having no babies !

Rekin there won't be no number seven then. The old man replies trying to get a stir out of the boy.

How come you ain't got no TV Deuce? , can i call you Deuce?

What's Deuce mean anyway.?

Slow down boy , i can't hear 'em as fast as you can spit 'em out. I ain't got no TV cause it will rot your brain.

NUH UH !

Yep anything that flies through the air that you can't see ,swat ,or shoot at ,cain't be good for you. Yes you can call me Deuce , everybody does . Deuce in a deck of cards means the number two, my dad was the first Frank ,so we called him Ace , My son was the third one so i called him Tripps, he named your grand pa Quattro or four and he named your dad Nickel cause he was the fifth one . I guess we can call you nickel and a penny if you want.

No i like Six better. Are me and you kin ?

Yep ,, your my great great grand son.

What does great great mean .

After grandson we use great to separate one generation from the next. Your dad is my great grand son so that makes you my great, great.

So my dad is kin to you ?

Yep,, i rekin.

You don't like him much do you ?

Kiddo why don't you just look at the stuff on the walls, i gotta go feed my critters .

Critters ? What's critters ?

Ha ha! The old man responded as he shook his head in amazement at how quickly the boy could come up with questions .Boy , you sure do gotta know everything don't you ? Critters is like pets , only you don't let 'em in the house.

Oh , i didn't mean to make you mad.

You didn't . I'm just not used to so much conversation. I haven't been around little ones in a long time.

It would be difficult for anyone who hadn't been around children much to keep good patients .But this wasn't no ordinary child , he had lots of questions and he wanted answers to all of them . Deuce went outside and feed his animals like he did every day and left Six to himself. After he feed his chickens , pigs, cows , and other animals he made his way back to the house . He stepped softly on the front porch and entered the house ,as he did, he found the boy looking at a pair of old pistols in their holsters on the table .

WHOOOOAAA!! BOY!!! Don't touch them ,them ain't toys !

Deuce made his way to the table as quick as he could . He wasn't trying too ,but he startled and scared the boy and he was a little startled himself. The boy had a few tears building up in his eyes and he was about to cry.

Hold on there son, i didn't mean to scare you and i didn't mean you couldn't look at'em. I just got to unload'em is all .They're older than me and you put together , both of'em got hair triggers and they ain't real safe. They been hanging on that wall more than forty year, them ain't look at's, that's just where i hung'em last time i took'em off. Bout all i do is keep the dust off of'em from time to time.

You mean you used to wear these guns?

Yep , and my pa wore'em afor i did.

Was ya'll cowboys or something?

Nope , not like in the movies anyway . My pa was a gub'ment marshal .

Was you a marshal ?

Nope, i was a bounty hunter.

Wow, a bounty hunter ?

Yep, best in these parts , some say all over. My pa always said i could track a squirrel through the trees if need be. I been doing it ever since i was about nine years old i guess.

Wow ! Is nine a lot older than me ?

Not too much ,a little bigger ,but a whole lot less questions, i rekin.

My dad says i'm always talking too much too , he says i'm always rattin on him. What ever that means ?

Long as you're doing it to him, it ain't no bad thing.

You never did tell me why you don't like my dad.

Tain't my place too , long as you like 'em i got no call to say nuttin. Never speak bad about a man to his son . Even if you are kin, it don't make for a good blood line. Me and you are what you call a blood line and your dad is in that bloodline ,same as me and you.

The boy had a blank look on his face he sort of rolled his eyes back in his head and appeared to be confused. He didn't know what to say , it was clear to Deuce that no one had ever told him about anything like this.

You don't understand anything i'm saying ,do you kiddo?

No sir.

First we gotta leave off that sir part . All right i'll do my best , i ain't dreckly your pa , but in a way i'm more than that . Let me back up some, let's look at them pictures up there .You see how's there's you then your dad then your grandpa "

Yeh "

Well that's all most folks know about their blood line or kinfolks that came before 'em .Most folks never see their great grand parents and if they do they don't remember them because they were too little .Now you know your grand pa don't ya ?

Yeh , he comes to pick me up when my dad takes off .

Ok your grand pa's dad is my son , and my son is your dad's great grandpa , my dad is your grandpa's great grand pa. Now do you get it?

Nuh uh . But we are all family ain't we .

Yep and i rekin that's good enough , anyway that's a blood line.
How come there ain't no women in the blood line ?

There is, you gotta have a women to make a blood line , But when a woman is born it messes up the blood line, so we have to shoot 'em till we get a boy to keep the bloodline going.

Nuh uh !

We don't shoot'em right away , we see if they can cook and clean and stuff like that . But the first sign of trouble, we gotta get rid of'em. HAAA! HAA! Don't get all fly eyed on me boy , i was just kidding.

How come you don't wear them guns no more ?

Rekin i done killed every body i don't like. There you go giving me that look again.

You didn't really kill no one, did you?

Would you believe about three hundred men?
Nuh uh .

Yeh, that was a little much ,wuddin it? I did a couple of times, i didn't want too but there wasn't any other choice and i ain't proud of it. Have you got time to listen to this story ? If you ain't going no where, i'll tell it to you.

Deuce i'm six years old ,i ain't got nuttin but time . And i am too little to go anywhere .

Yep i guess you're right. Anyway i guess it was about eighteen ninety eight ,i was about nine or ten. I was out at the barn doing some of my chores when Miss Pearl came riding up hollerin her head off like some kinda wild cat. We called all single women Miss back then.

DUECE !!! DEUCE!!!

That's all folks called me back then ,,she kept hollerin my name till i answered her . WHAT ?!! PEARL !!

MARSHAL ACE,, SAYS YOU NEED TO PACK A TOTE AND COME TO TOWN . HE SAYS HE'LL TELL YOU WHAT HE WANTS WHEN YOU GET THERE , HE SAYS YOU NEED TO GET STEPPEN ,HE AIN'T WAITING ON YOU ALL DAY!!

Pearl was kinda pretty, but that didn't mean much to me back then. She was taller than me and about two years older than me .Every time i turned around she was whooping me over something .Seems to me like we couldn't get along if our lives depended on it . She was always calling me names like scrawnie and runt and sometimes when i passed by the field between her house and mine she would hide in the ditch and throw dirt clods at me.

Boy she was mean ,wudden she ?

Yep , that's her in that picture up there , had she a lived, we would have been married seventy five years next month. Anyhow i packed a tote and high tailed it to town like my pa said .When he said get steppen that meant run as fast as you can and that's what i did. It was about ten mile to town and i got there pretty quick ,Pearl had a horse, but didn't wait on me so i could ride. When i got there i could see through the window my pa was talking to these two men. So i eased up on the wooden walk that ran in front of my pa's office , jumped up and kicked the door open, like i was busten into the place. My pa and them other two men like'ta came unglued . I thought they was gonna shoot me or something the way they jumped back.

YEH ACE ,WHAT YOU WANT!!! I hollerd as i came running in the door.

BOY!! HOW MANY TIMES I TELL YOU TO STOP DOING THAT !! ONE OF THESE DAYS I'M GONNA BLOW YOUR HEAD CLEAN OFF!!

Sorry pa . I said, corse i wuddin sorry, but it kept me from getten a whoopin for laughing .

Look Deuce ,these two fellers need our help findin couple boys what ain't no good.

Hell Marshal, we was told you had a tracker , this ain't nothing but a boy.

Mister, Deuce here can find a fallen star, if i tell'im to. This ain't the first time he's had to look for someone for me. Last year he found this little girl that strayed off from her parents at a picnic and got lost in the woods. We looked for her for two days and figured a panther drug her off .Then i let Deuce look for her by hisself ,cause he wouldn't leave me alone about it . He found her in a half a day , he's got some kinda gift for
it. If any body can find the men your lookin for, Deuce can.

Look kid , the men we're looking for.

Name's Deuce, Mister!!

Yeh ok , these men escaped from a Mississippi Prison , we been tracking them three weeks and can't catch 'em .

You know why you can't Mister ?

Hold your tongue Deuce ! Ain't no call to be smart mouthen strangers.

Can i tell' em why when i find the escapers and get my reward pa?
There is a reward ain't there?

Yeh kid we'll give you fifty dollars if you can find'em and we catch'em.

Now i knew they'd pay more if they really wanted to catch 'em and they had badges, so i know'd they had to find'em .

Mister. My name is Deuce, and the reward will be a hundred and fifty dollars or you can find them yourself!

Marshal you need to teach this boy some manners. For two bits i'll do it myself, with a mouth like he's got.

My pa looked at him and smiled, then he threw a quarter on the desk. Have at it mister, i been trying to shut his mouth since he was real little ,and i cain't do it. Doubt you can either.

Marshal this won't take but a second . I'll show you how to wisen him up .I been handling prisoners fifteen years and i don't take no lip from none of them.

'Alright boy' he said as he wretch down to take his gun off . Then he as he started to take his belt off i stuck my hand in my pocket and waited till he had both hands on it trying to get it out of the loops. He thought he was going to give me a whooping, but I changed his mind on that idea. Anyway,, then i snatched one of my big rooster cod sized, cat eye marbles out of my pocket and chunked it at him. I hit that sap sucker right between the eyes .That man's eyes went crossed and my pa laughed at him.

I TOLD YOU MY NAME IS DEUCE ! NOW DO YOU WANT MY HELP OR NOT?!! That man came back to his senses , he was mad but he didn't say nuttin else to me .

Deuce, here is what we want you to do, the other man said. We know they are somewhere in these parts .He pointed to a spot on a map. Find them and come back here and tell us where they are at ,we'll do the rest.

Ok but i need fifty dollars up front .

What the hell do you need that kind a money for Deuce ? My pa ask me.

I gotta get me some new britches pa .These hand mades that momma makes is ok for sloppen and chores . But they are too thin ,and the trees and briers will scratch me to pieces when i try to run in the woods. Besides that they ain't too warm at night.

You see Six my momma was a good woman, but she thought her hand made britches was the best thing since rubber tires .They was ok for running around ,but i wanted me a couple of new pairs of dark blue overalls they had at the store . Most folks wore 'em cause they had to .They lasted longer and held up good, in hard work. But i liked'em cause they had all kinda pockets in'em .They had two great ole big pockets in the hips . I could put my sling shot in one and a bottle of sass a frass in the other and still have plenty of room. On the side it had a hammer loop and a ruler pocket ,but i kept my knife in mine . In my right hip pocket i always kept a pocket full of of marbles, incase i needed one . I used to take old Matty Leddbetter's marbles all the time .He thought he was best in the loop, till i came around. In my chest pocket i kept me a chew and a pencil. My pa always said keep a pencil incase you gotta sign your name on something. I got my money and went and bought me some new tuff nutts and a pair of new shoes and a new shirt . The tuff nutts had a brand new pocket knife in'em ,so i had two knives . Anyway i gave my pa the rest of what i had left then i talked to the men one more time.

Deuce we know they was last seen here , then he pointed at that map again, i ain't ever read no map, so i nodded my head anyway. We asked some folks out by the river, but they would not talk to us .So go get your horse that will be the best place to start.

Mister, that's why ———

Deuce just go where the man told you and start there !! You know how to find'em, so just do it!!

I was gonna tell the man all he had to do was walk, because a horse makes too much noise in the woods. But my pa said never tell a trade secret and that way people will always hire you to do stuff that they could do themselves ,if they weren't so ignorant.

What's ignorant mean?

Ah, it's just a little smarter than stupid, but you cain't tell the difference in some folks.

Did you catch the bad guys?

I thought you said you had plenty of time?

I do got plenty of time.

Then wait on me to finish the story, it ain't like i got this wrote down or nuttin. I'm ninety five years old ,things like to run together in my head .I could get three or four stories mixed together and then you would be confused till you was thirty. The other day i got my memories messed up so bad, i already had my cow saddled afor i realized it. ha ha ha!

Anyway i got my new cloths and set out after the escapees .I ran about a half day to where they was last seen. They had left a trail in the woods that a blind Indian could have followed ,i trailed 'em bout two days then i saw they was hold up in this cave .I knew they weren't going anywhere, so i hightailed back to tell my pa and the two men,, where they were.

LOOK BOY ,I MEAN DEUCE ,WE WON'T NEVER FIND OUR WAY IN THEM WOODS, HOW ABOUT YOU COME AND SHOW US WHERE THEY ARE?

THAT WASN'T OUR DEAL MISTER. I didn't like these fellows but ,my pa says a lawman is lawman and you should respect them all of the time. Not me ,except for my pa, i didn't think much about the whole lot of them. Anyway back then i smart mouthed most folks, that thought they were better than me.

HOW DO WE KNOW THEY ARE STILL THERE? One of the men ask.

I stuck my hand back in my pocket and looked that man right in the eye.

But this time i had a hand full of marbles . Mister ,they are there because i said they was there, and they will still be there when ,you, get there. Now give my pa the rest of my money .

Wait ! boy, i mean Deuce!, Just leave them marbles in your pocket. Marshal if that boy had a gun he would have shot someone already.

Yeh i know, that's why i won't let him carry one.

Deuce how do you know they will still be there? My pa ask.

They cain't go no where Ace, i just took their horse and that old trail mule over to the livery stable .They had that mule loaded down ,so after they unloaded everything in the cave, i knew they was gonna be there awhile . I don't figure they can find their way out no better than you can find your'n in. That old trail mule has probably been in them woods a hundred times, the mule most likely took'em in there in the first place. I cut the mule loose and the horses followed us on their own and neither one of'em never made a noise. Besides all of that ,if you'll look on that hitching post out there you will see their shoes hanging there. Ain't nobody commin out of them woods without shoes on.

Marshal what have you been feeding this boy ,gun powder ? He's got a mean streak in him worse than a pole cat.

Nope! he get's that from his momma, a little red headed Irish woman. You boys follow the directions he gave you , you won't have any trouble finding them runaways.

They left and i guess they found 'em cause we never did hear anymore from them. They did pay my pa the rest of my money.

How did you know them men wasn't going to find the runaways with out your help.?

They wasn't dressed for hunting anything .They was all slickered up, so i knew they didn't want to get dirty .The shoes they was wearing was too fancy and shinny ,so i knew they wasn't gonna do no walking . And i knew the runaways wuddin gonna do no walking either. Horses leave deep tracks in the woods and they kick limbs and stuff everywhere. If they ain't careful, they'll just be following their on tracks after awhile. A man can move in the thick woods as fast as a horse and don't mess up near as many tracks or make near as many for that matter.

You sure did make a lot of money that day.

Yep !! my pa showed me how to do that about a year or two before. He told me the better a man dresses and the nicer his shoes are the more he'll pay you to do the stuff he don't want to, or cain't do. I would have looked for the men for five dollars , that's all my pa pays me when i help him. That was still a lot of money for a kid .I helped my pa from time to time when he needed me, but mostly i stayed here and worked this place. After a couple years my pa sent me to a private school to learn more and get more refined he called it. I stayed there about two years and came back home .One day my pa called me in the Marshals office .

Deuce you been to proper school and everthang else ,so why are you still wearing them overalls ? You got enough money to buy a good suit and what ever else you want .

Because i like to wear my overalls Ace .I was old enough that he let me call him Ace, like everyone else did. They're comfortable and they don't itch like them wool britches ,i had to wear in that proper school.

What's a proper school Deuce ?

It's kinda like a regular school, except you gotta pay more for someone to wack you with a stick ever time you turn around. Cost my dad five hundred dollars a year for some old bat to beat me near to death. Stand up straight , fork on the right ,spoon on the left , don't put your elbow on the table . We had to say stuff like "sea shells are sitting in the sand by the sea shore" that lady hit me so many times trying to say that real fast, i nearly got a brain tumor. I would get started trying to say it and it came out .She sells air sh##ing in the sand by the she sore. I didn't mind the book learning and all because they had a great ole big library, but that crazy lady tried to show me how to eat fried chicken with a knife and fork. That's as dumb as sucking giblet gravy through a straw . My momma said they'd been better off if they'd just sent my yeller cur dog, at least something in these parts would have some culture. Any how back to my pa . Deuce he said .

You got good book learnin ,something most folks around here ain't got and people respect that. Folks look up to people with a good education and they ask for your help because of it. But if you are going to keep wearing them overalls at least wear a clean shirt and a tie. Go get yourself some good shoes and keep them shined ,comb your hair and buy a nice hat ,a man's gotta have a good hat . Here i rekin your old enough for this now.

DID HE GIVE YOU A GUN !!??

No a badge. You gonna let me tell this story or not!!?

Ok Deuce ,but you sure are grippie!

HAAAA ! I like that kiddo, you got grit.

Deuce i rekin you can get a salary for helping me now .There's a lot more people coming around here now and i need more full time help. Could make for you getting elected Sherriff one day. The job pays twenty five dollars a month and you get to carry a gun. But if you shoot a man you had dern sure better be in the right, cause i'll arrest you same as anyone. What are you rattling there ? You still got that pocket full of marbles?

Yep ,i can chunck one of them ,faster than i can pull a gun.

When you can pull a gun as fast as you can throw one of them marbles, then you will be the man to rekin with around these parts.

What about the bounties ?

You can still have them, long as you ain't wearing a badge ,saves me time anyway, i got enough to do with out chasing hoodlums all over the country. I had to go find two last month and i'm getten too old for all that running .There's one hanging up on the board right now someone needs to go after.

How much bounty Ace ?

None Deuce, Marshals get paid a salary catching crooks, it's part of the job.

I'll help you if you want, but i ain't wearing no badge Ace.

My pa didn't like it cause i turned the badge down, after that the only way he would give me the rewards, is if i helped him with the regular ones too. I kept the badge in my other pocket and most folks knew i was his son ,so they didn't give me no trouble when i went after them. Mostly all i had to do was go get someone that didn't pay a gub'ment tax or something . I made a thousand dollars the first three months plus my salary. I caught most everybody i went after, they had trouble getting away from me . I didn't chase'em like a lot of bounty hunters do, that was too dangerous. I just followed 'em till i figured out where they was going, then i got ahead of'em and waited on them to come to me. Most all of 'em was real predictable .If there was a bar or a cheep motel or an abandon shack, i knew that's where they'd be . I knew the whole area better than anyone .

Six sat there and listened with his chin propped up on both hands like he was watching television. Deuce could tell he was getting tired and sleepy the way his head dropped a few times, then he quickly snapped it back up like nothing happened.

AAAAAhhhhhhh Six yawned and stretched .

You sleppy boy ?

Yeh Deuce, a little.

Why don't you go get washed up and i'll fix you a place to sleep .Where do you want to bed down at ,the barn ,or the chicken coop, i know how about in the back of my truck ,you can see the stars real good from there.

Deuce i cain't sleep in no barn or truck !

Yep your right, might be allergic to hay ,i guess the chicken coop will have to do. ha ha ha!

Deuce slowly walked out to his truck and got the boy's bag of clothing . By the time he made it back inside he found Six asleep in a large padded chair . He covered him up and left him there, then Deuce went back outside and sat on the porch. It was a good calm cool night in the hills where he lived. Most people would be sitting close to the television this time of night watching some sit com or game show. Not Deuce ,he seemed best entertained by nature's orchestra, frogs , crickets, owls whoing on que , and the occasional moo of a lonely cow . He could hear the wings flapping in the chicken coop as the chickens settle in. All of these things seemed to calm him as he took a large pinch of tobacco and poked it in one side of his mouth. Then he sat there chewing and spitting and listening as all the animals played their tunes, each one keeping perfect timing with the other. He sat there for an hour or more watching the stars twinkle and he'd follow the occasional blinking lights of an airplane as it slowly flew across the sky. He decided it was time for him to go to bed so he went in side leaving all the doors open, except an old rickady screen door to keep what ever bugs out,, that may be around.

He was awaken early the next morning by the phone ringing . By his nature the phone seemed out of place in his house .There wasn't much in the way of modern day appliances in his house . An old refrigerator and stove . A long string of lights ran down the center of the house was the only attempt at keeping up with the times. He answered the phone and anyone could tell he didn't get many calls.

Yeh ,uh ,hello ?

Deuce this is Marion Frank Four .

I know who it is !! One and three are dead , Six is here asleep and five is probably all hopped on dope somewhere!! So that leaves two and four and i know which one i am!!

You mean to tell me ,Six is there with you ?

Yep, Nickel left him here yesterday.

I'm sorry grand dad i'll get there as fast as i can to get him. I think Nickel is in jail ,i got a call awhile a go from the Sherriff two counties over. But i couldn't find out where Six was. Nickel normally leaves him with widow May ,but she ain't in good health. I sure am glad you got him, i was getting worried. Grand dad don't tell him about his dad until i get there.

Yeh ok how long will you be? I need to fix this boy some breakfast.

About an hour grand dad.

Deuce walked over to the chair and started to wake Six up then he looked at how peaceful he was and decided to leave him be. He went outside to do some of his early morning chores. Sometime passes and he is sitting back on the front porch staring down the long dirt road waiting on his grandson to arrive. About an hour later he sees a large pickup coming down the road. As it makes it's way to the drive the old man stands up and waits for the driver to get out. He seemed glad to see his grandson, though he was in his sixties he open the door and gets out.

Well if it ain't ole Forty Four get out and sit down.

How's he doing granddad ?

Tain't nothing wrong with him, if that's what you're asking.

No granddad ,i mean emotionally.

He's six years old ,i think that as long as some one don't tell him that Superman ain't real he'll be fine. He's still asleep in the front room.

Well i guess i need to get him ready to go ,i have a lot to do today. We had a big to do in town last night and we had to put a bunch in jail ,so i got a ton of paper work to complete. First i'll have to take him to a sitter ain't no telling when Nickel will show back up.

If your so busy ,why don't you just leave the boy here?
I don't want to trouble you none granddad, i know your old and it takes a lot to keep up with a six year old .

No Marion you're old ,i'm an icon, they don't even make birthday cards for anyone over eighty, they just send you one of them i didn't know you were still alive cards. Just leave the boy here and do what you got to do. If you remember, i took care of you and your son.

All right granddad if you insist , just give me call if you need anything or anything happens .

The only thing that can happen ,is i might get a bowel movement ,you want to know about that? ha ha Just be careful going back to town.
Ha ha ,I'll be back later grand dad .

Deuce stands up on the porch and waves as Marion drives off.

I wish them boys would stop saying that . "I'll be back in an hour or two" is getting real old. Deuce says to himself as he goes back in the house. As he walks in he notices the boy is waking up, so he decided to make him some breakfast. A few minutes pass and Deuce is standing at the stove cooking and the boy walks up and leans against his leg and lays his head against his hip. Not really knowing what to do Deuce gently drops his arm and reluctantly pats the boy on the head .Affection like that wasn't something Deuce was used to giving.

You are gonna have to let go of my leg before this hot grease pops out on you. Go wash up and when you get done, well be ready to eat.
Then we need to go to town and buy some get by's.

Get by's ?What's that Deuce?

That's when you buy enough groceries to get by until you go again.
Me ,i buy enough to get by about two weeks.

Deuce and Six are eating their breakfast when Deuce notices Six is having trouble cutting his bacon with his fork.

What the hell are you doing Six?
I'm trying to cut this bacon proper ,but it won't work.

Didn't any one ever show you how to eat breakfast properly?
No not really.

Well here is how you do it . Are you right or left handed ?
I'm this one .

Good right handed , take the knife in your right hand and the fork in your left . Good, now spin the knife around and pinch the blade between your thumb and forefinger. Good, just like that . Are you ready ?
Yeh Deuce.

Then chunck that knife at that wall over there. Look ,,anything you cain't pinch or sop up with a biscuit, pick it up and eat it with your fingers , that's the proper way to eat breakfast.

What's the fork for ?

That's in case someone tries to grab something off your plate ,then you can just job'em with the fork. Ha! ha ! You ain't gotta look pretty to eat breakfast ,you just gotta get full .

They finished eating their breakfast and changed clothing .Sense the boy didn't change the night before, Deuce had him put on a clean pair of short britches and shirt. Deuce in his normal dress put on a fairly new pair of overalls . Beneath them ,he wore his usual bright white shirt and black tie and covered his head with a new Fedora. He carried all the normal stuff in his pockets ,pocket watch and small knife ,small change ,wallet , a buckeye for arthritis and on the dresser he kept a bowl of marbles in which he grabbed a handful and put in his pocket as well.

SIX !!? He yelled out .

Yeh Deuce ? He answered as he went to where Deuce is.

Here kiddo put a hand full of these in your pocket , just in case you need one.

What will i need a marble for Deuce?

You don't never know ,but they always come in handy for something. Now are you ready to go?

Yes sir , are we going in that old truck?

Yep , i'm too old to ride the horse and the horse is too old to ride me.

Ain't'cha gonna lock your house Deuce ? The boy ask as they stepped off the porch.

Nope, just leave it like it is ,won't nobody mess with it. How old did you say you was kiddo?

I'm six years old .

Good you'll have to drive ,i don't see so good no more.

I'M TOO LITTLE TO DRIVE DEUCE!

No Six, you're too little to pay taxes , if you can see over the steering wheel, you can drive, beside that there ain't nothing to it. Get in ,pull that lever down, and hang on .

Deuce i can't see over the steering wheel, how will i know if i hit something?

There won't be no question about it, if you hit something , you will know it ,it will leave a big ole dent in the truck. Here sit on this tool box , now can you see better?

Yes, but i can't reach the pedals .

It don't matter none , this thing ain't got but one gear left anyhow . Just pull that lever down and let it go on it's own .

Which way do i go ?

Look straight across that field , do you see that big gate way over yonder?

Yes sir .

Well we got about seven of them to go through, there all in a straight line . Don't be so scared kiddo there's three basic rules to driving .One don't hit anything , two if you do ,don't tell anybody and three if the person in front of you don't use a signal, ram in to their rear end they'll learn better next time. ha ha! Six there a few bull holes and a ditch or two just stay out of them and we'll be fine. All of these gates lead up to the back of the store, i had'em put in so i don't have to get on the highway. I got this bad habit of running into the rear end of other cars.

Six is real nervous as he drives across the pasture, but he calms down after a second or two .

DEUCE HOW AM I GOING TO STOP? WE ARE GOING TO HIT THAT GAIT !!

Don't worry about it , it'll stop when it runs out of gas .

DEUCE?!!

I got the hand brake kiddo , i'll stop us when it's time. See all i had to do was pull this handle .

WOOO DEUCE, I THOUGHT WE WAS GONNA HIT IT!!

As they walk in the store you can see the usual people there sitting and playing dominoes, and loafing.

Dewy ,Luke ,Jeb, Walt . How you boys doing today?

Hello Deuce ! We ain't seen you sense Tricky Dick was in office. Where you been keeping your self? Hey ,who's the two footer ?

He's my great grandson. We call him Six. Clark me and the boy here need some viddles ,about two weeks worth and put us some of that hard candy in it. Also Clark i'll need two boxes of forty four shells ,a box of them big cat eye marbles , two of them high powered sling shots. Have you got any britches to fit the boy here ? Put me a new pair or two in there as well.

You boys figurein on hunten are you?

Yeh Luke, i ain't shot my pa's pistols in awhile.

hahahhahh,, IN ABOUT LIKE ,FIFTY YEARS WOULDN'T YOU SAY? One of the men remarked.

Yep , give or take.

Clark can you send all that out to my place, me and the boy gotta to down to the feed store and get some grub for my critters.

Yeh sure Deuce, we always do.

I appreciate it,, just take that off my account.

Deuce your the only man i know saves money by paying for stuff long before you need it. You must have money on account in every store in this county.

Yep , that way some big shot banker cain't tell me i cain't have my money when i want it. Long as i got money on account here cain't nobody shut Clark down like they been doing to other small stores to build them big world marts. Long as we got money, he can stay in business. They tell you about that interest, 19 percent, then they charge you twenty percent for spending your money. I went to draw out ten thousand dollars one time ,the feller told me it would take three to four hours , didn't take but three minutes for them to put my money in the bank. Then the fellow said what do you want it for , i need to know so the gub'ment knows your going to do something legal with it. I told him it wasn't none of his dad blame bid'nuss ,just give me my money. Long as you boys got my money on account ,won't neither one of us be broke.

Deuce and Six went back to the house where the food was sitting on the front porch waiting on them .They got all of the food put away and fed all the animals and decided to sit on the porch a while. Deuce got his guns and started cleaning them .

Deuce did you ever have to go after any real bad guys?

Yep i did once .These was the meanest i ever saw . Believe it or not their last name was Outlaw .The whole family was meaner than a hemd up panther . Some folks say that's where the word outlaw came from, was their last name. These folks rob and steal ,murder ,cheat, you name it they did it. Tain't none round here no more though.

Why? Did you run them off ?

Kinda, but not really.

This story is pretty violent , are you sure you want to hear it?

Yeh, i see it all the time on TV!

Well this is the real thang and it's a whole lot different.

Ok let me hear it .

Alright then i'll start from the beginning.

DEUCE ! DEUCE!!

WHAT PEARL ! I yelled back at her.

YOU NEED TO COME TO TOWN RIGHT NOW, IT'S YOUR PA !!

WHAT'S WRONG WITH ACE ,PEARL?!

JUST GO DEUCE ,TAKE YOUR HORSE AND GET GOING!!

I jumped on my horse and hightailed to towns as fast as i could get that mare to run. When i got there my pa was in Della's Wet Cha Whistle laying on the floor. I was scared my pa was dead, there was blood on the floor, on him , on the chairs and on the bar. People was standing all around him. Some of them was trying to help him.

WHAT HAPPENED HERE DELLA ? WHO SHOT ACE?

Deuce it was two of them Outlaw brothers ,they came in drunk on moonshine and started trouble with Issack Calmly and Jubel Mays. Your pa came to break it up and Thomas Outlaw got behind him, next thing i know your pa's on the floor.

Deuce? A real low voice calls out

Yeh pa ?

Go put your badge on and come back here and get my guns.

What do i need my badge for ? Why can't i just save time and go after them from here?

The voice is still soft but it gets a little louder as he responds.

DEUCE , YOU ARE A LAWMAN COUGH!! COUGH!! EVEN IF YOU ARE HUNTING A BOUNTY. DEUCE THESE BOYS ARE MEAN, YOU WILL NEED THE LAW ON YOUR SIDE!!

Deuce has a few tears in his eyes, but he's restraining to keep them from showing.

The law on your side,, didn't do you no good this time pa .

DAMMIT DEUCE!! HERE ME BOY !

I never heard my pa cuss out loud like that ,but he was getting mad at me .

Deuce this can't be about revenge or your temper, if you go off from here like i know you want to, it will start a war among the shiners. We can't stand a war like that in these parts, too many people will get hurt. Deuce that's what this is all about, moonshine. There are some city boys here from somewhere and they are moving in on the small timers. There's some family from the city called Gottaveechie .They have hired the Outlaws to do their dirty work, they want the small stills gone from here. Now you are wasting time standing here ,go get your badge out of my desk and swear in the boys that are down there waiting on you.

Are you gonna be ok pa ?

Yep, just get going they are already way ahead of you. COUGH! COUGH! COUGH!!

Ok pa i'll be right back , Della is the doc on his way?

Yeh Deuce he should be here any time.

When i got back to Della's ,my pa was dead and covered up with a table cloth. I changed my mind and waited to go after them, i knew that there was a bunch of them and we needed to thin them out some. The Outlaw family themselves was a slick bunch and they knew the woods as good as i did. So it wasn't real smart for me to just go running in the woods after them. After we buried my pa and had his wake, i had all the other deputies meet me at the Marshals office. I had about seven of them deputized, but the more i thought about it ,the more it became a family matter.

Fellows it's going to get rough from here on out ,if we are not very careful some of us will be shot or killed trying to do what my pa did lawfully and you will act lawfully .Wallace you were pa's right hand man , you will take over till his replacement gets here. Then i took my badge off and handed it to Wallace. Them city boys is trying to take over here and i ain't going to let them. But i cain't stop 'em as a marshal , people been making shine in these parts for years, but this prohibition done turned everybody into criminals. You boys go start shutting down the stills on the out skirts of the woods before the revenuers get to them or there will be too much bloodshed, them shiners will fight back. As for me i can't do what i need to do with this badge. Let me forewarn everyone to stay out of the deep woods ,i will bring whoever i catch to the outside, and tie them to a tree, you all just keep on the look out for them . Anyone that resist local or not ,shoot them ,you don't know who your enemies are now. Now fellows,, get going.

Was there a bunch of'em Deuce?

Yep, But the worst problem we had was, we didn't really know who was against us. Some of these folks we had known for years and they just turned on us. I don't know if it was money ,fear from the city boys or they didn't know who they could trust .The first couple of days, i didn't have much trouble, most of 'em just gave up and walked out on their own. They knew why i was in there anyway. One day i found an old road that i didn't even know was there, it hadn't been used in so long. There was ruts cut in the mud that no horse or mules could have made .I decided to follow the road, but i stayed on the inside of the trees . I knew a lot of activity was going on up there ,but i didn't know by who. I hadn't walked more than a mile when i saw this city boy all gussied up like he was going to a wedding and a funeral. He was standing by this big black Ford all by himself. I could tell he had a gun by the way his coat stuck out. I knew i had to get the jump on him ,because if i shot him ,i didn't know how many would come out of the woods. I stuck my hand in my pocket and grabbed about three marbles then i threw one way then one to the left of that then another to the left of that. I had that big fat city boy spinning in a circles .I said to myself ; Yep, city boy thinks he hears something.

I kinda laughed to myself, took off my tie and dirtied my shirt up some ,then i snuck up on him some, staying in the bushes until he turned his head .I chuncked another one of these big fellows here and knocked the fire right out 'a his ass with that marble.

OWE!! MOTHER OF GOD!! WHAT WAS THAT?!!

Then he started rubbing the back of his head and shaking it, like it was full of marbles .That ole boy had enough oil on his head to fry deer horns.

PUT YOUR HANDS IN THE AIR CITY BOY , !! I AIN'T TELLING YOU BUT ONE TIME.THEN I'M GONNA PUT A BULLET RIGHT IN THAT BIG LUMPY SPOT YOU GOT.!!

Then he started getting sassy, but it didn't matter none ,i still had the gun on him.

Mister you don't know who you are messing with.

Your right i don't , and i don't care. Now slowly take that gun out of your coat ,put it on the hood of your car and step away.

I got his gun, then i gave him a wack on the head with my pistol. Them Italian people are some of the hardest headed people i ever saw. I had to wack him twice before he fell. I tied him up and hid him behind the car, then i put his coat on and stood there and waited on the rest of them to come out. The trees was pretty thick and it was hard to see anyone till they got close to you. I stood there a few minutes and out came two more city boys and a local. All of them was caring a couple cases of pure moonshine, apiece.

All clear !! One of them yelled out.

Yeh come on, i yelled back . They didn't recognize me, so i waited on them, by the time they got to me i had both guns pulled and pointed at them.

JUST KEEP CARRING THEM CASES THIS WAY FELLORS. IF ANY ONE GETS STUPID AND TRIES SOMETHING , I'LL SHOOT THE SHINE, AND WE ALL KNOW WHAT HAPPENS IF IT MAKES A SPARK.

I made 'em tie one another up and load the big one in the car ,then i drove them to the out shirts and wedged the car in between two trees. Of course i busted all of the moonshine first ,i figured i don't drink it, i don't need it. I walked about a mile or so straight back up in the woods when i came across three more hid in a hollow, running another still. I watched them a few minutes to make sure no one else was there .I grabbed a whole hand full of marbles and throwed them at the still, it sounded like hail hitten a tin roof, them boys jumped up and grabbed their guns .One of them had a shot gun, so i had to shoot him and the other two had pistols. After i shot the one, the others gave up pretty quick ,they didn't know how many more there was with me. So i yelled out like i had a whole posse with me.

OK YA'LL KEEP ME COVERED!!

Over the next several days we rounded up about twenty or so ,but still no Outlaw brothers, I decided it was time to start asking questions. I stopped by Clarks store and picked up some more supplies before i went to the abandon barn outside of town.

Mr. Corbit ? That was Clarks dad, Mr. Corbit . I said. I need two boxes of them new cat eyes you got up there .Them slang shots you got pretty stought?

Yeh ,Deuce, Taylor just made 'em couple days ago.

Good ,let me have two of them ,case i break one.

Little bit too big to be playing with marbles and slang shots , ain't cha Deuce? Mr. Corbit asks me .

I AIN'T A GONNA BE PLAYING THIS TIME MISTER CORBIT!! There was this little kid in the store , i cain't remember his name but i sent him to the marshal's office.

You want to make two dollars boy?

Yeh Deuce what do i gotta do?

Just go to the marshals office and tell Wallace to bring one of the local boys to Mason's old barn, and it don't matter which one . Now hurry up ,here's your money. Once you tell him, get on home.

You ever shoot a slang shot, Six?

No why?

Go in there and get me them two slang shots off the table. I'll show you how, then you'll know , i don't know how a kid ever gets by with out one.

Six does as he is told and brings back two large sling shots and hands them to Deuce.

Six ,,,these here are two top of the line slang shots .They ain't like them cry baby sissy wire ones that they sell at a toy store ,or them break your dad blame wrists fancy pants ones that they sell in a sports shop. These here are made out of genuine hickory. The ole boy that made these learned from his grandpa .He cut the fork from the top of the tree and used the straightest limbs possible .Then he cuts the rubber from an old tire tube just long enough that when you pull the strap back to your chin to aim, it is stretched all the way out ,with your arm stretched all the way out. Alright first you put the marble in the pinch strap ,or the cradle some like to call it .Then you pull it back as far as you can and line the cradle up right in the center of the forks and watch that rascal fly. Now you can use a rock or anything that you can put in the cradle , but nothing will fly as straight and fast as a marble. Here shoot at them crows over there by the hog trough.

Six pulled the rubber strap back as far as he could, almost straining as he held it long enough to aim, then all in one move he released the cradle.

DANG !! I MISSED!!

That's ok kiddo, you just gotta practice some ,but that was real close. See them crows came right back . A crow is so ignorant they don't even know what's going on. What did we say ignorant meant?

Just a little smarter than stupid Deuce.

Yep ,good you're listening , but actually it just means you don't know something. A crow is one of them that you can't tell if if he's ignorant or stupid .You can shoot at them all day long and they will keep coming back. That's how i got so good at shooting a slang shot.

The boy kept shooting marbles and with each one he became better .

HEY LOOK DEUCE, I HIT ONE!!

ALRIGHT, GOOD JOB!! He won't be coming back for awhile.

What happened to the man at the barn Deuce?

Well i had Wallace bring him down to the barn and i tied him in an old chair. I started questioning two or three of them, but they didn't want to give me any information. So i figured it was time to get tough.

Delbert where is the Outlaw brothers?

I don't know Deuce!

You're lying Delbert ! I pulled those rubber straps back all the way to my chin ,i thought they was gonna break i pulled them back so far . Then i let that marble go .SWOOSH!! I could hear it fly through the air.

Owe!! Deuce i swear i don't know where they are!

I caught that scoundrel right in the forehead, a great ole big fat pump knot instantly swelled up on his head, i sort'a felt sorry for him and i hated to shoot him twice, but i knew he knew something.

WACK!! OK DEUCE ,OK !! They said they was going to the city to make some kind'a deal.

Which city?

I don't know Deuce!! WACK !! OUGH!! DEUCE I SWEAR I DON'T KNOW WHICH CITY ,PLEASE DON'T SHOOT ME AGIAN!!

I drew the cradle back one more time . I didn't know how many more times Delbert could take getting hit with marbles. But i knew he was about to break. His head was getting lumpier than an a four day old squash.

NO DEUCE !!THE FELLOR IN THE PIN STRIPE, HE'S THE ONE IN CHARGE ,HE KNOWS WHERE THEY ARE AT!!

WHAT'S HIS NAME ?

I don't know ,honest .They call him three fingers cause that's all he has on his right hand. He's real mean Deuce , he won't talk.

I pointed my finger at him and looked him straight'na eye. He'd better talk Delbert and he'd better be the leader, or i'm gonna bring you back in here and turn your lumpy head into a wash board. Wallace bring me the one with the fancy suit .We'll just start from the top down , one of'ems bound to be a coward.

They brought the big fellow in ,and he was tough at first . I didn't think he was gonna say anything .

Your a pretty big fellor ain't cha? I ask him trying to size him up some.

Let me up and i'll show you how big i am !

If i do that ,then i'll just have to kill ya. You're big , but i don't expect you are too awe fully tough without one of your buddies holding me. NOW WHERE IS THOMAS OUTLAW AND HIS BROTHER? !!

I ain't telling you nothing ,you country schmuck!

I don't know what schmuck means, but i do know ,it better not be worse than ignorant.

WACK !! Like i said Six .Them Italians got the hardest heads of anyone i have ever seen.

That the best you got hillbilly? You see these two missing fingers ,i had them cut off to show my loyalty , and your country corn bread eating ass ain't gonna break me.

Take his shoes off Wallace!

You ain't gonna do what i think you are Deuce?

Yep , feet tenderizer. Big ole fat spaghetti eater like this one will be glad to talk before too long.

Wait ,!! What are you doing?

I put about five or six marbles in each one of his fancy winged tip shoes, then we put them back on him .

Tie him to that mule over there Wallace. Once that mule drags him around about twenty or thirty minutes with his shoes full of marbles ,we won't be able to shut him up.

Sure enough ,after about twenty minutes we could see his feet swelling up inside his shoes, he went to talking. I knew the ole boy had a soft spot somewhere , it sure wuddn't on that big ole head of his.

ALRIGHT !, THEY WENT TO ST.LOUIS TO GET SOME MORE ORDERS FOR WHISKEY AND PICK UP THEIR PAY FOR THE LAST ONE.!! WE DIDN'T HAVE NOTHING TO DO WITH THE MARSHALS DEATH .THAT WAS ALL THEIR IDEA.THEY WILL BE BACK TOMORROW.

Well ,we'll just have to leave them shoes on incase he's lying.

I am not lying mister!

Wallace did you know everybody that has ever told a lie, started off by saying" i ain't lying," first . Why is that? Done got so you cain't tell if a liar is being honest or not. I'll bet you if i shoot him with one of these big marbles now, he'll swear up and down he's telling the truth.

Who did the shooting of my pa , city boy?

Thomas shot your pa , he said with him out of the way you would be easy to handle. He said you don't go after nobody without a bounty on them.

Well he's stupid and wrong .How ignorant do you gotta be, to think i ain't going to find my pa's killer. You see Wallace ,it's people like them that give hillbillys a bad name. Now city boy you got two choices, one of them is you won't ever leave this barn alive. You want to know what the other one is?

He nodded his head yes.

You will send one of your boys out to get how ever many you got left in the woods and bring them back here. Then you are gonna call who ever your boss is and tell him that there ain't nothing left for y'all around here. If not, i will kill all of you right where you are. You see fellow i am a bounty hunter and i'm sure ya'll got plenty of money lying around somewhere. I can get to each one of you one by one, and i can do the same thing in the city ,that i can do out here,,, you boys ain't that hard to find. NOW WHICH DO YOU WANT? I WANT THE OUTLAWS AND YOU CAN GO SOMEWHERE ELSE.

What did they do Deuce?

They went back to the city.

Did you get the Outlaw ?

Yep, I killed Thomas and we put his brother in prison. Then we put their ma and pa and the rest of their family on a train and sent them away from here. Some of the other people burned their house and barn down so they didn't have no reason to come back .That's why they ain't here no more around here.

Where are they at now Deuce ?

Six there's Outlaws all over the world ,some by name and some of'em not.

When did you marry Pearl?

It wuddin too long after that , then about a year later we had Tripp.

What happened to him ?

WORLD WAR TWO ! Here boy you ready to shoot these pistols?

Yeh, can i shoot at them crows?

No , i just like to shoot marbles at'em ain't no need to kill'em for no reason. Shoot at that fence post over there .Here look right down the barrel and gently pull the trigger. Wait i better help you, when that thing kicks it's lobble to bop you on the noggen.

What's a noggen?

When you get bopped in it, you'll know, because you'll be rubbing it for a week. ha ha ha !

The two of them spent a lot of time with each other over the next couple of days .Six followed him and asked as many questions as he could , expecting answers to all of them. One afternoon Deuce was in the house and left Six outside practicing with his slingshot. He heard the boy crying and screaming at someone, but he hadn't heard anyone drive up. Deuce made it to the front door as fast as he could to see what was going on .

STOP SHOOTING ME WITH THEM MARBLES , SIX ,THAT HURTS! WACK , !! WACK !! He shot him again and again as fast as he could reload.

When Deuce got to the front door he saw his grandson and great grandson trying to stop Six from shooting more marbles at his dad.

MARION FRANK !! GET UP HERE ON THE PORCH AND STAY OUT OF IT, THIS IS BETWEEN THEM TWO.!!

GRAND DAD HE'S GONNA HURT SOME ONE WITH ONE OF THEM MARBLES!!

I SAID STAY OUT OF IT FOUR , HE CAN'T HURT HIM NEAR AS MUCH AS NICKEL HAS CAUSED HIM PAIN!!

YOU CAIN'T KEEP LEAVEING ME DAD,, I DIDN'T KNOW WHERE YOU WAS!!

PLEASE SIX, STOP SHOOTING ME WITH THOSE MARBLES, I WON'T LEAVE YOU ANYMORE ,I PROMISE!!

He shot another one at his dad , YOU SAY THAT ALL THE TIME !! The boy was crying and his dad was starting to cry too.

Six you gotta stop, i was in jail , i couldn't come back.

Six dropped to his knees crying and sobbing loudly as he grabbed little fists full of dirt, just as his grand pa started to go after him Deuce grabbed him by the shoulder and pulled him back.

You gotta let them work it out Marion, we won't be around long enough to keep fixing things .That boy told me he didn't ever want to have kids, because of the way his dad does him, he's too young to think that way.

Nickel bent down and picked his son up and hugged him tight , tears was still streaming down both of their faces as the boy looked into his dads eyes again.

You cain't leave me no more dad , there won't be no one around to take care of me! Mom has done and overdosed and Deuce is real nice and so is grandpa ,but they are getting too old.

I'm sorry son !

All four of what was left of their family stood on the porch as the three were getting ready to leave .They were happy and getting along for the first time in years, Deuce looks at his grandson .

See i told you a long time ago four, but you didn't listen. Always carry a pocket full of marbles and a sling shot, you don't ever know when you might need one.

THE END

The Bunkhouse

This story is fictional

WRITTEN BY WILLIAM CAMPBELL
'BOOTHEEL WILL'

The bulldozers are entering through the tall archway on large trucks .The archways stand tall and strong against the moisture less winds of the western Oklahoma ,,Kansas plains .The posts that held the large arched sign ,marking the entry way to an abandon, forgotten ranch ,obviously came from somewhere else. The plains were baron and only held the occasional patch of knotty entangled scrub oak trees that nearly drowned in a sea of knee high yellowish green prairie grass. Connected to the tall posts were partial strands of rusty, knotty ,entangled barbed wire that lay weaved in the tall grass below. Only a few fence post remain to outline any kind of a border or indication of how large this ranch might have been. The posts standing spuractic and scattered across the rolling plains ,would be connected to strands of barbed wire. It wasn't clear which was holding the other up to stand and face the elements that abused it's condition yearly. The only apparent conclusion is that neither would stand without the other.

As far as the eye could see ,nothing but a broken horizon and a dim faded view of mountains ,indicated any real beauty to this isolated ,boring parcel of land . Scattered about the ground lay bone and sculls of cattle, long since perished, bleached brilliant white under the high noon sun. The bones seemed to sparkle and glitter in the sun, almost reflecting it's rays and directing them to other locations about the ranch.

Off in the distance sat an old barn ,surrounded by a skeleton of a corral .The way the barn leaned to one side it was only a matter of time that a brief wind ,surely would collapse it within itself. Several yards from the barn, lay a large pile of stones indicating that a large and tall fireplace once stood there possibly to provide heat for a very large home. The stones was the only evidence that a house may have even been there, other than some metal debris that lay strewn about . To the right of the barn and even twice as far away from it, as the pile of stone, sat a long and wide structure that seemed to be preserved from an era long sense over ,and only remembered by someone that may have read about it. A bunkhouse no doubt ,was the purpose for this building even being there . Obviously near as old as any other structure there . Why did it survive?

Centered between the barn and the bunkhouse stood an old metal windmill that squeaked as it tried to turn in the slight breeze . It's efforts were hindered as most of it's wooden blades were ether rotted or broken away from it's rusty frame. This could be the only evidence ,that any attempt at modernizing this ranch, had even been made. Reminates of an old wooden wagon sat under the eave of the bunkhouse, cracked and dry rotted ,it appeared that the only thing that held it standing, was the large metal rings that bound the wheels of wood together, and even then the slightest shove could tumble it to the ground ,like a fallen house made from a deck of playing cards.

Where do you want me to unload the equipment dad ? J.W. calls out as he steps out on the running board of his large semi truck.

Put everything over there by that bunkhouse son it will be safe until morning.

Both of them unloaded the dozers and other equipment they would need to excavate the land ,and place it in a neat line in front of the building.

Too bad we have got tear all of this down dad. The sign when we came in said, Three X Two Bar Ranch .Est. 1851 . That's pretty old ,even for a ranch in these parts.

I know son ,but the rich people have got to have their golf courses, and we have got to eat. I think i'm going back to the shop .Are you coming soon or are you going to stay here and look around?

You know me dad ,if there is a junk pile, there is a gold mine just waiting for me to find it. There is no telling what i could find in a place like this. I'll see you back at the shop later .

J.W.'S dad get into his truck ,waves by to his son and slowly drives it back under the archway and makes his way to the narrow highway ahead.

J.W. walks over to the pile of stone and moves a few only to find a few pieces of charred wood in the rubble. Then he walks over to the barn and peeks into the doorway openings to get a glance at what ever might be left inside. He was nervous and avoided entering the barn because he knew it wasn't safe. As he looked inside he could only make out shadows of a few post and horse stalls that remained. He knew his best option was to wait until they pushed it down with the dozers. He makes his way to the bunkhouse to see what reward it may hold and as he props his foot on the wagon tongue and it becomes rickety and one of the wheels come apart. He laughs and shakes his head from side to side and goes to the doorway of the bunkhouse.

It took some effort for him to open the door as the cast steel hinges were near rusted into one solid piece. The planks used to make the door were thick and heavy and J.W. give it one final shove only to push the entire thing to the floor of the building. J.W. steps inside slowly as he is aware of the loose and warped boards that make up the surface of the floor .It was apparent that the floor had been put in at a later date , because the post that held the building up ran through the floor and anchored into the ground. This only gave him an idea that who ever lived here, at one time, tried to maintain the place. It was clear that the bunkhouse had nothing but a dirt floor in it's beginning. J.W. used caution as he stepped from board to board not knowing if either one would carry his average weight. The floor creaked and squeaked as he stepped across it .The walls of the bunkhouse had no evidence of any glass windows ,it appeared that the only protection it's interior had, was the broken shutters that seemed riddled with bullet holes. Leavening nothing to indicate why. Perhaps over time someone had just used them as a target to practice shooting on. In the center of the large open room stood an old cast iron stove ,over four foot tall and as wide as an oil drum, it too had many piercing of holes in it's torso .

Though J.W was young ,his investigation skills were sharp and he seemed to have a lot of knowledge of metal and antiques, as it would be common for someone that had collected artifacts from old to have. J.W pokes his finger into one of the hole in the stove and begins to mumble to himself as he tries to rationalize his find.

Hum? Cast iron breaks when it's hit with another metal object ,unless it was red hot when it was hit. So that could only mean someone was here when these shots were fired and the stove had a fire going in it. This is strange though ,this coffee pot has holes in it too , but these streams of rust are deeper and thicker as they run down the side of the stove. This could only mean that who ever did the shooting wasn't expected and suddenly attacked who ever was in here. I bet these guys didn't even stand a chance.

J.W. begins to look around on the floor and as quick as he does he notices little areas of wood that were darker than the rest of the planks used to cover the floor.

WAIT A MINUTE ! He says to himself. There are one ,two, six he continues to count . DANG!! There's got to be twelve different appears to be puddles of dry blood stains on the floor, all of them by or under what seems like where a bed used to set. By the looks of this place, they were bunk beds and it held at least fifteen people .These poor bastards were asleep when they were shot. By the look of the puddles under the table, two of them must have been awake and sitting there drinking coffee waiting on the others to wake up. Let me see,, fourteen blood stains and fifteen sleeping spaces there's one missing .So either he killed them all or there were only fourteen here.

J.W. didn't think much more about it as he inspected the rest of the room .Two rows of columns stood in a straight line down the center of the room .Each column held a large rafter suspended in air and the columns separated the room into thirds ,leavening a wide walk way between the rows of bunks on either side of the room. The end of the room was dark and only lit by the two window openings in the front of the bunkhouse .On a pole at the very end of the room hung a large dark object, that became more apparent as a saddle, the closer J.W. came to it. J.W. Walks up to the black leather saddle covered with many layers of dust and dirt for a closer look . He was reluctant to touch it, for fear that it may be overly fragile from years of exposure . But his curiosity was getting the best of him because this may very well be his gold mine so to speak. In most cases a common saddle would not hold much value as they are not that rare. However J.W decides to wipe some of the dust from the wide ,long thick straps, that held the stirrups and sintching belts to the base of the saddle.

He took the forearm portion of his sleeve and began to gently wipe off the dust. The more he wiped, the more he began to reveal some letters and numbers branded into the strap. Though only barely visible he could hardly make the items out and decided to go to his truck and get some oil to brighten the surface. J.W. returned from his truck with a small can of leather cleaner he had found under his seat while looking for the oil. The saddle begins to brighten and shine revealing the brass studs that had been attached all the way around the shape of the saddle, and bringing out even clearer the letters and numbers branded to it's side. The first peace of J.W'S mystery had fell into place. He now knew who the saddle once belong to . The first three letters revealed were, C.S.A.then CORP. THOMAS J. KILBOURNE came into plane view as well. 43RD.TENN.INFATRY 1864. This being the last brand ,J.W. now knew he had a place to start. Even knowing this it still didn't set him at ease as to why only one saddle remained and nothing else to clue him in on the rest of any story that might be present.

Further inspection gave J.W. confidence that he could remove the saddle from the post without harming it anymore than it already was. J.W. removes the saddle and puts it into his truck realizing that it was the only item in any kind of shape to keep. Most of the other items like badly rusted straight razors, metal plates ,a belt buckle and shell casings ,he placed in a bag knowing that they had no value, other that the fact that they were just old.

Later that evening he calls a friend that he sometimes hunt antiques with, and asks him about the saddle . He is informed that most of the surviving saddles are owned by avid civil war collectors or museums. He also told him that his find was traceable and only required some searching on some web sites and the history of it's owner could be easily found with the information he had. J.W. spends several hours browsing different related sites, but he has no luck .Several days pass and J.W. and his dad continue with their job in removing the abandon barn and stones ,burring what they could and burning the rest. They still dug up small items of no real consequence until most everything was down and level, but the bunkhouse.

The week end came on and J.W. tells his dad that he wants to keep some of the wood from the bunkhouse to remodel his basement and he would take it apart himself by hand until he had what he wanted.
His dad agrees and leaves him to work alone once again .The first day he stands on top of the bunkhouse removing planks from the rafters and sweat begins to roll from his forehead and drip in his eyes . He takes a rag from his pocket and turns his head sideways and suddenly catches a glimpse of several high mounds off in a distance. It didn't make any since that they were there, because they didn't fit with the contour of the rest of the land. Just as suddenly as he spotted them he remembered that he had found the blood stains on the floor and began to count the mounds. The number matched his count of dried blood stains to an even fourteen .This now making his first investigation correct, he began to wonder if in fact there was a fifteenth person. J.W. kept working until he was down to just the walls and floor of the building and decided that the best lumber left was some scattered out planks in the floor that could be refinished with a little extra work. J.W. tears up several planks and as he does more and more light shines on the ground beneath the floor.

WELL I 'LL BE SON OF A GUN !!! IT'S A SKELETON !!! He screams out as he is startled, and quickly jumps back to catch his breath and regain his composer. He steps back up to where he was and slowly removes more planks revealing even more of the remains of a human .There wasn't a doubt in his mind now, that there was a fifteenth person. Now he was even more confused than before . He knew that he needed to report something like this to the authorities, but he wanted a closer look before he did. When J.W.removed everything that was in the way leaving the skeleton in a wide open and clear space .He takes a broom from his truck and slowly sweeps dust and drifted in dirt from around the remains. The more he sweeps even more of his mystery is being unfolded and leaves him even more baffled. He had seen many programs on things of this nature, and though they were just TV. shows, he knew how to reveal the evidence without further damaging the bones. As he had all of the dirt removed he began talking out a scenario to himself once again as he often did.

He gets a piece of paper from his truck and makes notes as he talks to himself. Length approximately five foot ten .He has his left hand on his chest as if that was where he may have been shot. He still has his gun in his holster on his left side ,his right arm is extended to full length and another pistol lay on top of his palm as if he had been using it before he passed. Wait there are still bullets lodged in various places and in some of his bones. Judging by the two bullets laying on the ground beneath his ribcage he must have been shot in the stomach twice and in the leg once. One of his ribs in his back is displaced and it appears that he was shot in the back at least one time. One bullet is lodged in his left arm and it appears that one entered the center of his chest judging by the hole in his leather shirt. Which is the only remaining article of clothing. His feet still inserted in his boots and a knife remains in a slot to one side of his right boot. I wonder if he's the owner of the saddle ? J.W. ask himself. It makes sense because he must have been the one to burry the others and apparently their belongings with them. Poor guy, there was no one left to burry him, he must have lay here and ———

J.W. stops what he is doing and decides that no one was going to be looking for him ,and removes his gun holsters and knife. He knew that calling the police would delay he and his dad's work, possibly for several days and this would put them way behind on their project. J.W. gets a small tarp from the storage compartment of the truck to wrap the bones in so he can burry it over with the others. He bends down to place the bones on the tarp in the same order that he picks them up in and just as he lifts the leather shirt ,out falls a book of some kind to the ground. It couldn't be clearer to him that this book was important to it's owner, if it in fact was the owner, that he was about to burry. He did know that it stopped one of the bullets that had been fired into him. Because the bullet was still trapped in the pages as he carefully thumbed through it. After placing everything that he had found on the front seat of his truck, he had to make sure that there is nothing left to find, and buries the body in the tarp along side what obviously, must have been this fellows friends. After he completed the chores that he thought would never happen to him, and he sets the remaining part of the bunkhouse on fire and watches it burn to ashes, before he goes home. As dry as all the wood was, it burned in just a few minutes leaving him plenty of time to sit in his truck and inspect his newest find.

Later that night J.W. decides to see if he can read anything from the book ,like anyone in his place would. 'A gift to my son on his thirteenth birthday' was the first passage, on the first page of this book. The first several pages was very difficult to read because the pages were brittle and faded and he was afraid of damaging them anymore. J.W skips into the book several pages and begins to read almost an entire historyof one mans life. He would then later know what a sad life could be placed on one person. The more he read the more J.W. 'S eyes begin to fill with tears and as hard as he tries, he can't make himself put the book down.

FEB 1 1863 DEAR JOURNAL ;

IT'S BEEN THREE WEEKS SINSE BEING SET ASEA BY MY GRANDMOTHER AND GRANDFATHER. I AM STILL VERY SADDENED AT THE PASSING OF MY BELOVED PARENTS SOME TIME BACK. IT APPEARS THAT THE BLITE HAS TAKEN AN ENORMOUS TOOL ON ALL THAT SURVIVED . LEAVEING THE ONES THAT REMAIN TO SUFFER THE DISEASE THAT CONTINUES TO ATTACK WHOMEVER IS IN ITS PATH.

MARCH 2 1863 DEAR JOURNAL ;

I HAVE MET MANY PEOPLE ABOARD MY BOAT AND ALL SEEM IN FAIR GRACES .THE CAPTIAN BARES THE SAME SIR NAME AS MY GRANDFATHER THOUGH HE SAYS HE DOESN'T KNOW HIM , HE SAYS HE KNOWS OF THE CLAN OF WHICH I WAS BORN TO. AND SAYS THEY ARE A DREADED LOT TO PESTER. MY CONDITION IMPROVES AS TIME GIVES ME NEW THINGS TO THINK ABOUT.

THOUGH MY HEART IS STILL SOMETIMES HEAVY, FOR I AM ALONE HEADING TO A STRANGE LAND. I HAVE HEARD MANY THINGS SAID ABOUT THIS UNITED STATES, BUT I AM STILL SKEPTICAL THAT ANY PLACE COULD BE AS GOOD AS ALL I HAVE HEARD MENTIONED ON IT'S BEHALF . I SHALL KEEP AN OPEN MIND AND SEE FOR MYSELF.

APRIL 6 1863 DEAR JOURNAL;

THE CAPTIAN HAS INFORMED US THAT AFTER OUR DELAYS AT SEA WE SHOULD ARRIVE AT A PLACE CALLED VIRGINIA SOON. IT SEEMS THAT ALL I CONTINUE TO HEAR ABOUT THESE UNITED STATES TELLS ME THAT, EVERYTHING PLACE THERE IS NAMED AFTER SOME PLACE WHERE I CAME FROM. IT APPEARS THAT THEY CALL EVERY TOWN "NEW" SOMETHING OR ANOTHER. I MUST WONDER WHY ANYONE CAME IN THE FIRST PLACE. I SIT OUT ON THE BOW OF THE SHIP AND GAZE ACROSS THE HORIZON AND THERE IS NOTHING TO LOOK AT BUT WATER. TODAY IS MY BIRTHDAY AND I EXPECT THAT ALL THAT WILL FOLLOW, TO BE AS, THIS ONE IS .

WE SAW A LARGE ODD LOOKING FISH TODAY IT JUMPED IN AND OUT OF THE OCEAN FOR WHAT SEEMED LIKE HOURS IN FRONT OF THE SHIP. THE CAPTIAN WAS RATHER PLEASED

AND GAVE US THE IMPRESSION THAT IT WAS A SIGN OF GOOD LUCK. HE CALLED IT'S NAME A DOLPHIN .I EXPECT THAT THE LARGER THE FISH THE ODDER IT'S NAME. ALONE AND WITH OUT FAMILY . I EXPECT THAT ALL MY BIRTHDAYS FROM HERE ON WILL LEAVE ME WITH SAD MEMORIES LUCK IS SOMETHING THAT I WILL LEAVE TO THE CAPTIAN AND HIS CELEBRATING CREW TO BELIEVE IN .

APRIL 9 1863 DEAR JOURNAL ;

WE HAVE LANDED AT A PLACE CALLED HAMPTON HARBOR THE CAPTIAN HAS GIVEN ME MORE MONEY THAN I EVER KNEW EXISTED. FIVE POUNDS THREE CHILLINGS AND TEN PENTS AND A LETTER TO CARRY TO A LOCAL INN KEEPER FROM MY GRANDPARENTS REGUARDING A PLACE TO LIVE .THOUGH I'LL HAVE TO EARN MY KEEP, IT SHOULD NOT BE NEAR AS DIFFACULT AS IT WAS BACK IN SCOTTLAND. I STOOD ON THE DOCK AND WATCHED ALL THE PEOPLE SCURRING ABOUT, AND IT SEEMS THAT NO ONE HAD TIME TO TELL ME MY WAY TO THE INN . I HAPPENED ON IT BY MY OWN ACCORD, AS IT WAS ONLY A BRIEF WALK INTO THE MAIN PART OF TOWN. I HANDED MR. MC'CORD MY LETTER AND HE PUT ME TO LABOR RIGHT OFF.

MARCH 10 1863 DEAR JOURNAL;

I HAVE NEVER SEEN A MAN AS MEAN AND BRASH AS MR. MCCORD HE SEEMS TO NEVER STOP YELLING AT ME, AND TODAY HE DREW HIS HAND BACK AS IF TO HIT ME . MY LIVING QUARTERS ARE NOTHING MORE THAN A SHED AND MY PAY IS VERY MEAGER .TWO PENTS A DAY FOR FOURTEEN HOURS LABOR PLUSS BOARD AND TWO MEALS . HE SAYS THAT I SHOULD BE GLAD THAT HE HAS OFFERED HIS CHARITY AND BE PROUD TO BE IN AMERICA . MY ONLY REPLY CAN BE .THAT ALL I HAVE SEEN ABOUT AMERICA IS THE INSIDE OF A WOODEN PRIVY AND SLOPPING HIS SWINES . I PRAY THAT THE REST OF AMERICA DOESN'T LOOK LIKE A FEW BOARDS NAILED TOGETHER, TO BLOCK OFF AS MUCH RAIN AS IT CAN. HOWEVER MY LIVING CONDITIONS CAN BE IMPROVED IT'S MRS. MCCORD THAT WILL NEVER CHANGE . MY FATHER USED TO SAY THAT WOMAN HAS A TOUNGE AS SHARP AS A BATTLE AXE ,AND A HEAD TWICE AS BROAD. HE'D SAY IT MAKES MY HEAD WANT TO FALL OFF JUST LISTENING TO HER TALK . I HAD NO IDEA THAT HE WOULD BE TALKING ABOUT MRS. MCCORD. THE

GOOD BOOK SAYS WE SHOULDN'T MAKE JUDGEMENTS ON OTHER PEOPLE, BUT IT IS QUITE CLEAR TO ME THAT SHE IS THE MOST BITTER AND SPITEFUL PERSON I HAVE EVER MET.

J.W. takes a break in reading for several minutes, then continues on, only this time he starts to see a mental picture of what's happening to this young man . Already in just a few pages of this young boys journal J. W. may well wish he had never found his book.

DEC 15 1863 DEAR JOURNAL;

I AM SORRY THAT SO MUCH TIME HAS LAPSED SINSE WE LAST TALKED ,I HAVE MISSED OUR CONVERSATION VERY MUCH . AS YOU KNOW ,YOU ARE THE ONLY CONFIDENCE I HAVE. I FEAR I

HAVE MADE A VERY TERRIBLE MISTAKE TODAY AND MY REGRET IS ,THAT IT WAS OUT OF MY CONTROLL. SINSE I LAST WROTE YOU, I HAVE HAD NEWS OF MY ONLY KNOWN FAMILY PASSING . MR. MCCORD INFERED THAT NO GOOD CAN COME OF MY THINKING ABOUT IT. HE WAS EVEN A COLDER MAN THAN I FIRST THOUGHT. I HAVE NOW RESOLVED ANY FURTHER COMMENTS FROM HIM .THE DAY AFTER MY LAST PASSAGE HE FORCEABLY REMOVED YOU FROM MY POSSESSION .THOUGH I FOUGHT BACK ,HIS STRENGTH LEFT ME POWERLESS. HIS OPINION WAS THAT ONLY A MAN OF ESTABLISHED AND DISTINGUISHED CHARACTOR SHOULD KEEP SUCH NOTES. IT WAS HIS OPINION THAT I WASN'T OF ANY IMPORTENCE AND NO ONE WILL WANT TO READ MY THOUGHTS. A SLOPPER OF SWINE HE CALLED ME . A PEASANT WITH NO REASON TO RECORD THOUGHT . IN JEST, I DO NOT WANT ANYONE READING MY THOUGHTS. I HAVE WITHSTOOD AS MUCH FROM THIS MAN AS I OR ANY OTHER POSSABLY MIGHT INDURE. I HAD NO IDEA THAT A MAN MY GRANDPARENTS TRUSTED WOULD TURN OUT TO BE A SILENT ENEMY OF MY FAMILY BACK IN SCOTTLAND.

You will not be writing in this book anymore boy .I should burn it, so you can't dwell on the past .Don't look so teary eyed. I will take this from you for your own good ,now come and remove my boots, before i give you a lashing you'll not want to write down . Your trembling boy ,are you afraid of me . Well you had better be ! Them CAMPBELL'S that you are so proud of, are a nasty lot and you'll not have any reign here.

Today for the last time, i have taken cold water to sooth my wounds . My shirt is clinging to my upper torso,, as it is moistened with a mixture of blood and clear liquid that ooze from my shredded skin. I have survived many of these beatings in the months gone by ,and this man may well have killed me, had i not laced him to his bed and returned the favor of the beatings i have received. I do not know why i could not stop ,but as the last breath exited his body, i felt relieved and took you back from his possession. I ask that god have mercy upon me, for i have broken one of his most cherished rules.

APRIL 6 1864 DEAR JOURNAL

I am happy today, because i have treated myself to a present on my fourteenth birthday. I have taken a job delivering goods all along the coast . My overseer pays me fairly and i have purchased my first gun and sheath . It appears that the constables are too busy with the war, and no search for me has been attempted. I guess my partial Irish blood brings me luck as i sit and gaze across these mountains of the handsomest blue i have ever seen. It's ridges seem to have a layer of smoke that rest atop them , just below the clouds. I am at peace and feel secure in now being alone, because trust is something i can no longer give away. I have seen a lot of these Negros that everyone is talking about . I guess some folks will fight over anything . Even other people.

JAN. 2 1865 DEAR JOURNAL;

It has been six months since i have been, inhaled into a war i know nothing about. Just like home in Scotland everyone wants to rule over, everyone else. I had no idea i was crossing back and forth from one country to another, as i thought America was but one place. Most people here chose a side to fight with, for what ever the many different reasons they have . As for me , i was chosen by a side and just do as i am told. Day before yesterday the rank of corporal was bestowed on me. I have no real count on how many of the bullets i have fired, actually hit someone . My fourth face to face kill in this war saved my captain's life and he gave me my rank in appreciation of my bravery.

CAPTIAN!! I screamed out as i sprang up from the trench and thrusted myself in a panicked dash across an already blood soaked field. He sat atop his horse yelling orders and slinging his saber about wildly . WATCH YOUR FLANKS MEN !!He yelled as he impaled his saber into the chest of a Yankee soldier. RETREAT !!! RETREAT !! I heard him yell just as he turned his horse . No sooner had i fired my pistol to shoot a rider from his horse. Another horse and rider was running at him in full stride, and just before the rider fired his pistol, i hurled myself in the smoke filled air. My shoulder sank deep into his ribcage as he and i hit the ground with such force, that i had no air to exhale from my lungs. I lay there on top of him as the rider passes by, and while trying desperately to take in a breath, i hear the captains pistol fire and it deafens me, as the soldier falls to the ground.

I am in your debt soldier! He calmly states as he rolled me off of him. Thank you corporal Kilbourne . NOW LETS GET THE HELL OUT OF HERE ,WHILE WE STILL CAN. We'll face them another time. The captain and i became friends after that and i fought beside him for the next four months. We traveled back and forth fighting and everywhere we went. Destruction had all but taken a final toll on an entire ,separated nation.

APRIL 9 1865 DEAR JOURNAL;

I stood beside the captain in our final act of war today, as we stand just inside the court house in Appomatics .Generals Lee and Grant were staring each other down like two roosters captive in the same coop .They all but had talons ready to flog one another, when Grant handed Lee the quill . Lee gently lay his saber and side arm on the table in front of Grant ,before he accepted the quill . Though i couldn't hear what they were saying, they did exchange words . The entire room was silent as we all anticipated Lee's signature . He rest his elbow on the table and crooked his arm and his face became even sadder as he wrote his name on the documents of surrender. Several more men signed it as witnesses i suppose, then both men stood erect, extended their arms and shook hands. No one knew what to do, then Grant picked up Lee's saber and side arms held them out in front of Lee .

Accept your weapons back as my gesture of good faith , there is no dishonor in surrender as long as we can rebuild all that we have destroyed . I do not know what the future holds ,but for now .

Then Grant pauses and looks all around the room . THE WAR IS OVER GENTLEMEN, GO HOME TO YOUR FAMILIES ,REBUILD YOUR FARMS AND BE PROUD FOR ALL HAVE FOUGHT WELL ,FOR WHAT EVER REASON.!!!

HAPPY BIRTHDAY CORPRAL The captain says as he hands me the reigns to a black horse. I could not believe it, the saddle had brass studs patterned all the way around it's shape.

I had your name branded in the saddle, it was my spare, because i had been issued one by the C.S.A.The horse became attached to mine , i expect she is in the female way and ready to start again. So where are you headed Thomas ?

I do not know sir, i have not thought any on it . I can not stay in the east for fear a recourse from my past will haunt me. Perhaps i'll go to Atlanta or farther south .

Why don't you come with me back west, i have a ranch in the Oklahoma Territory i could use your help . It's a small place ,but i intend to rebuild my heard and make it larger . Won't be easy though, that's still hostile country

. These yanks ain't nothing like them Indians out there.

Sure captain i can not think of anything else better .

We received our pay allotted to us and headed west . We crossed back over some of the same places that we had fought so hard to stay alive in . My memories seemed to become alive . I sat by a fire one night a watched as the swift water of The Mississippi river flowed by .I am quite impressed at it's girth, even in pure darkness, it's wider than i have ever seen. We made it to Memphis and was awaiting a clear day to cross the river . My dreams, awake or a sleep, were haunting me . I am fifteen years old and already my pistols had six notches in it's handles. They were not there for bragging, but for me to remember how easy it had became for me to out draw and kill a man just by reaction alone. The war had made me faster than anyone i knew .The captain continuously tells me to be cautious because where we are going, men build reputations from how fast they can kill. He says there is always someone that wants to challenge you ,once they hear of you. It is not my wish to harm anyone else ,but it saddens me that i know i can ,without putting two thoughts toward it. The water was very high on the river and we had to follow it's banks to St. Louis just to cross. It wasn't bad as i thought it might be, because the land had flattened some and we found plenty of game to eat . We both had fattened ourselves up some, because the war had left us thin . When we reached St. Louis i went into a saloon for my first time . My first drink nearly drowned me and i choked on the whiskey as it burned all the way to my gut .This trip gave me many firsts. I had been in America little more than a year and enjoyed the pleasures of a city for my first time. You can buy food already skinned and cooked and someone will bring it out to you . Clothing sits in racks made up and ready to wear . The hat i purchased resembled the ones that the General wore and i felt very proud when i put it on. I couldn't sit still as the man cut about my hair wildly snip!! snip !!snip!! The closer to my neck he came ,,the more uneasy ,,i became .

Give us a shave there barber ,the captain said with confidence. I ain't had a steaming shave in a very long time .Hell the boy ain't never ,had one .ha ha ha !!

HOLY MOTHER OF GOD BOY !! TAKE THAT GUN OUT FROM UNDER HIS CHIN THOMAS ,HE AIN'T GONNA HURT YOU NONE .

HE'S GOT A KNIFE AT MY THROAT SIR !!.I yelled shaking as i pulled the hammer back and readied to fire .He done burned me with that hot rag !!

NO CORPRAL WAIT !!YOU AIN'T NEVER HAD A SHAVE HAVE YOU ? I was just teasing when i said that .I should have explained it to you

,all he is going to do is cut the hairs from your face .NOW TAKE THE GUN DOWN AND TRUST HIM .!! Don't be afraid ,you'll start looking forward to one of these each week.

Hang on a minute young man while i get my nerve back. We don't want my hands shaking anymore than they already are now do we?

No , i'm sorry sir .I just didn't know what you were doing is all.

I just received my first shave and i must say my face feels better and i look much better. I said to the captain as we strolled down the street.

Where are we going now captain ?

Well Thomas we'll need some more cattle to take back to Oklahoma and the stock yard here in St. Louis is the best place to get'em .Then we'll get us some fresh horses and ammo and hire two men to help us get 'em there.

July 3 1865 Dear Journal;

We have been on trail now for six weeks, the blisters that arose on my arms and neck have healed well .The sun out here in the plains gets very hot during the day .You can sit atop your horse and see blankets of heat waves rippling across horizon, like the waves in the ocean that i came over here on. Moving cattle from one place to another takes a toll on a man after awhile . I know i value my solitude, but i have spent many hours alone on my horse at night watching over the herd . It seems the dreams that i have while awake, can sometimes be as troublesome, as the nightmares i have in my sleep. As of late i use the bottled spirits to put me asleep and lots of coffee to awaken me. The captain says the boy in me has found the man, and i should let the man take over. I don't know what that really means, but i expect i'll have no choice in my change. The captain doesn't read or write so well and everyday when i write he says to make sure i don't spell his name wrong . It makes me laugh at him, because how would he know anyway? The captain says we are only a few days from his place and the cattle will like the tall grass, that covers his land. I look forward to sleeping in doors again, because sense i left that inn, i have had no real shelter from anything .The two men that joined us in St.Louis have decided to stay on and the captain says our first chore will be to build a bunkhouse . I heard the captain talk about a celebration tomorrow . He calls it Independence Day. I really have to wonder who that's for .I have seen very little independence, at least not enough to celebrate about. The captain says we'll put on a good meal just the same.

OCT 3 1865 DEAR JOURNAL;

We put the last plank on the bunkhouse today ,and it makes me very happy that i now have a home for the first time, sense coming here to America . I am only now starting to realize why people are risking everything they have in the east, just to get a glimpse of the west. I must say with a heavy heart that i am glad that the bunkhouse is complete ,for i may have been living in it alone, had i listened to one more day of Rory Truelane's mouth. The captain says he deserved the licking i gave him, but i should never shoot a gun out of a mans hand like i did Mack Reedy's . He tells me that the next time i pull my gun, it should be to kill who ever is in front of it.

BAM!! BAM!!BAM!! Just that fast i fired three shots, two hitting his pistol and one hitting his palm as his gun flew from his hand. I don't know what happened ,one minute they were insulting me and the next, Mack drew down on me. I didn't see any need in killing him, i have already done enough of that . I just didn't want him to shoot me .

WHAT IN THE FIRE IN HELL !!!? IS GOING ON HERE? The captain yelled as he ran out of his house.

That crazy kid, shot me captain. I told Rory, that boy ain't right .We was just funnen at'em and he eyeballed me down, like he was gonna pull on me .

This true Thomas ?

Sort of sir, but i only eyed him down so he would back off, i had my arms crossed and i wasn't going to shoot him .I just wanted them to stop calling me names , don't give them no right to poke fun at me because they know things i don't .

Thomas you can't shoot a man for poken fun at you .

I know that sir, but don't no one say ,i'm the son of a dog . My mother was a good woman, captain .I could have just as easily put them bullets in his forehead, i just wanted them to shut up is all . Besides that he drew first.

You call him a son-of a bitch Mack ??

Well ,,pause yes sir ,but i didn't mean nothing by it .

You fight in the war Mack? The captain calmly ask.

No sir ,me and Rory was way west .Didn't even hear about it till it was nearly over.

Boys, one of the last things the yanks sometimes yelled just before they tried to kill you was . Kill that son-of -a bitch he ain't worth the mud he's standing in. Now that might not mean much to you, but if you had called me that . We would be putting dirt on your head right now, then we would put one of them little crosses on the dirt pile ,to prove someone as ignorant as you even existed. Rory wrap his hand up and you boys call it a day. Thomas you come with me to the house so we can talk.

I dropped my head , i was sort of ashamed and a little mad at the same time. I didn't know if the captain was going to let me have it or what. I knew he was disturbed by the way he kicked at the dirt when he walked back to the main house.

Sit down Thomas and take a snort of this . Burns don't it, son ?

Then i thought to myself he just called me son .That made me proud, i hadn't been called that in a long time.

Boy you ain't kidden sir,, haaa !! WHAT'S IN THERE ? TURPINTINE? No Thomas it's my pa's own mix. Listen Thomas the war is over, of course you know that .You got a man stuck in a boy's body, you can't play marbles anymore and you can't back down from anyone either . Your gonna meet people like them two everywhere .They're ignorant and don't have any manners about 'em. Might not be their fault, but that's just how it is . No one around here knows, that you have already done more than they will ever do. You done something back in the war that tells me you are a good man . You risked your life to save mine and that's rare . You see Thomas, i fought in that war, in the place of my brother. I don't really give a damn about, who owns that mud hole over there ,but he does and his life and lively hood depended on it. He took ill in sixty three so the general in charge gave me his rank and company .I did my best to stand good for his honor and i would do it again. A week or so ago i received a relay that some of his Negros need work, sense they are free and he can no longer keep his farm, he ask me to take them on here .

What i'm trying to say is, we all have to do things we do or don't like and the reasons we do or don't do them, change from day to day. It will never stop being that way . You are not a boy, and i don't care how old you are ,SO STOP ACTING LIKE IT!!. I don't know how to tell you to ease your troubles, but i can tell you how to stay alive until you figure it out. First of all ,and i don't want to hurt your feelings by saying this .I don't know what happened to you ,but you are a killer son ,it's just as true as the hair is standing up on my arm . You can drop a man in his tracks without a second thought. That will never be in your favor .Everything you do from now on must be out of honor , not pride.

Now secondly, we know the truth .How you use the burden, that has been given to you, is what's going to determine ,if you'll die a good man or not. I don't know if there's a good enough reason or a bad enough reason to kill another person ,i don't even know where the fine line is .I just know that sometimes we do . If Mack had killed you ,he would be going to town as we speak, so he could brag about it ,he's that kind of man ,before the night ends he would be dead, because as sad as it is . Out here there are men worse than him in nature and faster than you at gun play.

The captain walks over to his gun cabinet and opens the bottom cupboard, that apparently had been locked for quite sometime .The lock was stiff and difficult to turn the key way. He grabs two Colt revolvers and holsters turns back and throws them on the desk in front of Thomas. Blued to solid black the metal was still polished and shined as Thomas removed them from the holsters. He grips the white ivory handles and spins them on his fore finger, in one motion he lifts both of his thumbs and stops their spin in a ready to fire position.

That's right Thomas they are very well balanced, i had them special made ten years ago. They are yours now .

Thank you captain ! Thank you very much!

Don't thank me Thomas ,i ain't so sure i'm giving you a gift or a coffin spike. The only way i can repay you, is to teach you how to stay alive ,from here on out . You will have to be faster and more accurate than any other man alive. Before i took a bullet in the shoulder ,from a man that shot me from behind, i was faster than you. Not much, but still faster. Even though he didn't live to boast about it, i could never draw as fast again ,that's why i carry this long barrel. You have to be your own law out here ,next time a man draws on you kill him. You turned them two into cowards and one of them will shoot you in the back before it is all is over. I have to now, as bad as i hate to ,make you the foreman of my ranch . It won't be easy on you because you will have to demand respect. For some of them that won't come easy.

I was proud that the captain cared enough to explain things to me. I was even more proud that i now had a place to call my home, even if it was a bunkhouse in the middle of a prairie. By my being the foreman ,i chose the space farthest from the door and a single bed separated me from the other bunks. In the dimmest lit spot in the room, with no one at my back or above or below me, i could keep my edge by seeing the whole room. I learned that in the war. By sleeping with my head and body in line with a large tree ,no one could sneak up on me from behind. I returned back to the bunkhouse and sat at the table with my back at the wall.

Mack ,Rory the both of you are fired! Here is your pay you have coming and one week extra. Pick up your things and be off the ranch in less than an hour.

Thomas we was just funnin ya, i didn't really mean to draw down on ya .It was just a reaction you know a habit .Mack replied

Wait why me Thomas? I didn't do anything but tease at you. Rory said as if he was innocent.

You are as guilty as he is, you are both trouble makers . If you weren't ,you wouldn't be so easy to turn on each other the way you did Rory. You can't even trust each other and that makes for back stabbers . Now get your gear and leave, you other boys let them pass .

JAN. 7 1866 DEAR JOURNAL;

I went to Beaver City yesterday and picked up the four Negros ,that the captains brother sent out here .They were worse for wear and hungry, i expect the only thing that kept them from freezing to death, was some old quilts they had wrapped around them. Two of them was middle aged and two was my age or maybe just a little older. They didn't talk all the way back to the ranch, but i expect they had no reason to. They just seemed to stare off, like they was blind. They seemed real skiddish like a cat hemd up by dogs ,but i guess i would be too. When we got back to the ranch the captain says for me to put' em up with us in the bunkhouse .

Captain them men out there ain't gonna share their quarters with, no slaves. I been hearing talk of it already and a couple of them ain't real happy about them even being here.

I didn't want to be disrespectful to the captain but i had to speak up about it.

They will get used to it, or leave here !

Captain you fought for the south and so did i . Now i'm just supposed to say HOWDY BOYS YA'LL COME ON IN !! Like nothing ever happened.

Don't raise your voice at me Thomas ,i fought against a change of ideas backed by greed, not survival. Follow me outside and let me show you something.

We both walked outside ,though it puzzled me as to why. I could tell once again that the captain was mad at me by the way the captain was kicking the dirt like before. We reentered the bunkhouse and the captain slammed the door behind him. There is an extra two dollars a month in pay for any man that stays on and works with the new hands that just arrived. Starting now !!

Then the captain takes out twelve dollars for the six men and lays it on the table in two dollar increments. The room became quiet for a few seconds as the captain stares each one down. All six men hesitate momentarily, then one by one pick the money up from the table.

You four stand there in front of the wagon ,Jeb take the blankets and supplies in the bunkhouse. The captain says as he and, i walk outside and look at the new arrivals.

What i just did in there Thomas, was show you how cheap it was for a man to alter his high and mighty standards. Everyman has a price on his morals, but most will be stupid for nothing. Men can't resist, one upping someone all the time, it comes natural to them filled with false pride. What's even worse is, a man that don't know what he believes in, lives in fear of self destruction. Hatred is the best fuel for self destruction, most people that hates someone, does it because someone else did first. Hate is the only place to go for someone, that doesn't know where he came from, or where he's going. Stick out your finger like it was a gun.

Ok captain what now .

Stick it to your forehead like you was going to shoot yourself.

This feels strange captain, why am i doing it ? I said as i sort of resisted some.

The only thing that separates your finger from the most powerful weapon ever made, is a layer of skin and about a quarter inch of bone, called the scull. That's right Thomas your brain. Men that don't use it much, don't cause much harm .They are easily led ,but them that use it all the time for the wrong reasons, will destroy everything around them. If you use your brain the right way and do things for the right reasons, even if everyone doesn't like it ,you can't go wrong. When you don't put any thought into what you are doing or why you feel the way you do . You may as well put a gun in that hand and fire. That's the only way to stop the most dangerous weapon ever made. Let's look at something for a moment Thomas ? Without going into a lot of detail ,what's the difference between you and them .

I had to think about it for a second and so did the four men standing there. They're black and brown and i'm white .

No Thomas ,, that is the obvious part ,now just by looking at them tell me what they are thinking .Or tell me where they have been. Or tell me what kind of men they are.

I don't know sir, i would have to be a mind reader to do that.

No ,,Thomas you don't ! All you have to do is use your brain and think for a second. Take off your blouse.

Why sir? I don't feel very comfortable doing that.

It's ok ,i know what's behind it. Now you boys take yours off .

They all did as they were ask and all five of us stood there slightly confused.

Thomas you can't see them, but do you feel the bumps that i am touching on your back. They can't see them yet either .

Captain i don't feel so good about this ,how did you know about the scars on my back ?

Look in their eyes son ,they have the same look you do, a mans face scars long before his body ever gets the beating. Turn around fellows.

As they turn i noticed the webbed patterns of scars on the men's backs.

Now you turn around Thomas .

As i did as he asked, the other men's faces seemed to get bigger in awe .Though i was embarrassed i began to realize the point the captain was trying to make. Then the captain lowered his shirt from his shoulders and revealed some scars like me and the others had.

Captain i didn't know,, what happened to you ?

My pa was as mean as a hungry bear, he was always whooping on me or my brother . He thought if it wasn't beaten into you, you'd forget it. He was right, cause i ain't ever forgotten and i never will. Them four didn't have a choice, just like us, but we do now . Them men in that bunkhouse don't know and don't care ,their concern is money and that's it. Me, you and these four Negros will be here till this place rots to the ground .There will be a hundred like them come and go. So remember that. One last thing son, it's not the scars that you can see that makes a man dangerous ,it's the ones on the inside that you can't see, that make's him dangerous and that get's you killed.

The captain turned and walked back to the main house leaving the five of us standing there . After a few minutes i decided to ask them their names. The two older one's being Hesakia and Abel ,the two younger Zackeeus and Shadrack. They all went inside and the other men had separated the bunks, putting as much space between them and the, new hands as possable.

June 15 1866 DEAR JOURNAL;

The new hands have came along well ,i have learned to trust them as well as i do the captain. Hesakia and Abel mostly run herd at night and Zac and Shad range with me during the day. The other men have taken to them as well, given the exception that we have to fight Hesakia to get him to bathe. I don't know if he is afraid of water or he just thinks a man should smell like a bag of dung. Either way it takes most of us to wrestle him down to the troughs . On Sunday last, the captain had some of the other ranchers and their hands here for some friendly competitions and wagers. Everything went well and we all had fun ,first i can remember sense coming here. There was plenty of meat and whiskey going around and the drunker everyone became ,the closer the fun changed to more difficult competition. Duncan McDonald owns a ranch adjoining the captains, it seems they came out here together in the fifties .Duncan is the more boastful type and like's to make high wagers, which ain't wrong if you can pay.

We are pretty well head to head on the score Jed . Duncan calls out. How about we see how strong that buck you got over there is. I here tell he's the strongest man you got .

Yeh Duncan he ain't no push over. What you got in mind. But he'll have to agree on it of course.

HESAKIA !! Duncan has a wager in mind on your strength .
What is the challenge sir?

We'll boy, i'll wager that you can't hold them two burros over there still with one hand tied to that corner post and one hand tied to the burros. I'll pay twenty dollars in gold coin for each minute you hold'em and the captain pays twenty for each minute you don't ,inside five minutes of course.

You don't have to take a wager like that Hesakia . Duncan that's crazy, he could get his arms ripped right out of their sockets. I ain't seen no man, that strong.

Can you pay if i can't sir ? Hesakia asked. I don't know how much that is, but i ain't scared to try.

Yeh i can pay ,but you must know ,you can be wounded for life .
No offence sir ,but i'm already wounded for life.

Suit yourself Hesikia do the best you can, i'll pay the difference.
Don't get hurt on account of a bet ,when it gets too tough, stop.

If i go the whole time, how much money is that sir?
It's a hundred dollars, why ?

Can you buy a good horse for that ?
Yeh i suppose so, two good ones in fact .

Make it ten minutes then sir ,plus what ever my pay is for three months.
That's two hundred and thirty dollars ,are you sure ? Hesakia

Tie me up captain .

Well i think it's a fool thing to do, but ok ! Man knows his own strength i guess.

You seem awful set on getting them horses Hesakia. You figuring on leaving. You ain't happy here or something.

No it ain't nothing like that ,this is a good place to live and i like it here.

Except ?

Except what? ,tell me what's on your mind . Don't beat about the bush .

Sir being free means i can leave, when i want too, don't it?

Yes it does and a man needs that feeling .

Captain i don't want to leave, I just want to be able to, if i ever have to, is all. Besides that i ain't never owned anything. I hear tell of colored's owning their own land now too. That sure would be nice.

Hesakia owning your own land, ain't no bed of roses .You are always having to protect it and keep people from squatting on it. Owning your own anything can turn you into cold bitter man before you know it.

They had their contest , leaving the captain scratching his head in amazement.

We'll see you boys ,come round up and separation Jeb . Duncan said as he tipped his hat and he and his men slowly rode out .

Been a pleasure taking your money Duncan . Ya'll take care .

MAY 1866 DEAR JOURNAL;

Captain says this is the best round up yet ,he and Mr. McDonald sorted ,separated and split over five hundred new borns this year. I hate the smell of burned hide and fur ,it does something to my stomach that don't set right ,and i can't taste my grub. I guess i have complained it about some ,but no good has come from it. The captain says the food don't have to taste good, as long as the whiskey you wash it down with does. After the branding was done me and the boys went to Beaver city for some well needed saloon time. It seems the captain was right when he said he wasn't giving me no gifts sometime back. Even though i haven't drawn my gun at nothing more than a rattle snake for quite sometime and my reputation has overwhelmed me .I expect i will always have to be, who they think i am. This is however the first time i had to face someone that didn't know me, but knew about me.

Hello Jeb ! Duncan called out as me and the captain entered the saloon .

Hello Duncan, damn good round up this spring ,you agree?

This is my new hand Jeb , They call'em Missouri ,can't say as that i know why, but that's what he answers to. He's a damn good cow hand though.

How are you Thomas .He said as he looked at me .

I'm doing well Mr. McDonald sir. And you?

Right smart okee doekee boy , damn! Where is my manners ,set us all up here bar tender. Keep'em coming, tonight's on me.

We stood there at the bar and talked about regular stuff, cattlemen talk and such. Then Missouri decides to walk away.

Gentlemen i gotta step out back for a second .

He walked past me and stared right into my eyes . Something struck me funny about that ,because i got cold chills instantly. Almost the same way you feel when you walk up on a snake and you don't know if it is going to bite you or not. The captain notices the same thing looking at our reflection in the mirror on the wall behind the bar.

What about your man there Duncan ?The captain ask, What do you know about him?

Not much Jeb, he came riding up couple days ago, said he needed work and well i needed another hand or two. You know we got drive coming soon. I rekin you'll be putting a few on yourself.

Yeh i got a couple on their way out. Duncan something ain't right about him. We've seen his kind before.

You worry too much Jeb , he's just a kid like your Thomas there.
Hell they all want to be the big chicken now a days.

We decided to sit at a table ,and as we did Missouri came in wearing a duster buttoned in the front . We didn't pay it any mind at first, then he swung his leg over the back of a chair to sit with us. Then i caught a glimpse of two fancy guns like i wore. At first i didn't think anything about it . Then i happened to think . He wasn't wearing them when he left . It puzzled me that he had them on now. I was sitting next to Duncan and across from the captain when Missouri unbuttoned his duster. He tried to look uncomfortable and play it off as being too hot. As he pulled both wings of his duster back, i knew he was hooking them behind his guns like he was preparing for some one to confront him. Then he gave me that same look as before, only stronger this time. I remember Mack looking the same way just before he pulled on me.

Them's nice pointers your wearing Tom .Can i see one of 'em?
I'm not a fool Missouri, you seen 'em good enough, you been eye ballen them sense we came in. Just then he started to move his hand from the table, like he was going to ease it under the table.

Unless you got some kinda itch down there, i suggest them hands stay put.

Well look here Jeb ,we gotta strutten match going on. Just like two roosters .You two knock that s##t off!, me and Jeb's been friends for years.

This ain't no concern to you Mr. McDonald. I hear he likes shootin people in the hand, so they can't work. I also hear he likes firing good men for teasing him, Says his ma ain't no bit—-

Stop right there boy !! Jeb step back away from the table, get up slow , both of you keep them hands on the table and i'm gonna step back too. Sorry Jeb i realize who he is now. I heard Mack spouting off here while back about some brother . Said he was real fast . That worthless coward your brother boy!? I just figured he was braggen like normal .

Yeh ,he was my brother , and i mean 'was' . Because of Tom here, my brother was shot down two weeks ago in St. Louis by someone, that couldn't even shoot good. It seems when he tried to get his gun out ,his hand stiffened up . He didn't even start it. The same hand he shot .

Missouri pointed at me with his hands on the table.

Seems to me ,if he knew how to keep his mouth shut ,he would still have a good hand and still be alive. I said.

I already knew i could beat him , by the way his eyes changed from cold to sad . I remembered the captain telling me about revenge and how a man can't think straight if he's got his mind on something else . I knew that Missouri was fast because he was built for it. He was tall and long armed, so it didn't require a lot of movement for him to draw his gun all the way out. I had to assume that he couldn't be much different than his brother because bragging sometimes is a family trait and a character flaw. I also felt that he most likely killed in a gun fight, but the way he tried to take the edge right away, he wasn't real sure about himself. The captain and Mr. McDonald was getting real nervous now, and i knew i needed to stop a man from dieing if i could . It was strange that he didn't notice, that they already had their hands on their guns . It was the strangest thing, that he had that straight of vision .

Captain ,Mr. McDonald ? You two please stand down sirs . I don't want to kill him and he don't really want me to. Missouri your just sad right now, and i understand that .Your brother treated a lot of people bad , i know i seen it several times. He liked to get'em riled so they wanted to fight, that's what him and Truelane did to me. I whooped Truelane in a fare fight ,but Mack couldn't let it go. I still didn't want to shoot him, but he left me no choice.

Well alright then, i'm going to get me another drink . He said as he slowly stood up .I thought to my self that was too easy .Then as i watched him ease his way to the bar, i noticed he was looking at me in the large mirror. I stood like i was going to say something to the captain as just as i did .

DON'T DO IT!!! .BAM!! BAM!! BAM I YELLED and fired three times putting all three shots in his chest as he spun and drew on me. There wasn't any trouble from the marshal, but i knew my troubles had really began, because a saloon full of witnesses, now had proof of the rumors they had heard. Just as the captain said, i was now a killer of men, whether i liked it or not.

July 16 1866

I've been noticing the Indians have been moving about in the open more. Could be the buffalo soldiers are keeping them on the move rounding up the renagades.They don't seem hostile, and mostly walk with their heads down ,as if they were defeated or something. Day before yesterday i seen several walking and pulling carts south toward Texas. I can only presume that they are what's left, because only the old and real young were visible. Hesakia and the others are so proud of their horses, that we can't seem to get them off of them. Captain teases him all the time, and says we'll have to build his bunk bigger to hold both of them ,if the horse is going to get any rest. We put on two new hands to replace the ones that ran off after my incident in town here awhile back. They are taking to our situation well and accept Hesakia and the others . Zackeas and Shadrack are starting to get real curious at my books on my desk . Late today when i was coming in, i spotted them through the window looking at them .When i entered the door they scurried to their bunks, as if they had been there all the time. I didn't pay them no mind, because i knew it was a matter of time before they starting asking questions. Tomorrow we'll start moving the herd to water because our creaks are drying up do to a drought . We'll bring them back in September when the rains start coming back. I really dread sleeping out on the range and i made it real clear to the captain of how fond of my bed i am. He just laughed at me and says i'm spoiled ,but i have yet to find out what that means.

Late September 1866 DEAR JOURNL;

As i was sitting on my horse looking over the herd, i noticed the herd getting real restless. They were starting to move about more than normal .The bulls were on edge and kicking up a lot of dirt . Though we have several large and dominate bulls, all of them were acting strange. I was sitting higher up on a hill, but i still couldn't see over the next one. I decided to ride over to the next hill and see if there was anything there. I knew the bulls only acted like that when they were threatened by other bulls. As i got to the top of the hill i could smell another large herd of cattle. At first i didn't see anything, then all of the sudden the ground beneath me started shaking and i heard the loudest rumble i had ever heard. There must have been two thousand head of buffalo running at full speed north into Kansas. As fast as i saw them they were gone. I had never seen them before and the captain tells me they used to run in herds of ten thousand or more. But they keep getting killed off for their hides. He says who ever is killing them ,skins them and leaves the meat there to rot. Just one of them beasts could feed a man for months. I am growing to realize that the more i see men destroying themselves,and the more i see them destroying anything close to them. The more agitated at man i become.

Dec 12 1866 DEAR JOURNaL;

The captain calls me out from the warmth of the bunkhouse . THOMAS !! THOOOMMMMASSS!!!

I opened the door and just looked at him like he was crazy.

Why didn't you just come in captain ?

Because son what i have to say i need to say to you first . I received a wire earlier and i want to ask you to do something that's very dangerous this time of year.

Sure what ever you want i'll get my horse.

No Thomas ! Not yet, hear me out first . I have received news that up in Denver they have lots of snow this year and way below freezing temperatures .They have ask me to deliver three hundred head to them as soon as possible. It seems their own herds are freezing before they can get them to the slaughter house. Some of them are starving because they can't find grass .The snow is higher this year and they have ran through their hay supply quicker than usual. Thomas we are the closest large ranch to them and they need our help. This is a lot to ask and you don't have to do it if you don't want too. You could be risking your life as well .

I'll do it !!

Thomas are you sure? You could freeze to death ,yourself.

Captain are you trying to talk me into it, or out of it?

Neither son, i just want you to know what's involved .

Do you think i can do it?, you know that country up there.

I think if anyone can ,it's you ,if i say you can't do it, you'll break your neck trying. You'll need help, but they have to be volunteers on something like this. Take five with you ,the rest can help me here. Thomas you have to try and make twenty five mile a day, That gives you little more than ten days, them people will be desperate by then, the ones that are still alive that is. I went back into the bunkhouse and explained what the captain explained to me. The captain has been treating me like a son sense i met him, and even if i had to make this drive alone .I couldn't say no. In true nature Hesakia ,Zackieus ,Shadrack and Able instantly volunteered. William Webb stepped up to complete the amount of men needed. We spent the rest of the afternoon cutting out the best steers and heifers.

Dec 13 1866 DEAR JOURNAL;

I awoke earlier than normal this morning anticipating the short but tedious drive ahead. Quite to my surprise when i went outside to saddle my horse Hesakia and the others were already waiting on me. Then Hesikia nodded his head as if he wanted me to look behind him. Still half asleep i noticed a long line of wagons, all filled with bales of hay. It seems that during the night the news spread fast and all of the other ranchers wanted to help as well . Almost all of them owned small places ,but just providing the hey alone would make my trip much easier. The first two days of my trip went well ,there was still plenty of uncovered grass for the cattle to graze on. The third day we started to run into small patches of snow, but still had little trouble going on. We pressed on to the fifth day and the difficulty increased as new snow began to fall and the trail became difficult to follow. Luck would be good, as one of the wagon drivers new most of the way by land marks and the shape of the tops of the increasingly growing mountains. By the seventh day we had reached waist high snow and everywhere you looked ,you could see nothing but white. We had to put the largest and strongest cows three wide in the front so they could push a path wide enough for the wagons to go through.

By day nine we couldn't be more than two days out and the hills changed from rolling to steep as we entered the base of the mountains .I now had to push ahead of the others and leave a narrow trail for them to follow . Day eleven i sat on my horse looking across the horizon ,wondering why i couldn't see Denver, i knew we had came far enough. My worst fear was that we had passed it by. If that was the case , then we wouldn't know where to change our corse. My men were very tired and starting to get frost bite in the bitter cold. The cattle wasn't going to hold out much longer, because the snot and drool was freezing to their faces. We have emptied two wagons of hay already and if we stay out here much longer we are sure to loose the herd. I sent Hesakia and one other ahead to make a large circle in hopes that they might spot Denver .Day twelve i awoke from my bed roll early ,as it was too cold to sleep. I have found seven cattle dead and frozen solid, though it is normal for the weakest to go first . I know now that we have to press on and let the cattle walk them selves warm.

As i crawl in and out of little dug outs in the snow waking up the men i can hear someone hollering off in the distance. Then finally i began to make out my name in the voice.

THOOOOMMMMMAAASSS!

I knew that Hesakia had found Denver by the way he was riding in. Thomas, he said as he and his horse came sliding up to me. Just over that hill there is Denver. Thomas we have been less than three hours away the whole time .Thomas when we passed by, i didn't see much sign of life .There is no one moving around we have to hurry .

Just after noon we arrived in town, i expected a greeting of some sort but only one met us as we left the cattle standing in the streets.

Sherriff Crouwl ,he said as he shook my hand . Mister we sure are glad to see you boys. We have been out of meat two days now . All i've been able to feed the sick is some thinned down soup. We already have the saloon and several other businesses full of sick people and more are coming in every so often. The rest are running out of fire wood ,hourly it seems. I don't know how we are going to keep these cattle alive long enough to do any good.

The trains can't get up or down the pass and all of our supplies i had to seize and ration out.

Sherriff i can save the cattle and help you with these people, if you will trust me. Hesakia said.

Mister, i have done all i know to do . Anything will be appreciated .

Shad you and Zack go to the livery and clean up every stall , then climb up in the rafters and knock a hole in the roof. Sherriff once that is done move all the sick into the barn. The rest of you move all the stuff from the stores into one building. Then put the cattle in the empty buildings. Give them enough room to move around a little .

Hold on there fellow,! These people won't want you to destroy their businesses .

Sherriff i know this sounds like a lot to ask , but for a slave every winter is like this. Or at least it was. When they used to sell us in the winter time, they would sometimes put a hundred or more of us in a barn chained to post . They did not care if we had enough heat, to them we were worth nothing more than the very cattle we shared the barn with. We had to stay close together to stay warm. We would surround ourselves with the cattle and use their body heat for warmth. These cattle will keep each other warm, and the buildings will keep the wind off of them. They can always rebuild or repair what's damaged. This weather may not break up for another month or more. If we don't get these people out of that saloon to some fresh air, they won't need their stores anyway. My people have had to endure conditions like this, without the snow for years.

Allright Mister, what else do we need to do?

All of the people that are strong enough. Lets get this hay off these wagons, then take the wagons to the livery and use them as beds. Take the sides off them to make it easier to treat the sick. Then move all the sick to the barn ,build a fire in the middle of the floor, the hole in the roof will let the smoke out. Everything the sick touched will have to be burned as well . Sherriff we need to skin a couple of these cows as soon as we can . Then get some pots and start a broth boiling . I'm going to find some root and herbs to mix with the broth .The blankets they used must be boiled as well and give them fresh blankets.

I don't know how Hesakia did it ,but in less than two weeks he had all the sick out of danger and the weather started breaking a little . I hate to know what a man had to go through just to be able to figure out something like that as fast as he did. It was still cold but we were able to let the cattle roam out in the open. The ones that were able began putting their businesses back together and we returned back to the Three X Two Bar ranch.

April 30 1867 DEAR JOURNAL;

Springtime has finally found us and the newborns have started coming on a daily basis, our round up shouldn't last much longer and we will get some well needed recreation in town. This year most of the ranchers have decided to have an all out competition to establish who has the best cow hands. I don't really know why ,but the captain and Mr. McDonald are like two dogs fighting over the same bone . It's humoring to me that they are always at each other. It seems to be catching on in the bunkhouse ,because there is always some kind of contest there as well. It seems we have had to get smarter at bathing Hesakia ,and this time he was getting ranker than ever. We all needed a good bathing, but he obviously can't smell himself and most of us dread even eating at the same table with him.

YA'LL AINT DROWNDEN ME IN NO WATER !!! He yelled as the ropes tightened around his arms sintching him to the chair he always sat in .

THOMAS WHEN I GET LOOSE FROM HERE ,I'M GONNA GIVE YOU A WHOOPIN YOU AIN'T GONNA FORGET !! THE REST OF YOU HAD BETTER FIND SOME WHERE ELSE TO BE WHEN I GET DONE WITH HIM!!

IT'S JUST A LITTLE WATER HESAKIA ,I DON'T KNOW WHAT YOU ARE SO SCARED OF.

It took ten of us to wrestle him into the new horse trough this time .Of course we got the same bath he did, but when it came to the soaping, that's when he got real wild. One by one he threw us out of the trough . He hit me so hard, that i must have slid ten feet or more in the mud hole we made trying to keep him in the water. We all had our fun and later that evening we all sat at the table playing cards and nursing our wounds ,at least we smelled better . Zackeus had improved on his reading some and a few others as well.

What is pu gi list Tom ? he ask.

That's pugilist Zack , it's another word for fighter or fighting, only in a contest for a prize .One man tries to knock another man out or make him quit.

Well this paper here says this man is a champion ,what does that mean ?

It means he is the best, at what ever he does.

How can he be the best , he ain't fought Hesakia yet? It says here he will pay fifty dollars to anyone that can beat him . When we have our competitions in town next week ,he should try out Hesakia.

I don't want to hurt no one Zack . I got no reason to fight him .

It's ok Hesakia you only use your fist ,there are rules ,no kicking or biting ,nothing like that you just have to stand face to face and punch.

You don't have to be mad or nothing. Other than a few bruises no one gets hurt too bad. It mostly fun.

Don't make no sense two men fighting ,that ain't mad at each other.

MAY 7 1867 DEAR JOURNAL;

We woke early this morning and gathered our belongings we needed to stay in town a few days. Beaver City has never seen the festivities that's about to take place within it's limits. When we arrived it was very busy with people wandering about everywhere. Beaver City was a small place about two hundred or so, but this day brought people in from all over. Everywhere you looked some one was in a contest of some kind. The older men were throwing horse shoes at metal rods in the ground. Small children were rolling their marbles into a circle, some of the older ones were playing mumbly peg and you could hear one holler as he had to bend to pull a short length stick from the ground with his teeth. Me and the boys went into the saloon and met the captain and Mr. McDonald and some other ranchers who were already in a contest of drinking.

SOO JEBBB ,DO YOU SINK YOUR, NEGRO CAN BEAT THE SSHAMP? Mr. McDonald ask in a slur of words

I DON'T KNOW IF HE EVEN WANTS TO FIGHT OR NOT, BUT HE WILL BE IN SOME OF THE EVENTS.

Hello boyzz the captain said as we sat at a table. Bring my boyzzz a bottle bar keep and keep' em coming.

I seen your kind before, a man said as he walked up to Hesakia. You think just because your free you can sit with the white people and be proud.

Go away Mr. we don't want no trouble here .Let us buy you a drink and be friendly.

I ain't drinking with no upadee Negros, they belong to be working like they were chosen to do. I ain't got no respect for a white man that befriends one and he belongs to be whipped as well.

Mister, if you don't walk away from us right now —-

Of course he accepted my warning as a challenge and ask me to the street. How does this happen captain , a man walks up and starts insulting you right off, when you don't even know him? I asked in a confused tone. Hesakia didn't know him either and he ain't done nothing to him.

Didn't have to Tom ,the man knows you and you are the one he wants out there. He used Hesakia to stir you up. Now you have to face him, because he will torment you till you do. Be careful a man like him ain't alone .I don't see his friends, but you can bet they're here.

You boys get out of the street there ain't gonna be no killings this time !!

Just as the marshal finished his sentence the man drew his gun . I now had to sleep seeing the faces of four dead men each night. I wanted to take my guns off and throw them in the mud and never pick them up again, but i knew i wouldn't live throughout the night, that way. I had became the one, that half the people hated and the other half loved. At seventeen a bounty would be placed on my head by a man that just wanted to hang my guns on his trophy shelf. On the third day of our competitions we had won some and Mr. McDonald had won some as well as the other ranchers. The last afternoon an eat was put on and we all sat at tables in the street eating and drinking and bragging at our wins and losses. There wasn't any hard feelings among the locals because one or the other taught one of us how to do the things we knew how to do. All along the length of the table you could see the ranchers passing hand fulls of money and laughing it off. Challenges for the next one were already being made and we still had one final event left .

Alright Hesakia the man is big like you, but you can whop him ,remember he's been hit more times today than you have. I yelled out to him.

Then Hesakia stepped over a waist high rope tied in a square. It was not there to keep the fighters in but keep the spectators out.

Names Doris Macgregor and yours big fellow.

Hesakia Derribauwn sir .

The champion fighter wore a tartan over his back and a tam over his head. His kilt was striped of all colors red, green ,yellow and hints of blue criss crossed each other and i knew he was Scottish. The colors of his tartan signified the clan he was from in Scotland. My father used to wear one very much like it.

Have you ever had a bare knuckle fight before Hesakia?

No but i have fought plenty sir.

There's nothing to it, no hitting in me manly area and everything above the waist is considered fare the simplest way i can put it is ,we fight fist to fist. I'm not going to try to hurt you ,but i am going to knock you unconscious.

Ain't no man wearing a woman's garment, ever beat me at anything sir.

Dad! J.W. calls out as his dad gets out of his truck .

Good job son, i didn't think that old bunkhouse would be down yet .What did you do? Work all weak end?

No dad, but we have a problem we have to deal with.

What do you mean son ?

Look just to the right there ,do you see them twelve mounds ?

Yeh so what , the land is hilly around here.

No dad them are graves , and the men in them were murdered.

AWE BULLPUCKY SON ,NOW HOW DO YOU KNOW THAT?

Dad i buried the twelfth one yesterday, myself.

Son that would make them graves over one hundred years old and the bones you buried over one hundred years old. Explain to me how a body can lay here that long, with out anyone else finding it.

Dad the body was under the bunkhouse ,it was a boy only about seventeen .I found his journal still in his hands and i read it. This boy started life out, in a living hell.

How do you know he was murdered .

Dad he wrote about it ,right up to his last breath. Look here it's all in the journal.

Dammit boy !! This is going to slow us down a bunch.

I'm sorry dad .

Don't be sorry son, all i meant was we have to call the collage and the Sherriff and get the proper people involved so everything is legal. If you unearthed a hundred and thirty year old crime, people are going to want to know about it.

Hell me too, for that matter.

Two hours later.

Hello Buck, I see J.W. has been trying to do my job again.

Yeh he's got that Sherlock bone working .

What is it this time, Indian massacre ,or let me guess . He might have found some lost gold.ha ha ha!!

No Jarred he's got something real this time .And by the way he looks, it scared the hell out of him. He found a body and a book, says there are eleven others in them graves over there.

Just as Jarred from the college finished, another vehicle pulls up to them and stops quickly.

I got here as quick as i got your call Jarred .

Who's this? Buck ask.

Sorry Buck he's from the news paper archives . He does some research for me. What did you find out?

Well it's real sketchy ,but it seems three men were hanged in the old town of Beaver City which ain't even there no more. I got a paper that says the town dried up after some captain was killed. Apparently his ranch was what kept the town going .There was a big stink over it sometime later, because they thought some gun slinger went nuts and they hung the wrong men. They never really did come to any real conclusion. Don't guess we will ever really know what happened.

Don't be so sure , i know everything that happened.

Now how can you know that J.W ? You take some class we don't know about.

Jarred i heard your smart elic remark about the Indian massacre ,and if i hear anything else like that, you will not ever know the truth.!!

I was just teasing you J.W. How do you know the truth?

I found this book in the arms of the gunslinger, under the far corner of the bunkhouse. He wasn't really a gun slinger, he was just a kid that had to keep defending himself. Then he died doing it. Only he didn't die because of being shot———

May 8 1867 DEAR JOURNAL;

We had to patch Hesakia up some ,that champion fellow almost gave him his first whooping. But he fought real hard and after about twelve rounds, they call'em ,Hesakia hit the man about three real good times in the side of the head and he went down. Hesakia being the way he was tried to help the man up because he thought he hurt him . I noticed six men dressed real nice watching the fight, at first i didn't pay them no mind. There was a lot of men watching . Everywhere i went they were behind me ,or some place close. I sat down at a table and the telegraph man comes running in and hands the captain a note. He wads it up and get's real mad.

THREE X TWO BAR BOYS ,TIME TO GO BACK TO THE RANCH.!!! Everyone got up complaining that they had another day of rest coming. I didn't ask any questions i knew the captain and when he does things like that, he has good reasons. When we got back to the ranch i noticed the captain was real edgy and he kept his gun on which is something he almost never did.

What's going on captain, why are you wearing your guns in the house? There's gonna be big trouble son ,someone's got a bounty on your head.

Why captain? I ain't done nothing wrong.

Yes you have boy ,your fast with a gun and that makes everyone just like you ,your enemy. The cable i was handed today was meant for someone else, but the telegraph man gave it to me first.

What did it say ?

Ten thousand dollars for his pearl white guns. That was all it had to say .

They want you dead.

Well i did see six —-

I saw them too, and they ain't here to wish you luck.

MAY 10 1867 DEAR JOURNAL;

They came in sometime during the night . I came in off the range early this morning and found five of my men dead in their bunks. They didn't even know what happened to them. The window in front of the stove was left open, so i knew they didn't even come in the bunkhouse. I don't understand how someone i never met, would be so afraid, that they would shoot a man in his sleep. I found the captain over by the barn and his horse saddled as if he were trying to come warn me.

May 11 1867 DEAR JOURNAL;

I saw the smoke as i was riding back from Mr. McDonald's place . He said he would send some men just as soon as he got them sobered up enough to ride. I knew it had to be our place because there was nothing else that large around. I kicked my horse and we rushed back full stride. I found three sitting at the table, they hadn't even drawn their guns ,the coffee pot was still boiling and water was running out of the holes in it and steam was still coming from where the water ran down the side of the stove. I buried the three men with the others and looked for the other two . I sat at my desk all night, i knew they were coming back .It was clear that they wanted me alone, I hung my saddle on the post in front of me, so i could see them before they saw me in this dark corner. Three of them came rushing in the door shooting wildly as i stood and shot back. I grabbed my journal as i was hit in stomach and held it to my chest to keep any shots from hitting me there.

Two of them fell and a third was wounded, but i could hear several ride off as i made my way to the door to try and see who they were. It was the same ones we saw in town, but i was in such pain from the gun shot to my stomach i hadn't realized i was shot several times. I pulled the floor boards back and crawled under the bunkhouse. They had to know that i was alone by now and it was just a matter of time before they came back to finish me off. I knew that if i could hold out until night fall ,i could get to my horse and get some help. It saddened me deeply that i had to burry Hesikia and the others . He was a good friend to me and always showed me respect, even when i had him do the hardest work. It didn't seem to bother him that i was years younger than him. I wish now that i hadn't taken his place on the range. His face and ribs were badly bruised , he earned the few days rest i was trying to give him.

Everyman in the bunkhouse had more than doubled their wages betting on him .If i would have sent someone else and stayed where i was supposed to be, i would have been able to stop them. I can feel pain beginning to set in on my leg, but i can't tell which one it is. It has been at least four hours since i have crawled under here and now i know that i am hurt worse than i thought. I have been shot several times through out my body and i now only realize that i only have one hand to hold my gun in. I'll surly loose my grip in it, if the bleeding doesn't stop soon.

May 12 1867 DEAR JOURNAL;

ALRIGHT FELLOWS SPREAD OUT! I KNOW HE'S HERE SOME WHERE!! I heard the marshal yell.

Why would he kill his own men marshal? That just doesn't make any since. One of the men riding with him ask.

All i know is the fellow at the docs office said they came out here to buy some cattle .They got into an argument over the price . He lost his temper and started shooting. We already know that boy can't hold his temper. If it wasn't for the captain i would have ran him out of town a long time ago. I don't know if he did it and that ain't for me to decide. Now look and see if you can pick up his trail.

Marshal there ain't no trail ,all of the tracks lead to here and then back the way they came. Marshal you got this boy all wrong. The man replied.

This boy is a natural born killer , and i ain't wrong about that.

Why are you taking the word of some stranger over someone we know.

Because that stranger hasn't killed anyone in my town, that boy has. Now let's get back to Beaver City and ask the stranger some more questions.

I can hear them talking above me ,i tried to get their attention ,but they just didn't hear me. I have lost a lot of blood and i am in great pain. I can hear the marshal and the others riding away. I can't believe he thinks i killed

my friends. My eye's are beginning to blur and for some reason i am feeling very cold . I have never shivered like this before and now i can hardly feel my fingers on my good hand. Though the bleeding has
stopped. I am going to have to stop writing now, because i keep dropping my pen. I am so weak and they will kill me if , i, can't, wait , them—-
————So J.W. apparently two of the men burred over there are the killers.

Yes dad . But he didn't say who buried them.

Doesn't really matter, now, does it?

THE END

They Were the Last

This story is fictional ,but the battle at Shiloh was not. The opinions expressed herein are only that of what might have been expressed by someone from this era . None of these men ever actually existed, but what if they had. This is a different story of the Civil war and of six men that fought in it. Some of the opinions are based on actual letters written by some men that did fight in it, for either the north or the south.

WRITTEN BY WILLIAM A CAMPBELL
'BOOTHEELWILL'

He stood there on the edge of the cliff ,and gazed across the mountains as if he owned all he could see. It's no wonder he looked at it the way he did ,the scenery was breath taking. The sun had just reached , it's highest point in the sky, near noon i expected, and still his shadow cast on the ground ,was the size of any tree around us. His hair was shoulder length and was a mixture of red and grey ,though it was clear it had been faded by the sun, from years of exposure. His age was near apparent and just by the look in his eyes ,you could tell he had a long hard life. Times had changed without telling him ,because he was still wearing buck skin, that he without a doubt made himself. Draped across his back like a cape, a long and worn tartan that hang from his shoulders, and were as wide as a new four burner stove. It's colors were faded and the ends and hems were frayed and small holes and tears indicated he had worn it for many years.

Standing up beside me ,he was a head taller than me , me being an average size man put him well into the ,more than six foot tall range. His hand was resting on the muzzle of his rifle and it was near as long, as he was tall. It was a little outdated for the turn of the twentieth century , but it had been well cared for. Tucked in the front of his trousers was a shining Colt Revolver and strapped to his side a knife that Jim Bowie himself would admire and carry .He turned to me with rattling Scottish drawl in his voice.

Why did you say you were here boy?

Well sir , I'm here to write a story on men of the nineteenth century , namely pioneers sir.

There's been a lot of stories written on the men you're talking about. Most of them were highly exaggerated ,so why did you pick me?

Just by the way he looked at me ,i knew i had better have a good answer. Of course i was nervous and hesitated, but i replied just the same.

Well sir, i uh ,was rummaging through some old boxes in my grandmother's attic, when i came across an old journal with my grandfathers name on it. As i was reading it i saw your name many times ,among others, though most were only brief statements .I felt you would be perfect for my story. You see sir—-

Hey knock off that sir malarkey ! That's what they call English men who take the property of poor peasants that can't defend themselves and that's what the slaves had to call their owners ,so he could feel good about himself. AND I BOY, AM NEITHER ONE! He snapped back in a rather harsh voice.

I was only trying to be respectful . I said to myself in a low mumble.

I'm old boy ,not deaf . If you want to show a man respect look him straight in the eye and talk so he can hear you, and he doesn't have to try and figure out what you are talking about. Don't stammer or lie ,even if it's going to get his dander up. Only a man who thinks he's above everyone else, really wants to be called sir. Respect is a gift and once you give it ,you can never take it back. Everything else is bullshit and fear . You don't have to be afraid of anyone ,if you learn to tell the difference . Even if ,you are afraid ,don't show it.

I apologies Mr. Cam——-

Boy let me be plain spoken ? My name is WILLIAM WASHINGTON CAMPBELL! You can call me Will or Campbell, don't make no never mind to me .Always remember there's nothing a person loves more, than to hear his name being called out by a friend.

Campbell your a hard man to find ,if it wasn't for that old-timer at the railroad station ,i may not have found you. I am amazed at how much, you are like my grandfather described you to be ,a little older, but just like he said. My father told me stories about a half Scott and half Cherokee man from Tennessee , but i thought they were just made up stories .Then i read my grandfather's journal and you're a legend.

Hold on boy, last i knew,, legends were about dead men , as you can see i ain't dead yet. By the way boy what did you say your name was again?

I'm sorry , i have forgotten my manners . My name is Johansson Nathanial Garrett , Joe Nate for short.

He kind of laughed and with a mischievous grin . It's a good thing you got that for short on there Joe Nate, a man could get out winded if he had to say that very much. I'm just joshen ya Joe Nate ,i mean no offense. Don't get to have much fun, up here.

None taken Will, i said in return. Then it occurred to me this might be a good time to ask him to let me go with him and write his story. He must of been a mind reader or had some special Indian gift, before i could open my mouth. He turned to me and said.

If you're going with me boy ,you'd better lighten the load on that horse, this old mountain is steep and rocky, one stumble could kill you and the horse ,but even worse it could kill me. He let out a loud laugh that seemed to come from his gut.

I thought to myself ,boy Campbell you're a real knee slapper. Now not only was i nervous about him, but this mountain as well.

Joe?

Yes Will ,i replied .

Leave the saddle, and the stuff you don't need right off. We'll come back for it later. Put it behind those rocks behind you, it'll be safe there. Hurry boy ,OLD MAN MOUNTIAN gets cold and wet at night. We've got just enough time to get down before dark.

I can take my tablets and pens and clothing ? Can't i ?

YES! That's why you're leaving the saddle! Answering as if he were a little short on patients.

I did as he said and we started down the mountain. The trail was only as wide as the width of a horse, so we had to walk in single file. After a couple of hours or so ,i realized all i would have to look at ,was the tail end of his mule.

I must have stumbled half way down that mountain before Will realized i was having a hard time walking on the steep rocky surface. By now my ankles were sore and blisters had already begun to well on my heels. I couldn't believe how agile the old man was ,he had to be in his seventies and his horse and mule older than me.

Let's stop here and rest a spell Joe. We'll get them city boy feet of yours some proper foot wear.

We sat down on a large rock that lay next to the trail, he looked at me and i could tell he knew i was in pain.

Get them shoes off, tie the strings together and drape them over your horse. Stay down wind of me too boy, i can smell a rattlesnake fart from fifty paces, and you're feet will be no pleasure to my nose! HA!HA
HA——! Another gut wrenching laugh, that rattled your ears.

He walked over to his mule, untied a couple of furs ,wrapped them around my feet and tied them so they would not come off.

Up here Joe he paused a second,,,, If a man don't take care of his feet ,he'd just as well not have none. Well lets get on down the trail, we'll be there in an hour or two.

It was quiet the rest of the way down and the trail had flattened ,but i could tell we were still pretty high up on the mountain. As we approached a small winding stream, Will yelled out.

Here it is Joe!

Here what is Will?

My place ,don't you see it?

It took me a few seconds more, but as i focused beyond the stream, there nestled up in the trees, i could finally see a log cabin almost hidden in plain sight. Me being from the city, this was all new to me .

Will had a small barn, some livestock and fowl in a small corral. But of all things for a man like him to have, there were flowers everywhere, vines of roses of all colors grew up and over the cabin, except where the windows and door are.

Flowers Will?

I ask in surprise?

Yes he replied. If a man ain't got no woman , he has to have some beauty in his life, and that damn mule ain't nothing to look at.

With a near laugh he turned toward the cabin ,then he turned back to me.

Unload the horses and mule, then we'll eat, OH! also bring in an arm load of that split wood over there. Be cold tonight.

I did as he said and put the horses and mule in the corral, then went inside. I didn't expect to see what i saw, the entire cabin just one large room and areas only separated by handmade furniture. It's entirety rather clean for a single man, ,,,i hadn't expected this at all.

What's wrong boy, never seen a home before? I take baths too ,hell i even wash my hind end too, from time to time.

I meant no harm Will, i said a little embarrassed.

None taken boy ,now sit down and eat, stews been cookin all day, if this don't stick to your belly, nuttin will.

I hadn't ever eaten anything that tasted like this, it was a little spicy and had an unusual taste ,but good just the same. Trying to be polite and complimentary at the same time, i thought i had better ask what i was eating. After all this man was a mountain man. This stew is really good Will , what's in it?

Joe if i told you ,you wouldn't eat it. I know how squeamish you city people get.

After we ate and cleaned up our dishes , Will told me to join him outside. He already had a fire going and there were logs all around the fire as if he had a lot of company. I sat down across from him where he had already began to draw smoke from a pipe that ,appeared to be old and well used.

Smoke Joe?

Um, no thanks Will.

Then he pulled a jug from beside his leg where he sat half Indian style, hooked it with his thumb and flipped it across his elbow and drank as if he were dehydrated from thirst.

Drink Joe?

No thanks, I replied again

You a preacher, boy? Man that ain't got no vices ,might have a pretty dull life.

No, I have never tried the stuff, i have seen what it has done to some men. Quite frankly i don't see what they get from it.

Good nuff, stay that way, you'll do just fine. So tell me bout this here collage, you're going to?

I looked at him in a stare ,how did he know, I wasn't even sure if he even knew who i was.

Putcha eyes back in ya head Joe, i ain't no mind reader, your grandma wrote me some time back. She told me you was coming ,and i've been expecting you. By the way that old-timer at the station ,we call him "IUKA JACK" if he hadn't been there ,you woodna found me. Iuka does a lot for me and we've been friends for forty years or better. He brings me supplies and i run his traps for him.

Well Will, i want to go to YALE UNIVERSITY in the fall, they have a good history program and i want to be a history teacher. Sinse i was a small boy i have been interested in old stories and i have probably read every dime store novel ever written. If i write a good enough story, it will help me get into school ,i hope.

Let me tell you this Joe ,you can spit in one hand and hope in the other ,all you got left at the end is a hand full of spit. The only way to fill up both hands with something other than spit, is a lot of hard work. Let's get some shut eye Joe ,gonna be a long day ta mar and we got a lot to do.

By this time the fire had burned low and the air began to chill, i was real exhausted from the train ride and the hike on the trail.

You take that bed over there Joe.

Thanks Will.

I lay down and covered myself with furs that had been stitched together. The bed was soft and smelled like newly cut lumber, a pine scent almost , it was almost as if it had been built for me. I tossed and turned all night, i didn't know if it was from exhaustion or excitement of where i was at, or who i was with, but it didn't matter .I was too excited to care.

Get up Joe! he called out, time to meet 'THE OLDMAN".

We had breakfast and as i ate, all i could think about was the questions i was going to ask him. A flurry of thoughts were running through my head all at once, as I cleaned up the dishes and joined him outside ,where he already had the horses and mule bridled and ready.

So tell me about my grandfather, Will? I was real young when he died, and i don't know much about him.

In due time lad, in due time. Here i got you some proper footwear ,then he handed me a pair of knee high moccasins, just like the ones he had on.

Hey Will, they fit! I said all excited .

They should boy ,they were your grandpa's. He always kept an extra pair of shoes here.

Just then a chill or shiver came over me . I don't know if it was because i was surprised Will would even keep something like this, or if it was the fact that my grandfather wore these shoes long before i was born. It didn't matter ,i needed them just the same. We followed the stream the better part of the morning ,through passes and over light rapid banks .I was so bewildered at everything i saw, it seemed everywhere i looked a different color rock or cliff. The water was so clear, it was like an aquarium back home ,however there was nothing to match its beauty.

Time to get some work done Joe ,a mans gotta earn his keep.

He walked over to his mule and pulled out a revolver much like the one he carried.

Ever use one of these lad?

Sure Will ,a couple of times.

Well here then strap this one on, and don't shoot yourself , but more important than that don't shoot me. ha ha ha!!

There was that laugh of his again. I just knew before it was all over that mans sarcasm and that loud half a ha ha laugh was going to do me in.

Listen here Joe , what we are going to do,,,, is about a mile down this stream , i got my traps set out. Won't be no trouble findin'em , they'll have a critter in'em. What ever you do Joe don't step in one . Wouldn't
want to have to cut your foot off or shoot you or nuttin. ha ha ha ———
—-

Boy Will ,you're a real rib tickler. I replied

You work that side lad and i'll work this side, what ever it is in the trap ,knock it the head and drag it to the stream.

I started working my side like he said ,when i came across the first trap, and saw it had an animal in it and i was a little reluctant to knock anything in the head. After all, i wasn't a hunter. It was difficult at first to kill an animal, but i did, just the same. Each time i did it seemed to get a little easier, i knew there was purpose for it. As i neared the end of where he told me to stop, i knew there could not have been more than one or two traps left, so i continued my task like the proud hunter i was.

I had my gun ,my knife and a big stick . I said to myself, There ain't nothing to this mountain man stuff. I drew in a deep breath and spit just like i had seen Will do, HAAAAA!SPLAT! it felt good too. Not a moment or two later i noticed movement in a briar thicket just ahead of me, so i took off at a trot and right when i turned around the edge of the thicket. I retreated so fast i tripped over my own feet and landed flat of my back. The ugliest beast i ever saw, let out an ear piercing roar and so did i. HOLY MOTHER OF GOD!! WILL!,WILL!!!

WHAT BOY ? He yelled back.

BEAR, WILL! ITS A DAD BLAME BEAR!!

SHOOT LADD,! SHOOT'IM RIGHT BETWEEN THE SHOLDERS!! He ain't likely to be friendly.

I drew my gun ,but i was shaking so bad i missed the first shot. I pulled the hammer back and just as i readied to aim Will walked up behind me .

Shoot boy or you're gonna have to whoop his ass, that chain ain'na gonna hold much longer.

BAM! BAM! BAM! All three shots missed.

Damn boy ,i can do more damage with a rock.

Shoot him Will!!, come on !! Shoot him!

Cain't boy ,guns empty ,you got two shots left, make'm count.

I took a deep breath and aimed. BAM! BAM! Both shots, right in the center of the chest. The bear instantly went limp and fell to the ground.

I could feel the ground shake as it hit. I GOT HIM WILL!, I GOT HIM!

Good thing too lad ,he was about to get you. I ain't seen a bear eat a man in a long time, don't even know if i got the stomach for it.he,he,he, Let's get'im loaded up lad ,we'll skin'im later.

We tied the bear to the mule, dead man style, i noticed there were only enough furs to match the ones i killed. I gave Will a questionable stare as if where is yours? Before i could say anything he said.

Hell boy, i know how to hunt and besides, i'm getten too old for this stuff anyway.

We set out down the stream and stopped for a second, he held his hand up and started sniffing like he smelled something, then he turned and shoved me behind him and with the speed matching only that of a gun slinger and fired two shots .

Damn snakes ,there everywhere, you damn near stepped on that one.

Thanks Will. I said just before i got nervous and started to shake.

Don't mention it ,glad to do it lad.

We approached a clearing in the woods and then i remembered something he said earlier.

Will? I thought you said your gun was empty? He let out a laughter so loud, it scared the birds in the trees.

Hell boy i'd swear to Daniel Boone's grave ,a man be a damn fool to come up here with an empty gun.

He was still laughing as we entered the clearing and kept shaking his head from side to side laughing under his breath and talking to himself.

This visit is gonna be a real hoot . He said to himself .

HELLO ! ya'll wandering repabates. Will yelled out to some men sitting around a fire in the clearing.

HELLO CAMPBELL!! They yelled back, as if they weren't surprised we were here.

That him ? One of them asked.

It ain't Moses! Will replied with that nerve racking laugh. HAAAAAAAA!

He do that damn empty gun thing ,young man?

Yes sir.

Well you ain't the first one he's pulled that trick on. One of the others said. I thought about shootin him ,when did it to me, but then i'd hafta bury him.

After we unloaded the horses and mule, then Will introduced me to the four men sitting around the fire. Wasn't none of them much to look at .They were all unshaven ,scruffy and some what soiled, but they appeared to be friendly .That was good enough for me.

Joe, the fellow over on the far side is Mathias 'THE CAJUN' La' blanke, the man to his right is 'IRISH' John Duncan O'Conner , the only man i ever seen out drink me. Of course you know 'IUKA JACK' ,as you put it, the old timer at the station. And this here he said as he slapped him on the back, is the happiest damn Indian you'll ever meet, Charlie White Bear. Joe these men are the last of their kind, you will probably never meet anyone like them again. Very few men will ever live to see what we've seen ,in one man's life time nor will they survive, what we've survived, let alone, tell about it.

I shook their hands and we made small talk like ,did you drive an automobile ?And what is it like to live in New York city? Things like that. I was happy that they were interested and i answered their questions.

Will stood up and said, 'Charlie help me with that bear' .Charlie agreed and the two of them walked away. As they skinned it and cut up the meat, Mathias began to talk first.

Wait while i get my notepad and pin please? Sure he said, i sat back down ,ok i'm ready Mathias, anytime you are.

I was born around eighteen forty five in the fall i think, in Biloxi Mississippi. The stories you're gonna hear boy, you ain't never gonna forget. My folks were slaves on a plantation near Biloxi, when i was real little , they was sold to a cotton grower in Birmingham Alabama. They were only allowed to take me with them, sinse i was too small to do any work and weren't worth nuttin.The plantation owner wouldn't sell my brothers and sisters, so they had to be left behind. That's just how it was in them days. We lived on the La'blanke farm until the start of the war, Mr. La'blanke gave us our freedom, but by this time my folks were too old and too tired to move on anywhere else, so we stayed on to help Mr. La'blanke. He was a good man ,he didn't treat us bad and we ate good, so there wasn't no reason to go anywhere else. La'blanke needed help on his farm and the only way to get it, was slaves . Just before his death he gave my pa a small parcel of land, imagine that, a free black man with land .

As he lay on his death bed he said to me, Mathias in the free world a mans got to have a sir name, and i would be honored if you would take mine. I will not be needing it any longer. That was the last thing he said before he passed on, we buried him behind his house, next to a giant oak tree. Well it wasn't long after that the Yankee soldiers took everything he had, including his live stock. What ever animals they couldn't take with them they just killed and left them lay. Not only did they burn his whole farm, but they burned my folks as well. Because we resisted, they shot and killed my folks and left me for dead. I woke up after some time had passed ,i don't really know how long. I cleaned myself up and set out to find those yankee sons a bitches .I made it all the way to Corinth Mississippi, when i came up on a company of rebel scouts that were going to be sent to regiments all over the south.

When did you meet my grandfather?

Hang on boy i'm getten to it! When i walked into the camp you coulda heard fly crap hitten a dry leave. I walked on up to the table where you signed up at and there was this smart ellic soldier that thought he was somebody.

WATCHU WON'T HARE BOYA. He asked like he got his tooth stuck on a stump or something.

I want to join this here war, sir.

Ya'll hear that, he wants to join this here war. Why you got to be one stupid son of bitch, BOY.

Well they all had a big laugh out of that. Bout dat time i grabbed him by his shirt collar and snatched him out a his chair with one hand, i drew my fist back with the other ,i was just about to give him one right in the mouth, just as i did there was so many gun hammers clicking back ,it sounded like hail on a tin roof, and everyone was pointed at me. A man stepped out from behind the soldiers that were eager to shoot me.

WHATS GOING ON HERE? PUT HIM DOWN, MISTER! the man said ,so i did. Anyway i turned to see who was talking, and you can kiss my hind end if he wasn't the biggest damn man i ever saw.

Put them guns down men, there'll be killing soon enough, make your mark and give the corporal your name. SOMEBODY GET HIM SOME GRUB ,MAN CAIN'T FIGHT HALF STARVED, AND WE'LL NEED EVERY MAN WE CAN GET!!

One of the other soldiers spoke up and said, sir i ain't fighting with no nig.....

If you finish that sentence soldier ,I'LL BE THE ONLY FIGHT, YOU

WILL HAVE TO WORRY ABOUT IN THIS WAR!. IS THAT CLEAR?!

YES SIR!! The soldier replied and sat back down on a stump.

He stuck his hand out, Johanson, Sergeant Nathanial Johanson. I shook his hand and told him mine, he was the first white man ever shook my hand.

'You'll be scoutin for us, he said and i followed him over to the supply wagon, where he gave me a gun a uniform and the rest of what i needed, of course i ate too. The first i had in four days besides a few berries and some raw corn i found along the way.

Thanks for giving me a chance sir ,i never been a scout for nobody before, i'll do you proud.

Don't be so proud yet ,all a scout means ,is you could be one of the first som bitches to get shot. I already buried a half dozen proud scouts.

First couple a days i stayed to myself, didn't nobody say much to me anyway ,but i didn't care , i was used to it.

About the third or fourth day ,late in the afternoon two men came ridin into camp ,it was Charlie and that little scrawny mule dragger over there. He said as he pointed to Iuka.

Scrawny mule dragger? Why i have you know i saved your sorry cotton picking hind end, a time or two. IUKA snapped back.

Them two started in on each other and for ten minutes they went back and forth at each other, I was starting to get a little nervous, but then they started laughing ,then i realized they had probably been doing this for years.

After them two stopped picking at each other Iuka began talking.

Damn Cajuns ,their all alike ,jabber ,jabber ,jabber, don't ever say nutten. Me and White Bear had just rode into camp and there seemed to be riders coming in from all directions. We had been scoutin all night and we knew the yanks weren't more na day or so away. We had something to eat and got a few hours sleep .But it weren't long before i heard that voice, i dreaded to hear.

IUKA! I I I IUUUKKKKAAA!!! He yelled out. YES SIR ? I yelled back as i jumped up, like a spring loaded jack rabbit.

Take Charlie and La'blanke over there and find us some where to cross the Tennessee River. We'll be headed to Alabama soon as ya'll get back.

SIR YOU GOTTA BE PLUM OUT'TA YOUR GOARD! I told him. Explain your self Jack!! .He said to me ,i knew then i had his dander riled.

Well sarge ,you already got me riding with a head peeler ,now you want me to add a green broke buck to it .Then you want me to cross the river and look for the enemy . Hell sarge ,i ain't even sure who the enemy even is now. When i turned to walk away he called me again.

Iuka !!

Yeh serge ,i replied .

Stay down wind of them ,you should be safe then. ha ha! Oh and by the way Jack, when you get to the river ,try gettin some of that water on yourself . We'll all be safer then. ha! ha! ha !

Boy he's got some nerve talking to me that way, that ga damn crazy Dutchman's gonna get me killed ,for it's all over with. I said as i walked away talking to my self. Every man in hearin distance was laughing at me and i was gettin so mad, i could'a whooped a grizzly bear , with my bare hands. Even though i didn't like it ,i did as he told me to. When we got to the river we split up to look for the best way to cross. Anyway ,i was bent over fillin up my canteen , when out'ta nowhere this damn Indian came running at me with that hand axe he carries. He drew it back and flung it at me ,well that's what i thought at the time anyway. I grabbed for my pistol and just as i was about to shoot him ,i noticed one of Grant's boys layin there with an axe buried in his chest. Hell i should'a shot him anyway he's been a pain in my ass ever sinse. ha ha !! As i calmed down and made sure i hadn't crapped in my britches ,me and Bear heard a ruckus in the weeds and bushes several yards behind us. We ran there to see what was going on ,and there was Mathias .He had a yank lifted plum off his feet with one hand and i thought he was gonna squeeze his head like you'd squeeze juice from a tomader. Course i don't need to say what happened next ,you'll have to figure that one out on your own.

I knew right then, i would never be more safe ,than i was with these two. I thanked them and we returned to camp where they were all ready to march. Listen men ,your grand pa said ,we're gonna meet up with Crittendon's men and join Trabeu along the way, no unnecessary noise. We marched most of the night until we got to the river, then we followed the river north, even in the darkness you could see the ruts made by cannons and foot prints stomped deep in the near dry mud. Thousands of men had already been there and thousands more surely will follow. I knew then that the Corinth and Iuka Mississippi battles weren't near the devils wrath , we were about to face. Our horses even seem to be skiddish and difficult to handle. It was like they could smell what was coming to us.

Iuka paused for a minute ,his eyes seemed to be moistening up as he stood up ,he said in a low voice, All this talkins got me whistle dry. He walked over where Campbell and Charlie were working on the bear hide.

You boys gimmie some of that swamp water you been hoarden up over here , hell we don't need no half breed Scott or full blood Indian gettin drunk on us. ha ha ha!

How did you know my granddad ? MR. O'CONNER .I asked.

Well lets see——— ,i believe eighteen sixty five ,the war was nearly over, and i a scrappin lad hadn't seen much fighting and i was eager to get in on it. I didn't know much about why they were fighting and back then any reason was good enough for me. I hadn't been too long off the boat from Ireland, where i made my escape from starvation because of THE POTATO

FAMINE. Me mother and father weren't so lucky. Most of my folks didn't survive the famine. Some soldiers met me when i got off the boat and told me if i didn't join their war i wouldn't be allowed to stay, so i signed their paper, and they gave me some money and food and clothes, and said that i ,and the others would get the rest when we joined our rebel camp. I could tell the uniforms had been worn, they had bullet holes in them and still had dried blood on them. But i didn't care they were better than what i had on. I wound up in Appomatics a day or two before Lee's surrender at the courthouse, there were guns and cannons being fired every which way you looked . Soldiers were dropping dead all around me and the ones that weren't dead, had their arms or legs shot off or were bleeding so bad they couldn't live much longer. I heard someone yelling behind me FALL BACK! FALL BACK,, YA DAMN FOOL!! I turned and ran to the voice, then i dove into the trench beside it.

Names Duncan O'Conner sir.

Johanson, Lieutenant Johanson but soldier if you don't wise up, you won't be alive long enough to remember it.

Why you fightin sir ? I ask him, like it made some kind of damn difference.

Same as everyone else now ,to keep from being maggot dung. Listen Irish no matter how hard we fight now, we'll not hold out much longer ,we're surrounded on three sides ,and we've been here sinse dawn. We have nothing to do but retreat even farther back and Grant's men are closing that gap up fast. So just stay alive, that's an order.

YES SIR !I said. That day, ended any more thirst i might have had for war. LEE surrendered April ninth, eight sixty five at the courthouse in town. We were standing on the lawn when GRANT and LEE were going through the surrender process, with our heads hung low we knew that we would receive our pardons soon, so we could return home. For me i had one problem ,i didn't have a home, so i sat down on a fallen tree at the edge of town ,when your granddad stopped in front of me.

IRISH? he said.

YES SIR ?

Here is some of your pay ,also i have been commissioned to help the injured get home, there will be lots to do on the way ,and we're sure to pick up strays along the way, that will need tending too.

Well i got nothing else to do sir.

Knock off that sir malarkey ,Irish, the war is over, its just Nathanial now. It will still be dangerous ,a lot of men don't know the war is over and won't, till we tell them.

No matter Nathanial, anywhere's fine by me.

At daybreak we were issued our guns and ammo and a few provisions. Our wagons must have stretched out to cover more than a half mile ,loaded with blood soaked, near half dead men and boys. We wasn't more than a mile out of town when we happened on a reb who was burring the dead. He was knelt over a yank sobbing. Didn't make much sinse to me why a reb was crying over a yank but it did to your grand dad. Nathanial walked over and picked him up to his feet.

Who was he soldier? Nate asked .

He's my brother ,sir , he answered, just barely able to stand. I was fightin just over there by those trees day before yesterday, they charged us quick in a storm of smoke, all we could do was shoot their way .Sir i didn't really know where i was firing ,i was just shooting into the smoke like every one else.

Nearly curdled my blood, when he fell back to his knees praying to god, that it wasn't his bullet that killed his brother. We buried his brother and left him to himself, the last thing he said before we pulled out .

We only lived twenty mile apart and neither of us ,had any god damn slaves!! We didn't even know any.

Duncan decided to stop there. I guess the story was getting a little too sad to tell all at once, so we made some small talk and decided to get some sleep. We would start all over in the morning. I tossed and turned all night, all i could think about was how these five different men met and became best of friends. It was one of the most unusual things i had ever seen. When i awoke the next morning ,they were already sitting around the fire drinking coffee and reminiscing about days gone by. I joined them by the fire and everyone said their good mornings and kept on talking.

What about you Campbell? When did you, meet my grandfather? I sort of butted in.

Must have been about EIGHTTEEN FIFTY NINE, i was riding front for a wagon train headed for Colorado, when we arrived i took my pay and headed back to Tennessee. A day or so into my return, i was sitting by my fire eating a rabbit i killed for my evening meal. Dusk was falling fast and it appeared to me that i was alone, till i heard a voice off in the distance .

You ,by the fire! It said .

I could hardly make out the figure of a man on his horse so i yelled back, IF YOU'RE FRIENDLY? YOU'RE WELCOME, IF NOT ONE OF US WILL SURELY PARISH ! RIDE IN SLOWLY STRANGER, I HAVE SOME FOOD AND COFFEE LEFT OVER THAT YOU'RE WELCOME TO. The closer he came to me ,the smaller his horse looked and it wasn't a pony. He ate what was left and we talked for a bit ,the next morning while we were saddling our horses, he told me he needed a couple of men to help him deliver some cattle and wild horses to Oklahoma.

Will, i lost two men back on the trail ,if you're interested, the pays good and the foods not bad either. Won't take you too far out of your way back to Tennessee.

I agreed and decided that a little more money couldn't hurt. We joined up with the herd and finished the drive and collected our pay. Me being the connoisseur of fine American made huetch that i am, i told Nate to meet me at the saloon where i'd buy him a drink. We stood at the bar about an hour ,he told me his plans and i told him mine. Anyway a half dozen or so Calvary soldiers came in,,, ,after they poured enough liquid nerve in them selves they were looking for someone to fight. I reckin by this time the Indian in me done pissed off the Scottish in me and i was gettin a little on edge. Well, over in the far corner sitting by himself was this Indian and he weren't dressed like no Indian I ever saw, he really didn't look no different than no body else. He was so quiet, i didn't pay no attention to him, until those soldiers went over there and started jawen at him ,it all seemed harmless at first, till i heard one of them say to him.

We don't take kindly to no Indian drinkin in this here saloon.

That was all i needed to hear ,now both the Indian and the Scotsman in me was pissed off, i took my gun and knife and my tartan off, laid them on the bar ,stepped out to the middle of the room .Nate said, Let me know if you need a hand . Of course me being the way i am, i replied, ah hell there ain't but eight of em Nate, we don't need to out number'em. Then i hollered WHAT YOU BOYS GOT AGIANST INDIANS ? I had to get their attention so it would be a fair fight. LETS SEE WHAT YOU CAN DO WITH TWO INDIANS, YA BLUE BELLIES? so i squared off and the fight was on. We must'a went at it twenty minutes or more ,then they started gettin the best of us .Two of them had my arms behind my back and another was whaling the tar out of me .I yelled out HEY DUTCH I CAN USE THAT HAND, NOW! he rolled up his sleeves and took another drink of whiskey then he yelled back.

DON'T LET THEM HIT YOU IN THE FACE AND IF YOU CAN HELP IT, DON'T LET THEM HIT YOU AT ALL AND YOU'LL DO JUST FINE,HA! HA! HA!

THANKS DUTCH. I appreciate it.

DON'T MENTION IT, I'M GLAD TO DO IT!

Oh he had him a big smart ellic laugh. Then this lieutenant walked in shot his gun at the ceiling and broke everything up. Good thing too, I was just about to kick some blue belly butt. We left the saloon ,and the Indian followed us out, he told us his name and we told him ours.

White Bear he said ,Charlie White Bear, thank you for helping me out ,not many people in these parts got much help for Indians. Before i could say a word the DUTCHMAN spoke .

Don't mention it we were glad to help, then he turned to me and laughed. I looked at him cross eyed and just shook my head .I knew right then this friendship would never be boring. Me, Nate and Charlie stayed around for awhile and broke horses for the Army and local ranches ,i had quite a bit of money saved and, had just about all the cow shit and dust storms i could stand. The three of us was sitting by the fire one night and i told them what was on my mind.

Fellows i done had all i can take!. I'VE swallowed enough sand and dust, to crap my own state. No Offence BEAR, but the renegades, Mexicans, hard headed Indians and smart ellic cowboys can fight over this whole god forsaken sand bed, plum to the bloody ocean ,for all i care.

It was quiet for a minute or two, then BEAR asked me .

What are you going to do William?

A mans gotta settle down while he's still young ,i want a house with a barn and maybe a few critters running around the yard. Then i'll find me a wife and start a family while my loins are still working. They say that with all the people heading west ,that lands cheap over across THE BIG MUDDY in Tennessee and i have plenty of money saved. I want to be up in the hills so i can enjoy some peace and quiet for a change. Little did i know it wouldn't be long before i have to eat those words too. I decided to get some sleep ,so i would have an early start come sun up. The next morning i was awaken with horse slobber dripping on my face, Nate and Bear was lookin down at me with a goofy ass grin on their face.

Damit Will ,if you don't get moving, i'll be too damn old to help you build a house and barn, but you'll have to find your own woman ,won't be easy, ugly as you are.

Yeh WILL, i ain't gettin any whiter either you know, there ain't nothing worse than being a one Indian tribe. ha ha !!

Even Bear had a sense of humor, first time i'd seen Bear laugh. After i saddled my horse and doused the fire, we lit out like a bandit coon running from a blue tic hound. We went through HOT SPRINGS ARKANSAS, and then we took a boat plum to the Mississippi river. We got off the boat in Memphis and stood there on the bank. It was called Elizabethtown back then.

Smell that boys?

Smell what? Your stinkin hind end Will? Nate said.

No boys the air, there ain't no dust in it. And one more wise crack out a you and i'm half a mind to drowned you right here in this river.

We're sorry Will.

Sorry about what?

Both of them had another one of them grins they get when they're up to something.

We're sorry that you got half a mind and you need a bath. Right then they jumped on me and in the river, all three of us went, like three young boys playing in a creek. We traveled about three days east of Memphis, then we topped a hill and you could see the foggy mist laying just on top of the mountains. Most beautiful sight a man could see ,next to a woman, that is.

This is it boys we're here, lets find a land office, gotta be one back the way in Savannah City, i'm gonna buy the first place i can. We found a man in town and he told us about some land for sale near Hamburg Landing on Childers Hill. The three of us bought what land was available and set out to build our homes. With the three of us helping each other it didn't take us too long and we had a good time doing it. Wasn't too long before me and Nate found wives ,they were sisters to be a fact. Course we hung up our side arms and rifles and started our families like we intended to. Hell that butt ugly Indian over there even found him a wife.

Will slapped himself on the knee ,proud of the joke he had just made and we all had a good laugh. By this time it was mid afternoon and the mood seemed to change a little. Duncan stood up ,rolled his shoulders back as if he were in some sort of pain , then he stretched out his arms and flexed his back ,stuck both fists in the air in a pugilistic pose and with a boasting growl he said.

There'll not be a man alive, that can whup the likes of this Irishman in a tussle of Indian wrestling. I'm half badger and half bear ,panthers faint at my mere presents. I can eat saw dust and spit a fence post , you'll be much the man ,to throw this one down.

Not to be out done by this braggarts challenge Iuka stands up and gives his poetic cadence of acceptance . He rolled up his sleeves ,and then he seemed to pop every joint in his body. I got a little unnerved, as i thought these two were going to fight.

My name is" IUKA JACK", i've been to hell and back ,the waters of the Tennessee flow through my veins ,i can eat thunder storms and laugh lightning, i can give a bath to a mountain lion, and i'll turn my back to no man or beast.

They placed their right feet together, grabbed each others hand like they were going to shake hands ,then started pushing and pulling trying to throw one another off his feet, grimacing and grunting and staring each other down. It was apparent that neither would win, but still there was no ground to be given. One then the others took a turn, each with his boast of self praise each boast unique to fit the man.

Alright boy, get over here, you'll not be taken leave of an ass whopping today.

UH ,i've never done that before Duncan.

Nuttin to it laddy, just square off and prepare, to land on your city boy ass.

We grabbed each others hand ,as i began to learn what i was supposed to do, my confidence grew with each push .It was like i had been doing this for years, then all of the sudden he gave me a yank and on my face i went. White Bear picked me up from the ground and they all patted me on the back as if i had done a good job. They were laughing so hard i thought they were going to tears.

I don't understand, I was watching you fellows and none of you beat each other .I thought sure i had a chance to win. Then Mathias spoke up and said 'honor and pride doesn't come from winning a war ,you can win a thousand wars and not feel good about yourself. If a man does his best and fights for the right reasons ,whether he wins or not ,then and only then ,does true honor and pride come, even if it ends in a loss. But you did a good job just the same Joe .There's a trick to that game, and we all know it. We just didn't tell it to you. ha ha ha !

You show him yet KELT-A-KEE ? Bear asked.

No ,i figured we would all go in the morning, ain't no need in rushing it ,Will answered .

Show me what ?

YOU'LL FIND OUT SOON ENOUGH LADD, WILL REPLIED.

So tell me Iuka how did you meet THE DUTCHMAN ? I asked .

Then he took a drink from the jug just like i'd seen Will do on the trail.

Haaaaa—!!!Wooooo! that's, some, panther piss he said as he took the back of his hand and wiped his mouth and beard, then he let out a belch, that reeked of whiskey and what ever else he had brewing in his gut.

I was born Jackub Allen House near Iuka Mississippi ,i had seven brothers and six sisters. My dad was meaner than a rattlesnake and as awnery as the day is long, the man he worked for ,was just as mean as he was. When i was a boy it seemed ,if one wasn't whoopin the tar out me, the other one was . About fourteen or fifteen i decided i had all the ass whoopins and cotton picking i was gonna take. I took one of the farmers mules from the barn and high tailed it out a there ,never looking back. I made it to the Tennessee River, where i was gave a job on a river boat. I worked on the boat till i made enough money to buy me some traps and a gun. Then i was gonna make my fortune hunting and trapping. I hunted and trapped all up and down the river, i did good for a young boy. Well ,one day i was walking through the woods when i came on these three men cuttin timber and building a barn. Hey ya'll up at the barn? I yelled out.

What can we do for you stranger?

Mind if i come up and sit a spell?

Suit your self ,ain't no fence. One of them hollored back.

I went and sat down on a stump they left behind and watched as they worked. From time to time i would hand them something they needed , but mostly i just watched . Little did i know that these three men were doing what i always dreamed of. Having a nice place live and good friends. That afternoon they joined me by the fire i had built and i cooked up a couple rabbits ,i figured it was the least i could do. We got to know each other a little and the rest of the night was spent jawin back and to. The next morning i was about to leave and the Dutchman ask if i wanted some work, sure i said, whatcha got in mind?

We could use someone to remove all these stumps and help out where ever needed.

Well,, i worked on them dern stumps a solid week , when they finished the barn they decided to help me with the stumps, i kept on working and didn't pay them no attention . Next thing i knowed BAM!! BAM!! BAM!!!——ga damn stumps was flying everywhere ,hell one damn near landed on me. The three of them were hid behind a tree laughing their crazy heads off. YOU GA DAMN CRAZY SONS A BITCHES !!! WHAT YA'LL TRYING TO DO,, ,,,KILL ME? They came out from behind the tree laughing like one of them higheeners in a zoo.

Nate was always pulling some kind of trick on someone.
Sorry Jack ,we was just funnin ya ,besides we ain't got but one shovel any-how. Nate said still laughing.

How come ya didn't tell me you had dynamite?

You didn't ask ,Will said, like some kinda smart ass.

We finished all the houses and settled in for the winter . I bunked in with White Bear, when i wasn't runnin my traps. Sometime bout early spring we heard bout a war starting and how some states was splitten from the union. At first it wuddin much to us, so we didn't pay it no mind. Nate and Will came back from Savannah City where they were picking up supplies and gave us the news bout folks gettin their farms burned out and figured it might be wise to join .We talked about it that night and me and Bear made up our mind to join too.

Nate started talkin first.

Listen fellows? I can't tell another man his mind or what to believe ,but i will say this .Their telling us this war is about freeing slaves ,even though i don't believe in slavery, i know that there's more to it than that ,there always is. War ain't never about just one thing. Those men at the capitol decided to free theirs ,for what ever reason, it don't give them no call to start telling everybody else what they can or can't do. One more thing, ain't nobody and i mean nobody gonna tell me what i can and can't do on my land, not now, not never!!!. AND I AIN'T FOLLOWING NO HYPOCRITE!!

Your grandpa didn't get his dander up much but when he did it was Katie bar the door ,hells commin wide open. They put their wives on a train and sent them way north, away from where there might be any fighting, Nate had some family up there and knew they would be safe. We went and signed up all at once ,WILL and NATE became sergeants right off and you know about me and Bear, sorry, Mathias too.

Will went north into South Carolina. And we met up with our company ,right away ,Nate made a set of rules as plain as a frog bumps his ass.

Gather round soldiers ,Nate said, Most of you have never been in a fight, worse than getting your ass kicked by your sister. I've been in battles from the Mississippi River to the Pacific Ocean and from Mexico to Canada.

I've seen men die for nothing more than a few cents of gold dust. Greed will get you killed, or make you kill needlessly, our job is to prevent the freeing of slaves ,,,,or so we're told, i don't have any slaves, but i am here to protect my land and my lively hood. You'll do well to do the same. I'm only going to say this one time! Any man in my outfit that harms another man, who isn't trying to harm him, and i don't care if he's black ,white ,tan or red, i assure you ,you will not live to squander the spoils. We'll not burn farms or hinder animals, unless we're so ordered. Remember our job is to fight soldiers,, and that's what we'll do, believe me, you'll get all the killing and dieing you'll ever want to see, any soldier that doesn't like what i've said speak up now, or forever keep your mouth shut. Also we'll be leaving first light ,so get some sleep, that's all.

Joe we fought in Georgia ,Alabama, Mississippi ,Tennessee, Kentucky, Missouri and Arkansas and some places i never heard of.
How about you Will ? Where did you fight at?

He took a big swig from the jug and took a deep breath and paused a second before he answered. Any man that fought, in that war, fought from one end of it to the other, that is, those that lived. When i went to South Carolina i joined a company of soldiers and we fought our way back across Tennessee and Kentucky, but true to what your pa said ,this war would be about protecting your land. Little did we know the bloodiest battle of the war would be fought right here in our own back yard, of course i'm talking about the BATTLE OF SHILOH and believe it or not, the whole damn thing was named after a little old small church just over the hill there.

Fact is ,right here where we're sittin ,GENERAL GRANT had over forty thousand men held up and more on the way. GENERAL LEE had assembled near fifty thousand men at Corinth i rekin. After my company was defeated at Nashville we headed this way to help reinforce Lee at Shiloh. Hoards of men were already worn ,blistered, wounded and sick. Twenty five thousand men and young boys, some as young as twelve years old ,,dead ,in just several hours of fighting and near as many wounded or missing. After this battle there wasn't any doubt in any mans mind, that this war wasn't going to end anytime soon. Men were buried in the trenches where they fell near a thousand to a grave, i suppose. I fought near a year and a half, before i was captured and held in a prison camp in Virginia. Just like many, many other men i was wounded several times, only to just barely heal and go right back to fighting all over again. What was strange though as many men would die from typhoid fever ,small pox ,starvation or some other silent reaper of man. Than did in the war. Young boys that have never even been with a woman or got that first kiss from their first sweetheart, would be wasted to someone's misguided conception of right or wrong, mostly guided by greed and hatred, for some other mans quest for control and power. I'm not saying that slavery didn't need to end, because it did. What i'm saying is that there were men in the north involved in big industry and it was just starting to boom . There was all kind of new inventions being made ,and they needed somebody to work in there new factories and businesses. Sinse most people up there were already doing some type of work .The only way to get the labor force they needed ,was to free the slaves and offer them a paying job in the north. Mathias over there ,can tell you how all that turned out.

William then turned and walked away, tears were beginning to collect under his eyes ,as they were on all of us. The subject was changed after that ,to idle chatter and about the way things were then and are now, in general conversation was held to different hunts each had experienced and reminiscing about the good times they had had. We woke up early the next morning and gathered all our belongings and cleaned up the camp sight . After loading the horses and mules,, we once again started out in single file down the trail, that Will and I came in on. Of course i was still stuck in the back looking at the ass of another mans mule again. We stopped at Will's place only long enough to reinforce the supply of whiskey, and other needed supplies .Then continued down the creak and over several steep hills to what seemed like an endless trek. Then all of the sudden Bear, shouted out ,we are here Joe! This is what we wanted to show you.

I stood on a hill covered with vines and trees decorated with greens of moss, some hanging from the branches, like Christmas trees newly ornamented. I gazed across a span of land that showed signs of abandon, over taken with weeds and tall grass, i could tell that man, once had his hand on this land, for only nature could do better.

This land is beautiful fellows. I said in amazement.

No boy! Mathias said, go over there and pull that knot of vines back.

I walked over and began to remove the vines ,though it took some effort ,i managed ,as the vines were removed, i began to see the remnants of a rather large petrified log standing erect as if were a sentry standing guard over the field. The more vines i removed , the more words began to appear ,when i finally removed all the vines .Carved in this tombstone created from nature were some of the most meaningful words i had ever read.

LUET. NATHANIAL JOHANSON
" THE CRAZY DUTCHMAN"
BORN ABT.1833———1895

HERE HE LAY TO GUARD HIS LAND
ALL HE LOVED MORE THAN HIS FELLOW MAN
WAS HIS WIFE SARAH ANNE
HE HAD GREAT STRENGTH
HE LIVED WITHOUT FEAR
HE HELPED CLEAR THE WAY

TO A NEW FRONTEER
HE WORKED HARD ALL HIS LIFE
THAT'S WHY HE LAY HERE

I was over taken with emotion as i stood there ,it was like i too had became a statue, i began to regain my composure and noticed the shadows of a house among a group of trees. My blood began to hasten and my body cover with shivers.

Is that the Dutchman's place over there i ask ?

Yes Joe they all answered at once.

It's yours now, lad .Duncan said.

I looked down and saw several markers with names i didn't know, all surrounding the large headstone of praise.

Lets go to the house and show the boy around .

Ok Bear ,WILL said .

When we got to the house ,the vines had begun their journey up and over the house, the yard was covered with flowers of all shapes, sizes and colors and everything seemed to be growing as if were planted that way, perhaps it was. The inside of the house resembled that of Will's, only there were more beds and the rooms were larger. As i walked around the room and with each step, the floors would creek. Each board appeared to be shaved flat by hand and each one in it's own place.

There were items of all types hanging from the walls, spurs and pictures, traps, horns ,chains of claws and teeth hung with leather bindings, a cross of Christ hang above the mantle with a Bible centered just beneath it ,with the pages open to the Lords prayer. Small wooden toys sat neatly at the end of each small bed. A large table spanned the center of the room and two long half log benches complimented it's entire length. At each end of the table sat, almost throne like, a wooden chair. Etched in the center of the table was this prayer;

DEAR GOD SHOULD, I FORGET TO SAY MY GRACE,THIS IS MY REMINDER TO KEEP MY FAITH, AND I ONLY ASK FROM YOU TODAY, HELP ME KEEP FOOD ON MY FAMILIES PLATE.

Now, i had more questions than before, and i realized how much i didn't know about my grandfather. And i knew these men could answer them. We all sat at the table and true to their ways no one sat at either end. They took cups from the cupboard and began to fill them up, including the extra that sat in my grandfathers place. Duncan being the Irishman that he was ,stood up and said.

Lets drink to all things past, especially that Crazy Dutchman, who on more than one occasion ,saved my sorry ass, lets drink to his memory, his beliefs ,and the strength he put in all of us and last but not least ,lets drink because, i havn't had a drink all day.

That got a laugh out of all of us, and that seemed to be the most important thing to these men. As we all cheered, i grabbed my grandfathers' glass, took a deep breath and swallowed it's entire contents down. Just then i knew, why i didn't drink. They all patted me on the back and each would say atta boy, there's hope for you yet . I had never felt a burn like the one i had from my stomach to my throat. I tried to hide the feeling i had, but they knew and didn't say a word.

What about those graves i saw on the hill? I asked .Who are they ?

A real silence fell on the cabin for a moment, as if each one was afraid to speak. Will cleared his throat and slowly answered.

Those are the other children of your grandparents. Two were taken by the fever and the other by pneumonia , your mother was the only to survive. That's how it was after the war, you could walk outside and get sick, it seemed like there was a funeral every week for someone. We all, buried our wives and children in these hills ,from one reason or another, it got so your ma had all she could take ,she stayed on your pa, till he moved her back east, he stayed there for awhile, but he just couldn't take city life, so he came back here. They came to see each other every season end ,they loved each other very much ,but they were just cut from two different lives. I guess your pa always hoped she would move back here ,but she never did.

You boys talk for awhile, i'm going to put the animals down for the night. Will said as he got up from the table and went outside.

Each man finished their stories that were started a day or two before ,each unique in itself and each one ending up back here, though all yet to be complete.

Mathias told of his travels to Chicago and Detroit to work in various places , yet it was worse than he remembers living on a plantation and how they would pay less than you could get by on. Poverty was so bad ,that exslaves against their own nature ,had to take to crime and do things they would never have done before the war, just to survive.

Many a man has paid a price for freedom ,but it seems that only those that died actually have it, for as long as we live, there are those that will always control us, by what ever means. I wrote down these words of Mathias La'blanke and if anyone else would have said them they wouldn't be any truer. Charlie White Bear told of his going back west after the war, he also told how his parents died on THE TRAIL WHERE THEY CRIED, how he was raised by a minister and his wife. Bear was educated in the white mans ways ,but among the Indians, he really didn't know which tribe he was from or the type of Indian he was and he didn't care. Charlie wanted to educate the Indians and teach them the language of white man ,in hopes that they could better communicate with the people of an ever expanding country. He felt if they knew more of the white mans ways, that it would help save lives, of course it's no secret how all that turned out. Bear found a wife and moved her back to these hills where he knew he had true friends. And here is where he died.

IUKA JACK HOUSE would never marry, it seemed that he loved his solitude and the company of these mountains, that he knew so well.

John Duncan O'Connor ,he must have been part banny rooster and part mountain lion, this man couldn't sit still and tell a story, if he were strapped to a chair.

Laddy your pa had a soft spot for strays and those attacked by misfortune. When we were taking the soldiers home after the war our wagons were already loaded. We zig zaged across Tennessee and Kentucky ,it seemed that every patch of woods had a couple of weary worn soldiers in it's womb ,when we told these men that the war was over they would drop their coats on the ground, whether it was grey or blue and leave them right where they fell. All along the trail men would die and we buried each one, your pa over each grave placed a makeshift marker with the mans name on it and he'd say the same prayer over each one.

Dear god this man that lay beneath your sky is no longer a soldier of politics, but just a man of of misguided err , judge him not by his deeds of war ,but the man he truly is. Should you see your way clear, please take him into heaven and away from here. AMEN. I've heard that prayer a thousand times and it still raises the hair on my arms. We took each man home just as he said we would, we delivered the wagons to Memphis and collected our pay, while we were in the office of the officer in charge ,your pa took this list from his shirt tuck.

Sir he said ,I have made a list of the men we buried and where we buried them at ,i have also marked each grave. I ask that if you can would you see to it that they get laid to rest in the proper place, these men deserve that much.

Lieutenant Johanson the officer said. I will dispatch a company of men to do just that .We are already establishing cemeteries as we speak, if this war has done anything, it's created plenty of places to burry good people.

Thank you sir ,i'm going home to rebuild my place. Your pa said .They shook hands and that was that, we left the office, then i realized once again i had no idea of my next move, because i still didn't have a home.

Irish he said ,your welcome to come back to my place until you decide your path. And of course i did. We all rebuilt the places and repaired where needed .Your grandma and her sister came back home and everyone started all over again. Despite the death of your grandpa's children he never gave up. No one ever treated me as good as he did and that's why i never left these woods.

After John was through talking, we decided to go to sleep each one picking a spot to himself. The next morning when i awoke they were all gone except Will, and he was packing his mule and horse, readying to leave himself.

Where did every one go Will ?

Well, they come and go as they please, they all came a far peace to get here. I too have things to do, i'm going back to my place ,so i figure you'll want to stay here and get to know the place sinse it's yours now.

Mine, i asked in surprise?

Yes Joe, all this land and house belongs to you, these men that you've spent the last couple of days with, all were there when you were born, to them you couldn't be any more kin than blood. All of them are leaving their land to you, including myself. I know you havn't thought much about it, but i'm your great uncle, i married your grandmother's sister.

You're right Will, i hadn't thought about it until now.

Listen nephew, Will said for the first time.

I had cold shivers run through my whole body, i had never been called nephew by any one, i was so over come with joy,, that i nearly cried. It felt so good knowing that i had more family than just my grandmother, the security of knowing you're loved by more than one person and by people you didn't even know ,causes you to change your way of thinking and i certainly did mine.

Nephew if you take that path over there in the holler, it will take you right to my place, i'll see you on your way back, take care of yourself ,there's things in these woods that will eat a man your size ,and i ain't talking about chiggers either. So be careful, and by all means keep your guns loaded.

We shook hands ,and i watched him as he and his animals walked up the trail slowly disappearing into the trees. I was so overwhelmed with pride and i now had a feeling of what my place in this world could be. I also knew that i would do what ever it took, to achieve my dreams , just as those before me have. I stayed at my grandfathers place several more days to catch up on my writing and to do some well needed repairs, being alone in the woods gave me a sense that for the first time in my life, i was a man. It gave me a sense my character could only grow strong, that what I've learned from these men, could only make me smarter and more self sufficient. I must have looked at everything left in that house ten times or more, memorizing each piece, and it's location. It became obvious to me why these men fought so hard to build and keep the places they had. The beauty of the Tennessee hills and mountains was unlike any i had ever seen, and i too grew fond of this place.

Before going back to Will's, i stopped at the graves and removed all the weeds and vines and covered the whole area with rocks in hopes that the unwanted growth would not come back. I bid the house and land a farewell ,and began my way back to my uncle Will's place. After walking about a half day i finally reached my uncles house. Hi ya Will, i yelled out from a distance.

Hi ya back, he said happy as a banny among a new crop of hens.

If i didn't know better i'd say there was a mountain man stepping on my land. What they call you anyway? "CITY JOE GARRETTE"? He said jokingly.

That's got a ring to it, i thought to myself. Uncle you come up with that all by yourself? Then i let out a hearty laugh .

Don't get sassy boy, i still got a good ass kicken left in me. Haaaa!

I knew here is where i belonged ,but my other goals would postpone any desires i had to remain here. We spent the rest of our time picking at each other ,and Will showed me some things i needed to know to be a 'COILLTICH' Scottish for forest folk. He showed me how to tie certain knots, shod a horse, clean a gun, load traps and even how to tan hides. When he let me shoot his pistol at some tins on a fence post, i damn near shot his mule. Lets go inside boy for you kill every damn animal i got he said.

Once inside the house we sat down at the table then Will pulls a couple of rifle boxes from under the bed .

Got something to show you Joe.

Branded on the top of the boxes the name Lieut. Johanson C.S.A. .Will opened the box and took out two rifles, one was a black powder long rifle and the other an eighteen sixty seven lever action Winchester. He lay them on the table and pulled out a Colt Peacemaker still in it's holster with spare reloads all the way around the belt. After putting it beside the others ,then taking out a rather worn and tattered uniform ,though you could barely make out it's color of grey ,it was with out a doubt a Confederate uniform. Can i try it on WILL?

NO! he snapped back . A lot of good men died so no one would ever have to wear that uniform again!. I only kept it because your grandpa wore it . Those that wore this uniform after the war were just murderers, not soldiers. Promise you'll never wear it .

Ok, uncle i promise.

He removed several more items from the box ,a few coins, a cross ,knives ,and trinkets found along the way, but the one thing that interest me the most was a locket with my grandparents picture in it.

Carry this with you boy, your pa did, everyday, he loved your grandma very much. If you're going to catch that train in the morning boy. You'd better get some sleep .

I was awaken early the next morning by his shuffling around .

Get up boy, were burning daylight, they'll be here soon .

They who uncle?

Never you mind, boy, just get ready.

Will you got on a suit ?

Yeh lad ,mans gotta look respectable once in his life.

What's that awful racket i hear out side?, sounds like gun fire. I ask.

That'll be our ride to the station.

I was dumbfounded, WILL, we came here a foot . I returned.

You're right ,but we'll not go back that way, lets go ,get your stuff.

When we got outside it was almost carnival like, O'Conner and Mathias drove up in a brand new automobile.

Just came in on the train ,one of them yelled.

HOT DAMN ! Will , yelled nearly jumping off his feet.

Come on in O'Conner said ,Aint this fancy? Put your stuff in the back boy, this thing don't need no saddle.

THE CAJUN and THE IRISHMAN were dressed to the tee, you could hardly recognize ether one. The way both of them were cleaned up and civil looking.

Will if they ,got this off the train, won't we miss it?

Don't worry lad , Charlie and Iuka got that all taken care of O'CONNER said.

We rode down to the station hooping and hollering the whole way into town ,it didn't take but a few minutes , the IRISHMAN'S driving had a lot to be desired ,but we made it safe and sound. When we arrived at the station i saw the most amazing thing a person could ever see , White Bear dressed in full Indian dress, was astride his horse, across the tracks, he had on a full length Indian war bonnet, with his rifle propped on his hip and his horse painted with Indian symbols, it appeared that he was ready for a one Indian uprising.

The train engineer was pointing and cussing so hard at him that he turned as red in the face, as the caboose. Iuka was cussing back at the engineer.

I can't stop him or make him move, he done killed three engineers this week, already ,hell ,that damn red skin thinks has in Arizona.

I handed my stuff to the porter ,and all five man came up to me before i stepped on board .They said their farewells ,shook my hand and hugged me . Will was the last to walk away, before he did he handed me a somewhat heavy bag with all of their names on it .

Don't open this till your down the tracks a far piece, and wait until you're alone ,there some words on paper in there, but don't read them until you've gotten away from here. So long nephew .

So long uncle, till the next time.

Then the train began to slowly pull away, i knew i would miss them, as i already do. A porter approached me and ask.

Are you CITY JOE GARRETTE?

I thought for a few seconds, not instantly realizing the question, that was being ask was to me.

Ah , well ,,yes i guess i am .

Mr. Garrette i'm sorry but you are in the wrong seat ,we have a private booth reserved for you ,your baggage is already there ,if you will, follow me please?

Thank you sir i said .

Don't mention it ,it isn't any trouble at all ,not for the grandson of THE CRAZY DUTCHMAN.

When i opened the bags, there was several gold coins of many different values and five rolls of paper cash ,there was so much money ,that i didn't even count it. As i began to read Will's letter, my tears couldn't help but well up in my eyes. Never have so few words said so much.

Dear Joe you're the only kin i have left and i am proud to have spent these days with you ,i wish we would have had more time ,but your education is more important. There should be more than enough money for you to go to that collage of yours, I bid you good luck. So when you write your story remember, THEY WERE THE LAST, of their kind. Also to teach history, you must first have been part of it, then they will always remember what you have taught them.

SINCERALY

W. W. CAMPBELL

I went to collage and graduated ,then shortly after world war one broke out ,i joined the army and fought all over Europe .I was wounded twice in battle . When i returned home i became a teacher of history.
Sometime during my term at collage and my return from war all of these men had long sense been buried . I taught history for many years until my yern grew stronger and stronger to return to these hills and mountains of Tennessee. I did come back to this land left to me by the men ,i so loved, who bought it ,cleared it ,built on it ,and fought to protect it.

There grave markers all stand tall and in a straight line as if they are a force to reckin with. This is my last passage for them .

They overcame every obstacle put in their path .They over came every tragedy that saddened their day . They feared no man or task at hand . They were soldiers ,mountain men ,pioneers ,explorers ,husbands and fathers and all a different breed. But most of all ;" THEY WERE THE LAST"

CITY JOE GARRETTE

THE END

You Can See It From My Back Porch

THIS STORY IS FICTIONAL

WRITTEN BY WILLIAM CAMPBELL
' BOOTHEELWILL'

A young reporter knocks on the door of a home that appeared to be forgotten and over looked by time. Built out of necessity and not for style, it's up keep had been over looked as well. A log home somewhat large in size ,though rather well built ,it was clear that time and the elements had taken a harsh toll it's appearance. The rails on the front porch were loose and rickety and shook from each step taken on the warped and weathered creaking floor boards. After knocking and waiting patiently, expecting someone to answer the door quicker ,he decides to knock again. This time he knocks louder and harder skinning his knuckles on the layers and layers of pealing lead paint.

Hold your dad blame horses ! Is the reply he hears being yelled from the other side of the door.

As the creaking door slowly swings open , it becomes clear to him that he has the right place. A very old, weathered and worn man stands in the opening, though his greeting wasn't very pleasant. He offers his hand for the man to shake in a friendly posture . The man grabs his hand revealing the scars and calices that stood tall in the palms of his hands. The young man could feel some pain from the old man's very firm grip and strengthful shake. It was not at all what he expected from a man of his age.

Who the hell are you young fellow? The old man asked in a harsh and mean toned voice.

Sir my name is Howard Scarburo. Are you Thomas J. Campbell ?

Yes i am , why ?

I'm from the Memphis Historian and we do articles on historical people and events . Someone from the census department sent us your name and address because they thought you would make an interesting story for our magazine. We sent you a letter telling you i would be coming on this date . If it's ok, may i have an interview ?

Letter ? What letter ? Heavens boy i can't read !

Just then a loud and broken southern accented voice come from the other room.

Jefferson ! Stop lying to that boy , you been telling that same lie for seventy years ,it wasn't funny seventy years ago and it ain't funny now. we got your letter boy! Come on in and sit down we've been waiting on you . Thomas show some manners for once in your life ,invite the boy in.

Come on in boy . Thomas replies and then yells back to the other room . Sinse when did you start telling me what to do !?

Is that him sir ?

Him who boy !? Thomas asked as he slowly turned to walk back into the other room where the voice came from.

George Washington Brown sir ,that's why i'm here , he's why the census department sent us this story. Well not just him ,but both of you . He may very well be the last living exslave on record . Sir what is even more ironic than that, an exslave and his owner ,both one hundred years old, according to the records, living together on the same farm in the same house after all this time. Don't you think that's very odd ,for nine teen forty eight?

HA !HA! HA !EXSLAVE? HELL THAT AWNERY BASTARD AIN'T DONE ONE THING ANYONE HAS EVER TOLD HIM TO DO, IN EIGHTY FIVE YEARS! HELL BOY ,IF YOU WAS TO CUT HIS FOOT OFF ,HE
WOULDN'T BLEED, JUST TO MAKE YOU EVEN MADDER! Thomas said laughing and joking as he entered the other room pointing at George sitting in a chair.

Don't pay him no mind, young man ,come in here and sit down. If you got plenty of time ,we'll tell you what you want to know. Thomas open that shade ,so we can see .George ask.

There you go ! Telling me what to do again ,one of these days i'm going to teach you who's boss around here. Thomas said as he opened the stained and worn shades.

Howard seemed a little nervous at the way these two went back and forth at each other. Trying to understand their mood and behavior he didn't know how to break what seemed to be tension between them. He began to notice things in the room and ask questions about some of them, in hopes of altering the way they were acting . It became apparent to George that Howard was getting nervous and uneasy around the two of
them. So he decided to set him at ease.

Young fellow me and him been friends for over ninety years, and you are lobble to hear anything come out of our mouths. We are all the entertainment each other has ,so just over look it. Thomas ain't that mean no how ,he's just misunderstood.

This settled Howard down some and he began his interview with small talk and short questions. He takes out a pen and pad as he tries to decide where to start at.

Mr. Campbell i notice you have all kind of collectables hanging and laying about . Would you care to tell me about some of them?

Sure but unless you want me to keep calling you boy , you might want to tell me your name.

THOMAS HE SAID HIS NAME WAS HOWARD ,CANT YOU HEAR!? George hollered back at him.

Yes George i can hear ,i was just funnin the boy is all .Thomas replies as he hides his thumb and points it at George and in a low voice whispers to Howard . Howard you gotta look over George, he ain't got no sense of humor, some old people are like that you know? Then Thomas sits back up and acts as if he didn't say anything.

I got a real good sense of humor ,and yes i'm old ,but i ain't deaf! I just been listening to the same crap for ninety years, is all.

As these two continued to tease and pick at one another Howard became more aware that they had been this way for many years. Howard began to pick up little trinkets and what nots and they explained the meaning behind them, and where they came from.

You two have got a collection of everything here ,baseballs ,photographs, portraits, china, old toys , you name it , you two have got it. I am amazed at all this stuff .There has to be a fortune in all this stuff. One to be made too.

Hang on boy ! Them ain't collectables, them's part of our lives. Everything you see in here we used in some part of our lives. Like the baseballs ,George's grandson got them when he played in the negro leagues and some of them we used to toss back and forth when we was younger. Them photos and portraits is our families somewhere down line. Them toys ,one of our children or grandchildren or even one of us played with them too one time or another. Weren't nothing here collected ,all this stuff is what's left out of our lives. This furniture that we have, one or the other of our fathers made it by hand. Everything is directly connected to us .

As Howard turned and looked around he noticed a large curio cabinet sitting in a corner at the edge of the room. Made from cedar and cypress each joint seemed to be hand carved and fitted .The cabinet had wood grains of red and white running it's entire length and only stained enough to bring it's patterns out even bolder . Glass panes revealed it's contents as if they were in a picture frame ,magnifying each item causing it to stand out larger than normal. Some of the items that Howard saw, left a puzzled look on his face . He became quiet for a moment not knowing what to say next.

What's gotcha bewildered Howard ? George ask. Say what's on your mind.

Sir this cabinet is full of Confederate and Union memorabilia and artifacts .The records show that you were in the Civil war .But how did you get all this stuff? Sir you got bullets, knives ,pistols ,buttons, and some stuff i have never seen before. That little wooden box must have a hundred letters or more in it. Plus these that are in the frames, HEY WAIT A MINUTE THIS ONE HERE SAYS?!

I ARTHOR B. CAMPBELL DO HEREBY RELINQUISH ALL SAID OWNERSHIP RIGHTS AND DECLARE UNDER GOD AND WITTNESSES STATED HEREIN THAT GOERGE WASHINGTON BROWN BE INTITLED A FREE MAN.

A. B. CAMPBELL APRIL 1860

I'm sorry to carry on, but all of these in the frames are freedom papers. A museum would pay plenty for stuff like this.

Hold on boy! Thomas scolds once again. I done told you them ain't artifacts ,them's part of our lives .Our fathers wore them uniforms ,and them bullets was dug out of the walls of this house ,some of that stuff came right out of our yard. George's father nearly died to get them papers.

Calm down Thomas ,the boy don't know anything about that. George replies as he is trying to keep Thomas from being so defensive.

I know, but you would think i'd be over it by now. That stuff still hits a soft spot with me.

I'm sorry Mr. Campbell ,i got carried away. George are them your papers up there?

No ,them's my ma's and pa's, mine are in that box .Let me explain this to you ,my folks was freed long before them papers was writ, and long before the war said they was. If it weren't for them, we'd be just like everyone else, full of anger and hate. Thomas here gets upset sometimes because of the way people carry on.

I don't understand sir ? Howard ask .

Them papers, them uniforms and everything else would not mean a thing if a price hadn't been paid for them. You explain it to him Thomas.

Alright George, i'll do my best ,this done got my nose broke several times already. Howard in the years before the war, and for some time after,, it was really hard for people in these parts. This country was growing really fast. Immigrants and settlers were coming in from all over and there was a great need for farmers and crops of all kinds. They hadn't been long running the Indians off their land just so everybody had a place to go. People was clearing woods for farm land and roads. They were cutting trees for about anything you can imagine. This country was opening up and spreading out. My grandparents came here from Pennsylvania , which was getting over crowded in some places already. My dad hadn't had this place but a couple of years, when i was born.

The Scottish and Irish were coming in on boats by the thousands in the fifties. Not only them, but people was coming from everywhere in the world. I'd say for everyone that started a farm, there was five hundred that didn't .It was getting hard to feed all of the people .The more land my pa cleared, the more help he needed planting and harvesting. He could pick up help here and there, but for the most part people was just passing through to settle somewhere else. Me and my brothers and sisters were not old enough to help much yet. I guess when i was about five or so ,my pa went to Mississippi to buy some stock and find help working this place .Somewhere along the way he heard about gold being found in Georgia and decided to check it out for himself. He wasn‘t gone too awfully long when he found a small amount panning some hidden streams .My pa wasn't greedy and decided he had enough to help get by for a while or at least till he found someone to help. On his way back through Mississippi he stopped in this small town .I don't really remember where he said it was. But it was at a plantation where they were having a slave auction . Even though it disgusted him, he was kind of desperate. He watched as slave after slave was bought and sold. On his way out of the plantation he noticed a couple of slaves being whipped behind the barn away from the crowd. My dad didn't like it too much ,but all he could do was watch. This man wearing a large hat ,approached my pa and asked if he was interested in a slave in particular. At first he said no, but like i said, he needed help on our farm.

Hey wait Mister, what about them two ? He asked.

You don't want them two ,they done tried to escape several times and they got three small youngens that can't work either. The buck is a real trouble maker and won't do anything you tell him . Second time this month i had to give them a beating .

The more the man talked the madder my pa got. If i knowed my pa he wasn't far from putting that man on his hind end.

But you all had slaves ,so he must have bought them. Once again it appeared that Howard had hit a soft spot by the way Thomas looked at him .

Cough! cough !cough! Came deeply from Thomas's chest.

Are you sick Mr. Campbell ? Can i get you some water or something?

Thomas reached down beside him and picked up a mason gar full of a crystal clear liquid, took three small glasses from the shelf behind him and filled each one about half full. He handed one to George and slid the other over to Howard.

Take that glass there Howard ,this stuff will cure most anything that ails you.

Each one took his glass butted them together in a toast, then swallowed the entire content in one gulp.

GOD ALMIGHTY DOG !THAT STUFF IS POISON !He yelled out as he takes in a deep breath and clears his throat. Leavening Howard still trying to catch his breath, he looked at them in surprise and his eyes seemed to grow larger than they were.

POISON ? He ask as Thomas was patting him on the back trying to help him get his breath.

No boy, that's just a figure of speech. We started saying that when we was kids . Me and Thomas broke a bottle of this once ,and the grass died everywhere it landed .We been calling it poison ever sinse. George explained.

ARE YOU SICK MR. CAMPBELL? Howard asked once again . Slightly louder this time

No boy and i ain't deff either. HELL ,I'M ONE HUNDRED YEARS OLD ,I CAN TELL YOU WHAT AIN'T WRONG, A LOT FASTER THAN I CAN TELL YOU WHAT IS. So let's get back to the story.

Let me see where was we? Thomas asked, Oh yeh! My pa did buy them , that man dang near beat George's ma and pa to death, with George and his brother and sister watching.

Hold up there Mister. How much? How much for the whole family?

They ain't worth nuttin, hell my hogs probably won't even eat'em .But if you want' em ,i paid fifty dollars to catch'em .You can have'em for seventy five and i'll throw in a mule trailer to haul'em with. They won't be able to walk for a week any how.

I'll take them ,put them on the wagon and cover them up with something .Them little ones look like they ain't eaten in a week.

This ain't no charity farm Mister ,you don't work you don't eat.

For my pa that was all it took .He done had all the blood run straight to his eyes. My pa gave him the money and told the man to get him the papers. After he gave him the papers and put them in the wagon .
But the man just had to pour some more gas on the fire.

Mister, you don't know nothing about buying slaves————
My pa cut him off short.

Mister, if you say one more word, i'm going to knock you into next week! He woulda done it too. My pa said after that ,the man got real gun shy and walked off quickly. It took a spell for my pa to get them home and a lot longer to get them healed up. My ma weren't too happy about being no slave owner either. Seemed like she gave him a "what for" every time he turned around wrong. When that woman got that Celtic temper flared up ,we didn't stay in the same place she was. I mean we left in hurry .

Thomas had a look on his face that was apparent that he cared about his mother a lot . You could tell he missed her.

Anyhow Howard, they got them all healed up and ready for the season ahead. One morning my pa was working out in the barn sharpening tools, repairing harnesses ,what he called ‘ make work‘, when Big George walked in.

II'SS ready for work now sa .

Big George was about six, six or six ,seven and lanky as a split rail. He was stronger than any one i had ever seen. Pa didn't say much at first ,he was one of them that thought first ,then spoke. Cept when he got riled.

You been here about a month now, and i don't know your name.

Name sa?, i ain't got no name not one that I wants to repeat anyhow . Don't nobody talk to slaves ,they just point and you do what's expected.

Well what do you want to be called then? I can't go around holleren hey you ? Won't nobody know who i'm talking to. Pa was trying to make light of the situation and put him at ease some.

Don't really know sa, what ever you want to, i reckin.

This kindly stumped my pa . And he didn't really know what to say ,he kept on working while Big George stood there watching him .

Sa, you ain't told me nuttin to do .

All right i will ,but first we gotta clear the air about something . My pa paused for a second. The money i paid for you and your folks ,i found in gold chips. The way i see it, god put them there for me to find. So i gotta do what's right by him . I don't know nothing about slaves and such ,but i know right from wrong. And if you don't, you need to learn it.! A mans gotta earn his own way. If he's got a family, he's gotta earn theirs too, least ways till they can do it themselves. Look ? I try to be a good man , but i'm a stern man. When i tell you something ,you can take it for true. The money don't mean nuttin ,if it ain't used right. I paid seventy five dollars for your leave of the hell you was in. Plus me and my wife nursed you and your misses' wounds and fed ya.

I thank you for that sa.

I appreciate that ,but here is how it's going to be on this farm. Them's my family up there in that house. It's my place to feed and protect them, and you'll do well ,to do the same for yours. You and your folks can leave here now, and maybe make it way north and i'll burn them papers. God will give me my due. Or, you can stay here and pay me back what i'm out, and try to make a good living for your family. But if you do anything, in anyway to cause harm to my family , well i don't believe in even whopping a mule ,i will kill you without any warning. So if you want to leave ,do it now with my blessing. If you want to stay here ,then we got terms to make.

George then spoke up . Young man ,Thomas wasn't joking when he said his pa was a stern man. When he said something , he didn't change ,come hell or high water, that's how it was going to be. Big George had no idea how to make a decision for himself, that didn't end up in a whipping.

You called your dad Big George ?

YEP, that's how he wanted it. My dad was so happy when he picked a name for himself ,sometimes he would go around talking to his self just to hear it. Used to get Mr., Campbell laughing so hard he'd forget what he was doing.

How did he get his name ? George .

Well,, when Big George thought for a minute ,he really didn't know what to do. Sa he said ,i ain't ever did nuttin like this before .So what ever you think will be fine by me.

No it cain't work out right, if we do it that way. I'll try to explain it better, so sit down and listen close cause i'm not real good at this type of thing. Alright when you kept running away ,you was making a decision for yourself then . You knew that if you got caught ,what would happen. So you took a chance anyway. The same thing happens to free men, what ever happens to them ,happened because of the decision they made. Even for free men, things don't happen the way they want or expect. It's pretty simple ,if you decide to leave here and someone catches you or worse, they put you back in the same situation you was in , then it was your choice ,not mine. We all got to recken with god and i don't want this to be on my list. I done right by you so far, but if you decide to leave then there will be no hard feelings from me. I will only make this deal once ,stay and pay me back ,help me clear more land and get my crops in you can make some kind of life for your self. I will take a little off each season and give you a little to get by on till it's paid back. I will credit you some breeding stock for milk and eggs and there's plenty of wild game and fish for meat.

You can stay in the lean to barn that your in until you can cut logs and build you a proper place. This may sound mean, but the farm work and chores come first. The way i see it, slavery ain't going be around much longer. Every thing runs a course, then it dies out. You can get a head start, if you work hard enough. It aint' easy on free men either. I'll say this one last thing ,i don't have time to make you do anything, and i ain't gonna try. If you don't do your part, you don't stay, it's that plain and simple.

We work Monday through Friday from day light to dark , if there is work to be done . Saturday till the sun is straight over head .Then we get ready for the next week. On Sunday me and my folks learn gods word and fish and hunt. You and yours can do what you want , except when it's harvest time ,then we work until everything is harvested. Them's my terms, take 'em or leave' em .

Big George thought about it for a minute, but not long ,he was smart enough to know what was good and what wasn't.

What about them papers sa?

In due time , right now it's the only protection you have against winding up in the same shape you was in. When it's safe and you learn more ,i will give them to you. If you do me right ,you'll forget i even got'em.

OK Mr. Campbell ,i want to stay ,if you tell me the right things to do, i'll be glad to do'em.

Mr. Campbell stood up and stuck his hand out ,of course my pa didn't know what that meant either, but stuck his out just the same. He grabbed it with a firm grip and shook.

Good then 'by George' we got a deal. I been neglecting this barn for a long time you can start by cleaning and stacking hay.

My pa did as he was told ,but for the first time in his life, it was because he wanted to, not because he had to. After that he caught on to everything pretty quick and him and Mr. Campbell got along real good .That evening when they got done for the day my pa stood in the doorway of the barn and turned and looked at Mr. Campbell.

What's on your mind .

By George sa.

Huh ? he asked.

My name ,that's what i want to be called.

That sounds good, but how about i just call you 'Big George'? He said as he was laughing.

Yes sa, that'll be just fine , Big George it is.

After that both of them worked real hard with no trouble. Me and Thomas got older and stronger so we had to work too, every one did. It got so no one had to say anything, every one knew what to do and when and where. Every harvest and fur trade and anything to make a little money Mr. Campbell kept a tally and gave my pa his part. He taught my pa everything he needed to know about living free. When they were around other slave owners in town or somewhere they acted, like slave and owner . It kept trouble down that way. I guess i was bout ten or so when Mr. Campbell came up to the cabin my pa built ,of course he helped my pa some.

BIG GEORGE !! He yelled out while standing outside the fence pa built for my ma. Big George?

Yes sa Mr. Campbell? What's wrong? pa asked, cause he didn't bother us less something was wrong.

Nothing is wrong George ,you and your bunch come down to the dinner tree ,my misses got some food prepared. She says ya'll be quick about it, so it don't get cold. This was unusual cause as good as they were to each other ,we didn't bother each other on off days. It weren't anything bad that's just how it was back then. My pa always said if you leave good people alone, good people will leave you alone.

By this time i had nine brothers and sisters and Thomas had ten, so that was a bunch of people and a bunch of food. We got there quick as we could, cause my pa built our cabin about a half mile up in the trees over there. When we got there the Campbell's were already sitting around the table dressed in their Sunday best.

There was food of all kinds, some i never seen before. There was flowers on the table and a table cloth, it was as fancy as rich people had. The one thing i noticed above everything, was this fancy wooden box sitten in the middle of the table. This thing had a shine to like a mirror and designs etched deep into the grain. It had a lock and key slot, brass hinges and was big as a hat box. That's it over there . George pointed at the box in the curio cabinet.

What was in it George ? Howard asked

Tell him Thomas ,it still shakes me up a bit , but first give us a snort of that poison.

Thomas gladly did as he was asked and once again all three downed it in one gulp, setting Howard's stomach on fire for the second time.

Breath in deep boy ,you'll get used to it before long .Thomas said laughingly. My pa didn't say much when we was all eating, but he kept noticing George here eyeballing that wooden box. When pa was done eating and saw everyone else was done. He stood up and got our attention.

Ahum !Excuse me every one . I ain't good at speech making, but my misses says i got to!. Things has been pretty good here last couple years ,we didn't get rich but we made a fair profit. Big George. he said .Me and you made a deal, and you kept your end and it's time for me to keep mine. My father stuck his hand in the box and pulled out some papers. Big George these here is the papers i got when i bought you from that fellor in Mississippi. Then he handed them to Big George . He opened them, looked at 'em and hugged Georges ma . But you could tell he didn't know what he was looking at, by the look on his face.

Mister and, Misseress Campbell ,its cause i know you alls good people, that i believe what's writ on these papers, but to us we been free a long time. If you all will let us, we want to stay on here.

Wait George ,we ain't done yet .Them just the recipes from where i paid . We still got to write the freedom papers. That's what these blank pages are for. No one is saying you have to go anywhere. But things is different now. Mrs. Campbell still ain't none too happy about the position i put her in. There is something i have to tell every one. There's fixen to be a war ,it's only a matter of time now, before it will be here. Could be a week or a month or two years, but it's coming just the same. The north says it wrong to have slaves and Lincoln done let his free as well as many others in the north. There's some states splittin from the U.S. already. They are calling themselves Confederate States ,but the north is calling them rebels. Anyway George we are going to have a slew of trouble around here from both sides, cause Tennessee is joining the Confederates. It don't matter if your negro or not, you'll catch hell from one side or the other and most likely both.

Which side you gonna take Mr. Campbell ? George asked.

I ain't yet ,George its more complicated than that, if it were just about slavery it would be an easy decision, but it ain't never about one thing, when there's money and property involved. You'll have to make up your own mind, when it's time .George i know this sounds odd, but we need to fill out these papers, so we can stay within the law. We need to be prepared for what ever might happen. If the north wins, the laws will never stop changing and if the south wins we all may wind up slaves. Color don't matter when it comes to slavery and greed. There's some folks done set their slaves free down here. I been hearing about some Negros going north already, but the ones that ain't got no papers are getting hung on the spot ,cause there's some runaways going to join the north to fight. I'm not trying to scare you all, but you should know the truth.

We'll stay here till the end Mr. Campbell ,when you found us you gave us hope and a life ,that's all any one can ask for . At first i was trying to escape from something ,but if i was to go now ,i would just be running. For us, there ain't no place to run to.

My dad didn't believe you had to be a persons friend ,to be good to them, a good person is always good until you back him in a corner. My pa was tough and he would fight at the drop of a hat, when you got him riled. There was just certain lines you didn't cross with him.

Alright Big George, i just thought you should know . In the days to come we need to prepare for what ever might happen. We'll start storing potatoes, grain ,smoke meat and what ever else we might need. Now that you are going to stay let's get these papers filled out so you can learn more about being free. Then that way, Mrs. Campbell will stop reading that bible of hers, at me every time i turn around. She says slavery is slavery, and a man's soul dies long before he does, if he can't make his own choices.

Pa sat down ,took quill and paper and started writing. Me and my ma signed as witnesses and George and all his family, put their mark on them. Everybody was happy and having a good time . Pa put the papers in the box and gave it to Big George. Ma opened her bible and started reading it out loud .The way she read, put you at ease the same way a dove does when it coos and sings in the early morning. It was peaceful when she read . She loved to read from the Psalms on Sunday, but quoted something from the bible almost everyday .She could put a scripture with almost any situation that happened. Especially when pa veered astray. Sometimes i think if them words was willow switches, she would have beat us to death. hahaha!

THE LORD IS MY SHEPARD I SHALL NOT WANT————as she read from the twenty third Psalm everyone got quiet and listened. Big George seemed to melt in his chair, i never seen anyone pay that much attention to anything. When my ma stopped reading , Big George acted like some one was taking candy from a baby. She 'd read some more and he'd listen . She didn't care, as far as she was concerned, she was getting closer to god. It seemed like George memorized every word. Just before they went back to their cabin for the night Big George handed the box back to my pa.

What's wrong George ? Them's your papers now .

I know sa, but l can't read'em ,so i can't tell nobody about them or prove they's mine. As long as you got'em we'll still be safe and free.

Me personally, i think he was a little scared and overwhelmed about being free. Pa thought for a minute and looked at ma , of course she knew what he was thinking. She always did.

Alright George ,here's what were going to do . My ma said as she gave him that look she always gave me, just before she tore my butt up. Every Sunday you all come down here for bible reading. After that we'll teach you and your misses to read and write and add and subtract. There will be people that won't like it ,and you'll have to be careful when you are around anyone.

Every Sunday they came down just like clock work, rain or shine .On Saturday night George went hunting and kept our smoke house full of meat. It wasn,t long before Big George started getting like pa and had some kind a saying for everything. One of his favorite ones was if you didn't work for it, or pay for it, it ain't yours. Big George learned to read pretty fast and read just about everything he could get his hands on, including the bible, in which he read every night. One day him and my pa was fixing the roof on the barn and out of the blue he ask my pa .

A.B. ? George said, we ain't got no last name, Ain't all free people gotta have one?

I recken they do George and most of them got middle names too. That's how we tell who's who .There might be ten people with the same name, but they will have different middle names. Or they call them junior or senior and that's father and son.

Well mines gonna be Brown then. George Washington Brown, how does that sound?

It's got a ring to it. Any reason why, if i might ask?

Well i read about him and how he fought against a king and no matter what ,he didn't give up. And i just like the way Brown sounds. You know,, how are you today? Mr. Brown.

Pa shook his head ,laughed and said well get back to work then Mr. Brown. Yep your right , that does sound good. hahaha !

What about the war, Thomas ? What happened there? Howard ask.

Hum, Let me see ? Alright Howard, you can see the wildflowers from my back porch. Lets go sit out there. You ready to go sit outside for a spell ,George?

Yep, Thomas i am .I'm bout to get stiff as a cross tie, sitting here.

Thomas stood up slowly, cracking and popping in his joints . He leaned over and pulled a wool blanket from across George's legs and chair. As he did Howard seen the wheel chair that had just been revealed. Though it hadn't been apparent until now, but Howard noticed how thin and frail George was. Let me give you a hand ,Howard said as he stood up to help.

No boy, let him do it.! Thomas snapped back, it's the only walking he gets to do. Rest of the time i have to push him around in the chair. Thomas stood in front of George and braced himself by placing one of his feet far ahead of the other ALRIGHT GEORGE GIVE ME A SECOND TO GET MY STEADY ,Thomas said as he stuck his hand out. Then we'll jerk you right out of that chair. Ha ha ha! They grabbed each others forearm and pulled in opposite directions from one another, slowly George made his way up and out of the wheel chair.

Alright George take it slow now ,don't get your head spinning, just stand there a second ,get your bearings, then we'll go to the back porch.

You aren't afraid he's going to fall ?Howard asked.

I'm afraid he'll fall on me ,then we will both be stuck in the floor, and that won't be good for either of us.

Haven't you got anyone to take care of you two?

Who would that be young fellow? Our children are all dead, and most of our grandchildren as well. The ones that ain't, are in their sixties and in worse shape than we are. Hell Howard, our great grand children are in their fifties, some of them anyhow. Our wives died thirty years ago, so it's just me and him now. There's a few people that come by and check on us every now and then but not too often. I appreciate your concern though ,not many people got that now a days. We'll get by ,we always have.

As they walked to the back porch and opened the door ,the scenery was breath taking . Rolling hills sat on the horizon, with a light mist laying just atop the trees .The blues and reds the yellows ,all seemed to show up brighter as the sun shined it's late afternoon rays through the mist of clouds. The way it lit up an area at the bottom of the hill making brighter a very large clearing of land.

You see them wildflowers down there Howard?

Yes sir.

Well them's there for a reason. That's right ,that's the site of the bloodiest battle ever fought on American soil. That my boy, is the Shiloh Battle field of the Civil War . Well this end of it anyway. Yep, April six eighteen sixty two. Them wildflowers come back every April, just like clock work, they are fertilized from the blood of over one hundred thousand soldiers. Over twenty thousand of them died right down there. My ma used to say, them flowers are the souls of the soldiers coming back to clean up the mess they made. Me and George was working right down there at the bottom of the hill . We had just started turning the soil getting ready to plant our crop for the season. We noticed our mules were getting very nervous. Things just didn't seem right . The birds stopped making any noise and the rabbits didn't act like they even cared that we were there. They ran our way like they was glad we was there. It took us a few minutes to realize, what had them spooked. We looked to the south of us and it was awe full what we saw. Down in that gully right there. There must have been eighteen thousand rebels riding horses and marching south. They were so wore out and weary looking, it was a pitiful sight. Of course it didn't take no genius to realize we was in the war now. Big George and my pa heard what was going on ,and came running down the hill to where we was at.

You boys alright ? My pa asked.

Yes pa .What's going on ? Reckin where are they going ?

Corinth i expect son, but it won't be long till they'll be back here. When i was in Savannah City the other day, i heard they been zig zaggin all over the south. Mississippi ,Alabama and parts of the east are catching hell. They are burning farms and homes and destroying what ever's in their path. Listen you boys, go put the mules away, cause now we have other things that have to be done. George go and get your stuff at home, taken care of. Put all your valuables in a box and bury them deep beneath the floor of your cabin. Now ain't a good time to show them papers to no one. Bring all your folks to the barn ,anything that you don't want to lose, bury it. Keep out what ever your wife and youngens might need . I'll see ya'll at the barn, when you're done.

Big George did what pa told him and we was already at the barn when they got there.

Good everyone is here ,look George i started digging this cellar a while back. Now we have to make it bigger so we can hide the women and children ,if need be. There will be a lot more soldiers coming from both sides. We need to be nice to them all, but we can't trust any of them.

So everyone start moving the dirt out of here.

We kept seeing them heading south for a couple of days in and out of Mississippi .Sometimes it sounded like thunder the way they were marching. One day someone came riding up to the barn looking for my pa, when pa heard him ride up ,there was several soldiers with him.

You Campbell? He asked.

Yep, i reckin so . Who's asking? What's your business here?

I'm Major McCall, these men all tell me your right smart, a fighting man . The Confederates is losing men and we could use some one like you. We are forming a regiment from the people of these parts. You can take your buck there and stand him in with you if you want.

This fellow had brass buttons all over his uniform ,two pistols a saber and a rifle in his saddle.

I ain't interested in your proposal mister. I got my family to think about. Tain't my war no how.

Look Campbell ,This is every body's war, this side of the Mississippi River and parts on the other side. He said as he pointed his finger at my pa .Most soldiers got women and children to think about. The south's fixen to be a whole new country and you don't want to be one of the ones that didn't support it.

You threating me Mister? Cause me and you can fight a war right now.

No Campbell ,i don't have to do that, i'll just burn your place down for being a resister. Burn it down boys, all of it.

When he gave that order, i never seen my pa step back before.

But this time he did for a second.

Wait ! i know most of you men, some of you all my life, but if one of you touches my farm in harm ,you won't live to see the end of the day. I'll join your war ,but not because i want too. Because a lot of innocent boys will die if i don't.

I thought you'd see it my way ,so go get your gear.

MY pa did as he was asked, then he told us and my ma by, you could tell he was real mad.

Thomas you and Big George keep this farm going, till i get home.

George you gotta do my part too ,you boys help him.

Yes sa ,don't you worry none.

You could tell one of the men with the group didn't know much about my pa, because of what he said.

Mister, you act like you like that ni#*&!!^% or something?

Major, i ain't got no horse and i ain't walking, so i think i'll just take his.

Then pa walked over to the man, and grabbed his leg, pulled him off his horse and whooped the living tar out of him. Took three men to pull him off.

I'll tell all of you something right now ! I ain't taking no smart mouthing from no body. That includes you Major. By the way Major, next time you point something at me ,it better be loaded, AND READY TO SHOOT !!

My pa road off with him, even though it was against his grain. I guess that's how he saved our farm. He didn't want nothing to do with the war. He used to say that war is in a man's head ,once it gets there, it never leaves. Once a war starts it never stops ,cause there's always someone that wants to keep fighting it. The fight in a man, is in his heart and if his heart is strong the fighting will stop ,when its time. He also used to say if you want to get a war started, put two cowards in a room and let them try to decide what's right or wrong for everyone else. My pa didn't like slavery, but he didn't like no one telling him what he could or could not do either. Anyway we didn't see my pa for a long time, but we could see soldiers moving back and forth everywhere .They'd come in off the river and in and out of the woods. Sometimes at night you could hear gun fire way off in a distance. We woke up early one morning like we always did to start working in the fields. This time the air was different ,it smelled like wet wool or soured clothes ,it just wasn't the clean air we always smelled. Bout six o clock we heard the awfulest racket you ever heard. Screaming and hollering echoed all over these woods.

You could hear gun shots and cannons being fired all around us, the bullets was so think you could see them glowing as they flew through the air. Some folks said it was like a hornets nest being stirred up. In fact that's what they called it ,back up in them woods where Grant and his men were stove up, The Hornets Nest, right back over in them woods there .There were so many men hid out in them woods, there wasn't anywhere for them to go. The cannon balls were splintering trees in half, you could see the clearings form as they fell. The more that fell, the more of the fighting you could see, and the more men dieing .From this back porch right here, where we are setting ,you could see it.

Every now and then ,men would come running past the porch on their way down there, as they came off the river. Of course then the others would start firing this way toward the house. They fought about ten days back and forth, the soldiers ran out of the woods and back in again. When the shooting finally stopped, and we came up out of the cellar to see how bad it was. Young fellow, there was dead body's laying everywhere ,it looked like some one poured turpentine on an ant mound.

This made my ma scared and nervous and worried about my pa. Most of the soldiers were leaving ,at least the ones that could, but a few stayed behind to bury the dead. Over twenty three thousand died over something they didn't even know if they believed in or not.

Big George, you and the boys go down there and see if you can find him. My ma said. She just knowed he was dead.

Yes mam , ,he's going to be alright, he's tough and smart, take more than this to put him down. You'll see.

We made our way down there like ma said ,but when we got there we knew it weren't gonna be easy to find him. Like i said they was bodies laying everywhere , the ones that was still alive couldn't move, they was hurt so bad. Sometimes we would run across one of the dead that was holding a portrait or a letter in their hands. Many times we found little trinkets or crosses, lockets, any kind of keep sake, a person would carry to give him hope. My pa always carried a braided rope of our hair with him where ever he went .He said it reminded him ,why he was doing some of the things he did. We helped tote some of the bodies to the graves that had been dug after we checked to make sure it weren't pa. One day a Yankee soldier came up to us ,he too was wearing a bunch of them fancy buttons. Looks bad, don't it boys? Just wait till you go down by the Shiloh Church and Pittsburg Landing ,it's even worse there ,fact is ,their naming this whole battle after it.

Big fellow as you can see, we are loosing a lot of men, we could use your help. We are doing this for your people ,so they can be free.

This struck Big George as being wrong ,but he kept his restraint about him. Sa i can tell just by looking at you ,you don't give two spits about me, or my people. From what i can see laying here on this field ,don't no body care much about their own kind either. But i'll join any how, cause i do care about other people like me. Sa, just so you know, i been free a long time. First i gotta help this boy find his pa .

What did he look like?, Maybe i can help ,the officer asked.

Well Mister he had kinda red hair ,almost as tall as me ,but wider built. He wore a braided strap of hair on his belt. He had a temper like a hemd up coon ,when you got him riled. If you seen him you'd know it, he'd be the one, not backing down from any one.

I seen him, i think ,we picked him up yesterday, he was shot up a bit ,but he was alive. You sure ain't joshen about that temper. The way he was fighten back ,if he was healthy, we might not of captured him. I ain't seen no one with that much fight in a long time. We are patching him up some, before we take him to a prison camp.

Mister ,he's a good man ,if it weren't for this war, you would like him. Most everyone else does. The only reason he even got in it was to keep the rebels from burning his farm, in fact he whooped the hell out of one of them before he left.

Then Big George told the officer the whole story ,about how he got his freedom and how pa helped him learn .Then they chit chatted some. The officer told Big George and us to help bury dead bodies for a couple of days ,that he had an idea, but we would have to trust him. We did as he asked ,and it took us several days till we was done. Big George did as he said he would, and was ready to go with the officer when he came back. I done told my folks by already Big George said as a wagon came up by us.

Here's your pa boy ,but he ain't healing too well .He's got an infection real bad and probably won't make it to the camp anyway .Sinse he's near dead any way ,i'll just chalk him off as, dead. He can go home with you boys he can't hurt us none now. Big fellow i appreciate you joining us, but if you try to leave this war, i'll hunt you down for desertion. Then i'll hang you myself.

Big George went off with him ,and me and George took pa home. We didn't see Big George again till after the war. It took us awhile to get pa back to health. Ma would make up some kinda stuff and tell pa to drink it. She'd say little bit of this ,little bit a love and a whole lot of god will cure anything. Me and George kept working the farm as best we could, while pa healed up.

Weren't too much trouble after that except a few night riders after the war. We had to rebuild Big George's house and fix ours because of em.

Big George hadn't been home from the war long ,when bout eight of 'em rode up one night raising hell with their heads all covered up. They was shooting in the air and hollering at my pa and Big George. Then one of em throwed a torch at the barn, and my pa shot it straight out of the air putting the flame out at the same time. Then he shot the man that threw it ,when the man hit the ground his head covering came off revealing who it was. Believe it or not it was one of the men pa fought with.

Fellows you can leave them head coverings on, cause i now know who you are anyway. You see only wolfs, coyotes and cowards run in packs like this. If i see you on my farm, in your head gear or not, I'll start killing you all, till the last one is dead. Make up your minds, HOW IT'S GOING TO BE ,CAUSE I DONE MADE UP MINE!! This one last thing, a mans gotta right to like and not like who he wants, but he should be a man about it. I'll probably see ya'll in town when i buy supplies, but maybe you won't let on like it was one of you, what came here tonight. So pick up your friend here, and get him off my land.

Them boys high tailed it out of there and after that we didn't have no more night visitors.

Mr. Campbell ,Mr. Brown you two wasn't more than fifteen or sixteen and done seen more hell than most people ever do. And that's amazing.

Young man? George said as he cleared his throat, a lot of people died in that war that didn't hate no one, men ,women and children all good people ,died because of disease and many other things caused by the war. The typhoid was one of the biggest causes of death. For years after the war was over, it was still claiming lives. By the time you are my age someone will still be fighting that war, and won't even know why. In the future same as the past, someone will be misleading them. My pa would tell me, if you get mad about something or someone just fight your own battles, cause most people will fight for no reason at all, and lose doing it. Look down there where them wildflowers are growing and them graves ,there are as many as seven or eight hundred buried in one grave. Some from the south and some from the north, but they were still buried together.

Me and Thomas has seen many things, and been through many things ,World War One, World War Two, The Great Depression ,Indian wars in the west. We watched our children be born ,raised them ,and watched them pass on. We have heard thousands of praises from the mayors to the presidents, and watched them take them back. We've seen this country change many times over the years, and it will never stop changing. We worked hard and lived the way we was raised. We've been all over this country, and a few others besides ,but always came right back here. The only thing special we done, is live long enough to tell some one about the pain and sorrow we've seen.

I'll tell you what is special though, what we saw that hurt the most, "You could see it from my back porch."

THE END
BOOTHEEL WILL